Killer Sillage

Kat LaGue

Kathryn W. Patterson

For permissions, contact: katlagueauthor@gmail.com

ISBN 979-8-9999210-0-0 (paperback)

ISBN 979-8-9999210-2-4 (ebook)

Library of Congress Control Number: 2025918115

Cover and book design by Kathy Patterson (Minxgrafix)

Published by Guilford & Greenway

An Imprint of Kathryn W. Patterson

Baltimore, MD

https://katlague.com

In memory of my mom, Teresa Wielech.
She loved mysteries.
I think she'd be proud of me.

Contents

Sillage (see-yazh)

n. The lingering scent trail left in the air when someone wearing perfume passes by. From the French for "wake," as in the trail behind a boat. In perfumery, it's what remains. What follows. What betrays presence long after absence.

One

WITH THE FOLDED TOP of the small white paper bag clenched between her teeth, Clare Buchowski juggled her extra-large latte and ring of keys before managing to unlock the door. "Good boy!" she told her terrier mix, who had already sat at attention. Vetiver bounded through the entrance while Clare set the bag on the front counter beside a tray of perfume bottles. She slipped the leash from her wrist, then locked the door, leaving the bustle of Broadway Square behind.

It was a cool mid-October morning in Fells Point, the breeze off the Patapsco River sharp and fresh. Clare would have loved a few quiet minutes in the backyard with her coffee, but time was tight. According to the grandfather clock in the corner, she had about an hour to eat her pain au chocolat, fuel up on caffeine, and get yesterday's delivery unpacked and shelved before opening.

Scenting herself for the day was Clare's priority. She'd switch to something different before tonight's event, but for now she wanted light and floaty. She scanned the tidy shelves until her gaze landed on June Chapel *Lethis Water*. Perfect: submerged rose petals in glassy aquifers, cold light refracted through temple ruins. Bergamot, aldehydes, ozone, white rose, iris, mineral musk, and cedar, it was pale, pure, and just a little haunting.

Coffee still in hand, Clare went into the back room for Vetiver's water. Without putting the cup down, she pulled the bowl from the sink, filled it, and set it on the floor. She rewarded herself with a long sip before returning to the shop. With a sigh, she set the cup aside to pick up her trusty box cutter and slice open the waiting cartons. One held two new scents from a promising Italian indie house; the other, a new eau de parfum from the less-than-charming Baltimore-born perfumer, Guillermo Flares.

At first, Clare had been flattered that Guillermo chose Good Scents for his debut launch. But the more she thought about it, the more it made sense. Her boutique was the only niche perfume store in Fells Point—indeed, in all of Baltimore—and Guillermo had grown up in nearby Highlandtown.

Back then, he was William Leight. Clare and Billy had met in parochial school and bonded as outcasts, obsessed with Star Wars action figures, old comics, and, thanks to her grandmother, perfume. Busia Manya, as everyone in town called her, came from a long line of Polish herbalists and was the original owner of Good Scents. Though healing was her craft, she also dabbled in perfumery, keeping bottles of oils and fixatives in the back room for whenever inspiration struck. Clare and Billy were thrilled to serve as her lab assistants. They also loved sneaking into the local drugstore to test fragrances, though the clerks treated them like petty thieves if they came alone. More often than not, they had to coax Busia Manya out of the shop to chaperone. Afterward, the three would tumble back onto Broadway reeking of cheap perfume and carrying a bag of chocolate bars.

Years later, Clare was surprised to discover that the Billy Leight she knew and the perfumer Guillermo Flares were the same person. His new name certainly had more gravitas than his original and seemed to fit better within the pantheon of perfume gods he admired, creatives with elegant names like Étienne Valois, Delphine Sorelle, Wren Kalder, and Samine Moreau. Perhaps if she had followed Flares' popular Instagram account, @theguillermoflares, she might have made the connection earlier, but Clare tried to spend as little time on social media as possible. It was a time-suck, and she had a business to run. She knew she should post more to the store's account, @goodscentsbaltimore, but she figured she could never beat the dreaded algorithm. Her apathy for forums like Instagram notwithstanding, the store had a pretty decent following without her intercession, including Guillermo and several other independent perfumers.

As she unpacked the carton of *Lycoctonum*, Clare admired the posh packaging that must have set Flares back a pretty penny. The boxes were matte black-on-black with an embossed image of a wolf within a rectangle, the name of the perfume and its creator beneath in glossy ink. The bottle was a slim rectangular vessel capped with a silver sphere—pure elegance. And the fragrance itself, although not to her taste, was actually quite good in a witchy sort of way. It was rather dramatic, starting out tart and green, moving into bitter and dark, and would be the perfect scent for Lady Macbeth or Clare Underwood from House of Cards. Guillermo had brought her a lab sample of *Lycoctonum* when he stopped by early last month to propose that he introduce the fragrance at Good Scents.

The tall, dark-haired man had perused her wares at length before Clare recognized him. As he was spraying Midnight Black's *Silhouette Mourante*—a haunting bouquet of dried blood orange peel, Damask rose absolute, Lapsang Souchong, violet ink, sandalwood, myrrh, labdanum, patchouli, and a black dahlia accord—on a blotter, Clare approached. There was something familiar about him, and something unpleasant too. He wore no fragrance, yet Clare swore he emanated guilt. He was very well-dressed and highly polished, yet after a few moments of observation, Clare realized who he really was. "Is that you, Billy Leight?"

He turned to her. "Guillermo Flares," he corrected. Clare tilted her head one way and then the other, much as Vetiver did when he was trying to understand something. The man almost smiled. "Yes, Clare, it's me, Billy."

"But you're also Guillermo Flares? *The* Guillermo Flares?" Clare tilted her head yet again. He nodded. "You might say this is my *nom de plume*, if I were a writer. Though these days, I use Guillermo exclusively."

"Ah, your *nom de fumée*." She wasn't sure what else to say. Billy had been a cute kid—she'd always had a bit of a crush on him—but now he was a beautiful adult with ridiculously long eyelashes and a whisper of stubble on his angular jaw. "Let me tell you why I'm here, Clare. Good Scents is the perfect place to launch my newest and most magnificent creation. Think about how business will increase once *Lycoctonum* by Guillermo Flares is introduced to the world. People will flock here, to this lowly shop in a dying city, to experience the inception of greatness. I wouldn't be surprised if people erected a memorial here to commemorate the occasion." He gestured toward the front of the shop with a sweep of his arm.

Clare rolled her eyes. "Ah. I get it. You changed your personality along with your name. I'm giving it a 2 out of 10." When they were kids, one of their favorite pastimes was rating things on a scale of 1 to 10, mostly perfumes, but also food and people.

"I'm thinking the first weekend in October might be good."

Launch parties always drum up extra business, but that was the worst possible weekend to do anything in Fells Point. Clare practically shouted, "Are you kidding? That's the weekend of the annual Fun Festival. It's always total mayhem around here. There's too many people, not enough parking spaces, and most years it's either 1000 degrees or it rains buckets. Or both. And it's not all that much fun for those of us who live and work here near Broadway Square. Don't you remember that Busia Manya didn't even open the shop that weekend? I follow her example. I don't need browsers knocking over expensive bottles of perfume."

Guillermo sighed dramatically and threw up his hands. "Then let's do Halloween weekend. Even better."

"You'd think you didn't grow up around here, Bil...er, *Guillermo*. That's just as chaotic as the festival weekend, maybe even more so. At least the Halloween insanity goes on mostly in the evening, but I'm betting you don't want to have an afternoon party."

"Definitely not. It must start at dusk and will last for at least 2 hours."

"Then all I can give you is one of the three weekends between the festival and Halloween. How about the week ending the 18th? We could host the event on Thursday or Friday, when parking is a tad less impossible to find."

"That Thursday will be fine, I suppose." Guillermo didn't seem fond of not getting his way, but Clare wasn't about to let him step all over her.

Guillermo seemed to soften a bit, then, in a less-imperious tone, said, "I often think about coming here when Busia Manya was still around selling her remedies and fragrance oils. I loved hanging out in the shop and learning about the various ingredients she used. This place always smelled, I don't know... strange, but also wonderful, the air thick with scents of dried herbs and incense." He inhaled deeply, as if to find that long-gone aroma that once permeated the small storefront, then frowned. The shop had changed as much or more than he had over the years.

"Don't forget garlic. It always smelled of garlic here. It was Busia's favorite remedy for pretty much everything. Though we ate so much of it, it was probably just our breath." Clare chuckled nervously and thought to herself, "Ooh, awkward, Clare. Why did I say that?"

Though her childhood crush on Billy Leight was over a lifetime ago, and in the fifteen minutes he was in the shop she found herself on the verge of disliking him, she was touched that he shared her feelings of nostalgia for her grandmother's shop. Clare suspected that his affection for Busia Manya was the impetus behind his interest in perfumery. It was hers as well, though Clare wasn't artsy like Billy. Er, Guillermo. She thought it was important to approach fragrance scientifically and got her chemistry degree first before going to perfume school. Only, she didn't make it to perfume school. After suffering a severe concussion in a car accident on her way to Ocean City the summer after graduation, she was never quite the same. She lost her sense of smell entirely for several months; when it returned, it was patchy. Some smells were wrong; others didn't exist at all. Eventually, she started smelling things that weren't even there. The doctors referred to this peculiar symptom as "phantosmia."

Though the accident had ended Clare's dreams of being a perfumer, it didn't diminish her appreciation for fragrance. In some ways, she felt her sense of smell was even sharper than most. While she might not tell a Damask rose from a rose centifolia by scent alone, she could detect either, or both, by the way the odor made her feel. It wasn't synesthesia—where senses overlap, so tastes can be felt or smells can be heard—since it didn't affect any two senses in particular. One of her doctors called it psychosomatic sensory substitution: when the loss of one sense heightens the others to compensate. Whatever it was, it worked well enough that Clare could help customers choose perfumes without them ever knowing she had any issues. As long as she didn't blurt things like, "Gardenia looks like mossy blue spirals," or "Cetalox is a high, chalk-white hum." (Which had happened once.) That would be like telling people she could talk to ghosts. People already thought she was a little weird, no doubt in part because of the neon green She-Hulk t-shirt she wore to work regularly, often paired with a frayed denim mini-skirt.

Clare removed the remaining *Lycoctonum* packages from the carton, placing two on the counter and the others on the dedicated shelf. Guillermo had promised to bring a few more cartons later tonight, along with testers so the "teeming throngs eager to buy his fascinating new fragrance"—his words—could try before they bought. Fingers crossed there would be plenty of customers. At $190 for 50ml, it was hard to predict. Clare didn't expect it to be a crowd-pleaser, though there was a market for gothic scents. More likely, many attendees would just want to meet the handsome perfumer. Most of his Instagram posts were shadowy reels, the light catching his sculpted cheekbones as he spoke about his love of fragrance. Clare found them self-aggrandizing and dull. She guessed the bedroom-vibe of those videos was why he had so many followers.

She had spent countless childhood afternoons in this very store, staring at him while her grandmother taught them about natural ingredients. She shook her head. How had she not recognized him immediately?

After shoving the last bite of pain au chocolat in her mouth and washing it down with the dregs of her now-cold latte, Clare dusted off her hands and pulled up the shade on the front door. As she turned the "closed" sign around, her cousin Ivy, who worked with her, pushed the door open, nearly knocking Clare down.

"I'm so sorry I'm late! I stopped at Pitango to grab breakfast, and there was a longer line than usual. Here," pushing a small white bag into Clare's hands, "I got you something."

"Seems like bribery, but I'll take it." Despite having just finished her breakfast, Clare opened the bag and broke off a piece of chocolate chip scone, which she popped into her mouth. Speaking with her mouth full, she continued, "Actually, you're not late. The event's tonight, remember? We shifted your hours so you could work with me this evening."

"Dannnnnng. I totally forgot about Guillermo the Great. My bad. I'll stay late, maybe come in later tomorrow if that's okay?" Ivy picked up a newly unpacked box of *Lycoctonum* and ran her thumb over the raised wolf. "Cool." She put the perfume down and watched Clare cram a sizable chunk of scone into her mouth. "Do you actually think anyone will show up for this thing?"

"I hope so!" Clare frowned. "Billy, er, Guillermo will be even more insufferable if this is a flop. And for sure he'll blame me for not promoting the event enough."

Clare had considered taking out an ad in the recent addition to the local news scene, the online-only Baltimore Beacon, hoping that enough fragrance lovers would spot it between the news, sports, and slice-of-Baltimore-life stories, but it just wasn't a budget-friendly proposition. Instead, she promoted the event relentlessly for free to her 15,000 Instagram followers. Her posts—moody PR photos of the perfumer holding the bottle, accompanied by a caption meant to entice—had been shared by Guillermo to his stories, as well as by some of his followers. Surely this had widened their reach considerably.

NEW SCENT DROP

Introducing Lycoctonum by Baltimore's own Guillermo Flares. Exclusively at Good Scents. With notes of black rose, leather, oakmoss, and a rare hellebore accord. A fragrance that is as beautiful as it is dangerous. Bottled in shadows. Meant to linger. Limited quantities, available in-store only at our Fells Point boutique.

#goodscentsbaltimore #lycoctonum #indieperfumery #darkflorals #baltimoreboutiques #witchyaesthetic #guillermoflares

Over the past couple of weeks, Clare had received several comments to the effect of "I'll be there!" and "Reserve one for me, plz." which she did. So far, six of the dozen bottles she had received had been reserved, which was honestly not bad, considering. While she was eager to sell *Lycoctonum*, she was also hoping to get some other sales from tonight's attendees. There were plenty of great indie and niche brands to be discovered on the shelves at Good Scents, many that would be to the liking of a broader audience. Hopefully, there'd be some general fragrance fanatics in attendance and not just Guillermo Flares groupies who wanted selfies with the man.

Two

THE REST OF THE day went by uneventfully, and rather slowly, customer-wise. At one point, a couple of young women came in to browse. They asked Clare for several widely available designer fragrances and seemed disappointed that Good Scents didn't carry any of them. Ivy, sensing her cousin had other things on her mind, took over.

"You don't really want to wear something everyone else is wearing, do you? Let me show you some independent perfumes that share a similar vibe but are a little more special." She took a bottle of Half Moon Atelier's *Cloud Feeder* from a shelf and sprayed it generously on a blotter. As she shook the paper to dry the alcohol a bit, she said, "This one is a soft serve dream with jagged edges. It's marshmallow charred at the edges and just a hint of pistachio butter but balanced with subtle vegetal and musky notes of angelica and ambrette to give it lift and coolness." Ivy handed the strip to one woman before walking across the room to retrieve a bottle of June Chapel *Morning in Provence*. "And this one smells of untamed lavender dusted with citrus zest and softened with wild honey and golden hay, and orange blossom rendered earthy via smoky resin and sweetened with tonka. It's feminine and whispery, yet it roars."

One young woman looked puzzled. "What do you mean by 'it roars'?"

"Ah, sorry. I mean it has an amazing *sillage*. *Sillage* is the trail your perfume leaves behind. Like, you walk past someone and two seconds later they're still thinking about you. It's the reason some scents are date-night material, and some are just for yoga and errands."

It was amazing how easily Ivy conjured up such flowery descriptions, and how her words almost always led to sales. The young women tried a few other scents but went back to the ones Ivy had shown them first. One purchased *Cloud Feeder*, and the other asked for samples of both scents, promising to come back soon when she had more time to explore.

"Wow, Ivy. That was great. I was about to suggest they take their pedestrian tastes to the Sephora in Harbor East." Clare crossed her arms and rolled her eyes at the thought. She realized, however, that her lack of patience and overabundance of perfume snobbery would have lost her the sale and potential repeat customers.

Clare honestly didn't mind that people liked commercial fragrances, but it always surprised her they would expect to find them in a shop that had "Fine Fragrances from Independent and Artisan Perfumers" stenciled on the front window. She sometimes toyed with the idea of changing the name of the shop back to what it was in her grandma's day, "*Eliksiry Maryi*," or Mary's Elixirs, because it sounded far less commercial than the current name. There had been a much higher population of Polish-speaking residents in the Fells Point neighborhood of Baltimore during the first half of the 20th Century, when Busia Manya—Clare's and Ivy's grandmother—opened the place, but nowadays the relatively few Poles in the area were 2nd and 3rd generation and didn't speak the language, much less read it. Clare herself couldn't speak it particularly well, but she could mostly understand it. When she was young, her Busia spoke to her almost entirely in Polish. She saved her use of English for the customers, claiming it made her tired to think in another language, and Clare responded to her in English. Clare knew, even back then, that being fluent in another language could be a valuable skillset to have, but their half-and-half communication style worked well enough for the both of them. Besides, taking French in high school ended up being more useful to someone who planned on becoming a perfumer.

Because the day was shaping up to be so quiet, Clare thought it would be safe to close up shop for an hour in the afternoon so she and Ivy could grab something to eat. It didn't seem like they'd be able to have dinner at a normal hour, since Guillermo was insistent on having the event at dusk, which at this time of year happened around 6:30pm. It wasn't a terrible idea, as there would be more people stomping around in Fells Point in the evening than there usually were during the shop's normal opening hours. Hopefully, that would lead to potential customers finding the event accidentally. And Good Scents would be closed before the usual handful of overly inebriated bar patrons staggered about.

If tonight's schedule didn't include a special preview of a picky perfumer's newest creation, Clare would have no problem with eating lunch or dinner in the shop, but she was pretty sure that Guillermo would have a conniption if the air smelled anything like food. They could have gone up to her apartment over the shop to make something, but she was afraid that cooking smells could drift downstairs. Instead, she snapped on Vetiver's leash, and she and Ivy popped down the street to Barcocina to enjoy some tacos and margaritas at one of the outdoor tables. Clare had toyed with the idea of serving champagne at the event, but who was going to pay for it, for one thing, and for another, who was going to clean up the inevitable spills? The answer to both questions was "Clare," which made the decision easy. But she knew she was going to need a drink, and a pre-party margarita or two would do nicely.

"So. Cuz," Ivy began, "a little bird told me you once had a thing for Billy Leight."

"Guillermo Flares," Clare corrected. "I know I'm going to slip and call him Billy at some point." She sighed. "Who is this so-called little bird with the big mouth?"

"Your mom!" Ivy cackled as she shoved a tortilla chip loaded with chorizo-studded queso into her mouth. "When she dropped off the flyers last week, she stuck around for a little gossip sesh. I never realized that Aunt Terri was into spilling the tea. She could go into the blackmail business with what she knows."

"Well, you were a boy back then. Mom doesn't gossip with men. She gossips about men."

"And everyone else, too. So, you're not going to deny it, huh?"

"I thought everybody knew. It's not like I wasn't obvious about it." Clare chewed thoughtfully on a piece of fried calamari that she had dipped in guacamole. "We met in the third grade. He had just transferred from another school and didn't have friends at St Casimir's yet. Though I had been there since kindergarten and didn't have any, either." Clare shrugged as she swizzled her straw in her beverage. "So, we'd sit together at lunch. I'd share my pierogies, and he'd give me half of his bologna sandwich, you know, the usual charming kid-meets-kid story. Eventually, we became friends. I thought he was dreamy. Or as dreamy as a skinny schoolkid can be. He had long eyelashes and full lips, and he seemed really smart, though I was much better at math than he was." Clare stopped, lost in thought.

Ivy laughed at her cousin as she flagged down their server to order another blackberry sangria. "Do you want another margarita?"

"I'd better not. We need to stay focused tonight, so everything goes well this time."

"It wasn't your fault that the event for Lys & Fern went all to biscuits." Ivy said through a mouthful of duck birria taco, "Hey, do you want a bite of this? It's really good." Clare grabbed the last taco from Ivy's plate. "I said a bite, not the whole taco."

"Sorry." Clare took a big bite and set the rest down.

"I know, but I still feel bad," she said, pausing to sip her drink. "Fern Virelle flew all the way from San Francisco, but her shipment didn't arrive until two days after the event. Good thing I had a couple of bottles in stock so we could make decants for people. She was so nice about it, though, talking about her process and giving her sales pitch as if we had a whole shelf of her line."

As it turned out, her sunny, summer-ready perfume was a huge hit. Lys & Fern's PR material helped. The scent was described so evocatively that people would have been happy to blind-buy: "*Citrine Reverie* is bottled sunlight, the kind that dances on the rim of your teacup and brightens the darkest corners. Juicy Meyer lemon and sparkling bergamot burst at the top, softened by herbal lemongrass and tender mimosa. A heart of white tea and neroli whispers of breezy porches and linen dresses. The drydown is soft as driftwood and silken muslin. An optimistic scent for dreamers, letter-writers, and barefoot thinkers."

"It's so good," Ivy agreed. "Do we have any *Citrus Reverie* in stock? I want to spritz myself with it when we get back to the shop." She pulled a piece of duck out of her taco and fed it to an eager Vetiver, whose little nose had been wiggling non-stop, at least when he wasn't softly growling at the seagulls taking off and landing on Broadway Pier.

"No, we have to smell like *Lycoctonum*. Or something that won't compete with it." Clare frowned. "Please stop feeding him people food. And to go back to what we were discussing before..."

"Billllll-yyyyyy!" Ivy singsonged at her cousin.

"Yes, Billy. He started going with me to visit my grandmother at the shop. She took a real liking to him because he was always so polite and helpful. Eventually, he was there more often than I was. In fact, it was rare that I went to the shop and didn't find him pestering her with questions about ingredients while he was sweeping the floor or dusting the shelves. He was a good kid. I could tell that she loved his questions, and she loved him, too. His older sister Stephanie, on the other hand, was a pest. Busia was happy when that one took up the viola and was too busy with orchestra practice to be at the shop more than once every couple of weeks."

"Is Stephanie still a pain in the sticky buns?" Ivy accepted her fresh glass of sangria from the server and took a sip before setting it down on the table.

"Probably. Last I heard, she and Bil...Guillermo had a falling out, but that was forever ago at this point. Once both of them went off to college, I really didn't have much contact with either Leight sibling. I knew Guillermo had called Busia occasionally because she'd complain about how much he had changed, how he was no longer the sweet boy she remembered him to be. And the local rumor mill...."

Ivy interrupted her. "You mean your mother."

"Yes, my mother, but also your mother and their former St. Casimir's lunch lady buddies and even Mrs Leight offered conflicting stories about him working in New York or Rome, or attending perfume school in Grasse or at Pratt, being famous or infamous or quitting perfumery and becoming a stockbroker. But all of them agreed he had become difficult, snobbish, and just plain unpleasant. Which I learned firsthand when he contacted me about the launch party. He didn't even ask if I would be interested in hosting him, he basically told me I would. After he finished bragging about his talent and how his fragrance would be a bestseller, he then started making demands about rearranging the store and painting it a darker color so his dark boxes wouldn't contrast so much with the light walls. I mean, come on! Besides, why even have it here when he was allegedly big enough to have it anywhere? And then I realized: He's no big shot. Nobody really likes him. And then I felt sorry for him and agreed to host the event."

"So he's a jerk, but is he still cute?" Ivy wiggled her eyebrows up and down.

"Oh, come on. You've seen his Instagram reels."

"Yeah, but he sits in the shadows, talking in a low voice, like the love child of Asmodeus and Batman. I can't tell if he's really attractive or if it's just a 'demonspawn' filter."

"Then it seems appropriate to describe him as 'devilishly handsome.'" Clare added air quotes for emphasis. "Though he's not attractive enough to make up for his being so insufferable."

"Oh, goody." Ivy shoved a tortilla chip into her mouth. "Can't wait."

Three

At 5:30pm, the cousins arrived back at the shop where Clare's mom was waiting. She was taking Vetiver to her house for the night, as he didn't like crowds or noise and it wouldn't do to have him barking during the party. Once they left, Clare headed to the back room to freshen up after their taco feast. She spritzed herself with a dose of *Lycoctonum* from the lab sample she kept on a shelf littered with other samples before handing it to Ivy, who had just popped a breath mint. Clare thought if they both wore his scent, Guillermo would be flattered, and anything to keep him on his best behavior was a good thing.

"I'm not crazy about this stuff, to be honest. Whew." Ivy fanned the air in front of her face as they stepped back onto the shop floor.

"Get used to it, girlie. You should smell a lot of it tonight. Here's hoping." Clare continued, "It's not my favorite, either, but there's no denying it's a very good fragrance. I'm not going to say masterpiece, but..."

"...Guillermo will!" Ivy chimed in, and they both laughed. At that, they heard a rapping on the shop window. "Speaking of the devilishly handsome," Ivy snickered as she opened the door for Guillermo, closely followed by a gangly young man carrying a stack of boxes.

"Guillermo will what?" the perfumer asked as he swept into the shop.

"Be here any minute!" answered Clare, hoping that nothing else they said had been overheard.

Guillermo looked around the small fragrance boutique. "Where is the lit candelabrum?" he demanded. "The black velvet drapery on the tabletops? The blood-red roses I requested?"

"Dude. This is a tiny perfume shop full of flammable stuff. No candles will be lit in here, ever." Clare was peeved. She continued, "And where was I supposed to get the candelabrum? Liberace's been dead for ages. Also, who was going to pay for roses and black velvet? You want grandiose? Have your opening at Harrods next time. As far as I'm concerned, I'm doing you a favor here."

Guillermo snorted and said softly, "I was kidding." He then noticed Ivy and stared hard, as if trying to place her face. After a beat, he barked, "Chuck! Aren't you going to take the boxes from my assistant?" The young man, Efraim, had continued to stand by the door, arms still full.

"Ain't nobody here by that name going to help your flunky, Billy." Ivy bit out. "My name is Ivy, and I've been a woman for years. Well, since birth." She sniffed a bit and stomped into the back room.

"Honestly, I don't know why you had to start something. That was totally unnecessary. We want this evening to be as much of a success as you do. Being a hateful, pompous butthead isn't going to endear you to anyone. Especially not the people who you need the most. I expect you to apologize to Ivy."

Efraim cleared his throat. "Hi, um, where can I put these boxes? My arms are going numb." Clare gave Guillermo the eye, and he took two boxes from the young man, putting them on the counter as Clare took the other two.

Guillermo was about to say something else, but Clare brandished the box cutter in the air mock-threateningly before cutting into the first carton. She pulled out boxes of *Lycoctonum* and started arranging them on the narrow wooden console table in the center of the room. "Did you bring a tester? I'm not cutting into my profits by opening one of my packages."

"Oof, left them in the car. Be right back." Efraim ran out the door, eager to escape the air of tension in the room. At that point, Ivy emerged from the back. "Oh, I heard the door and hoped you had left," she said to Guillermo. Ivy took a deep breath and continued. "I know you're trying to cultivate the persona of a villain, and you're doing a fantastic job of it. So I'm going to be the grownup here, the professional, and pretend you didn't call me by my deadname."

Before Guillermo could say anything, Efraim returned with the testers. Packaged in plain cardboard boxes, these capless bottles were going to be the vehicle for getting the scent of *Lycoctonum* onto the hopefully many bodies that would visit the shop that evening. Clare put one on the counter next to the taxidermy raven she affectionately called Harbaugh, after the Baltimore Ravens longtime head coach, and another on the console table. "Ooh. Almost forgot something!" She scurried into the back room, returning with a small hand-lettered sign and an ornate easel, which she placed on the table next to the display of *Lycoctonum*.

INTRODUCING LYCOCTONUM
BY BALTIMORE-BORN ARTISAN PERFUMER
GUILLERMO FLARES
EXCLUSIVELY AT GOOD SCENTS
BLACK ROSE • OAKMOSS • TOLU BALSAM
AMBER • LEATHER • HELLEBORE ACCORD
DARK, BEWITCHING, AND NOT QUITE SAFE
CRAFTED FOR THOSE WHO CRAVE MYSTERY IN EVERY NOTE
A KILLER SILLAGE
SNIFF IF YOU DARE
LIMITED BOTTLES AVAILABLE

Guillermo shrugged at the sign, but Clare could tell that he loved it when he whispered, "10 out of 10."

Just before 6:30pm, a line of black-clad individuals was seen waiting patiently outside the door to Good Scents. Clare was pleasantly surprised that there were that many people interested in trying *Lycoctonum*. First in line was Jasmine Reed, fragrance blogger at *Black Narcisse*. She was the only person in the ever-growing line who was not clad from head to toe in black. Instead, she wore a smart orange leather jacket over a belted grey floral minidress, and over-the-knee boots in burnt umber suede. She wore her hair in a short blonde afro, and heavy Bottega Veneta-style teardrop-shaped earrings hung from her earlobes. Clare was happy to see Jasmine, because even a brief mention of Good Scents on the *Black Narcisse* blog or Instagram account will bring in a new customer or three.

Clare had met Jasmine years earlier on a now-defunct online forum dedicated to all things perfume. *Cognoscented* had been the perfect place for a budding perfumer to chat with like-minded individuals—until it wasn't. Most of the time, it was a pleasant space for nice conversations with nice people, but as in any social situation, online or in person, conflicts could arise.

Things turned particularly contentious when a controversial new member, Myrrhcury, who styled themself as a perfume critic, began trashing fragrances, including those that were considered classics. Feelings were hurt, arguments flared, and some participants were banned. Eventually, the site owner, tired of playing babysitter, shut it down. Before that, Clare had reveled in passionate discussions with a handful of people who became good friends, people she still chatted with and occasionally met in person, like her BFF Jorge Delgado. And Jasmine.

The blogger had been one of the people banned for taking arguments too far. In a way, it had been good for her. Jasmine discovered she had strong opinions that were as valid as anyone else's. Unlike Myrrhcury, however, she considered that perfumers were real people whose creations didn't deserve unmerciful savaging.

Sometimes she thought about Myrrhcury and wondered what had become of them. If she was honest, she rather missed their interactions. Though they had argued frequently on the forum, they also chatted regularly in direct messages. Their private discussions had been far more civilized. And stimulating. Part of Jasmine hoped Myrrhcury was male, imagining an in-person connection—but once the forum was gone, she could no longer find them.

Clare opened the front door a crack and gestured to Jasmine that she should come inside. A collective groan went up from the rest of the people gathered when they realized that they still weren't allowed to enter.

After embracing her friend and acknowledging Ivy, Jasmine asked Clare, "Is anyone else from *Cognoscented* going to show up tonight?"

"Not that I know of. Was hoping Jorge would show up, but he's having relationship issues. Again. And Esther is in Japan, looking for new scents to add to her decant site. I don't know about Damarion. Everybody was invited."

"We should reunite the gang for drinks some night, either here or in DC. It's been too long since we've gotten together and lamented about the 'good old days.'"

Clare, too, would love to spend some time with her old friends. Along with her grandmother, these were some of the very few people who encouraged her dream to be a perfumer, and they were there for her when that dream had been shattered. "That's a great idea. When I get a moment after this event, I'll send something out to the group chat."

Guillermo paced the shop, hands fidgeting at his sides. He was dressed for drama: a sharp black suit, black shirt open at the throat, and a dark red silk scarf tucked into his breast pocket. The only color in his ensemble, it seemed to vibrate with the tension in the room. His wavy black hair was slicked back from his widow's peak, giving him the look of a dashing vampire. Clare watched him straighten up and tug at his cuffs as if he were trying to force himself into composure. He moved with the restless energy of someone about to step into the spotlight. Any minute now, it would be showtime.

Moments before letting anyone into Good Scents, Clare pulled up a playlist of Adam Hurst's gothic cello pieces on her phone. As the haunting music filled the small room, guests stepped in quietly and almost respectfully, as if entering a house of worship. As Clare was about to say, "Welcome," Guillermo beat her to it, opening his arms theatrically and bowing his head in acknowledgment of his fans. Ivy elbowed her cousin and whispered, "Very Count Creepy. Why do I feel like something bad is about to happen?"

"Shhhh! Don't say that!" Clare admonished her assistant. "It's going to be a great event. We'll be talking about it for a long time."

Jasmine broke the somber atmosphere when she walked over to Guillermo and offered her hand. "I'm..."

"I know who you are," Guillermo interrupted her and took her hand, but rather than shaking it, he turned it slightly and kissed the back. Ivy rolled her eyes at Clare, who raised her eyebrows and shushed her before she could say anything snide. Still holding Jasmine's hand, the perfumer picked up the nearest tester of *Lycoctonum* and sprayed where he had kissed. "You will love it," he said, as he looked deeply into her eyes.

Jasmine nearly swooned. Those eyelashes! She held the back of her hand to her nose and took a deep sniff, as if trying to identify the top notes before they disappeared. She closed her eyes and sniffed again, one nostril at a time, looking for the heart notes. Jasmine then took several quick sniffs in a row, followed by another long one. Meanwhile, she had opened one eye the tiniest bit and searched for the sign listing the notes while trying to avoid looking at Guillermo. Spotting it on the console, she finally spoke. "I am loving the tart blackcurrant opening and the herbal green notes, moving into a dark and thorny rose, and an atmospheric moss. It speaks of the night and all its beauty. It's stunning, Guillermo, seriously." Jasmine hoped she got that right, lest he blow a gasket. Unlike Clare, she followed the perfumer's Instagram account and was captivated by his videos. She knew how exacting he could be and that he was not a fan of criticism of his work. She dared to look at his face but couldn't tell if he was pleased or not.

During her decade or so as a fragrance blogger/reviewer/social media influencer, Jasmine had the good fortune to meet several famous perfumers. Most of them were lovely and humble human beings. A scant few were prima donnas. Guillermo Flares was firmly in the latter category, despite not having many creations under his belt. His listing on the popular online fragrance forum *Scentology* comprised only three perfumes, each of which had been created with other better-known noses. None of them had been big hits. Jasmine was curious about why Guillermo had struck out on his own in the field of perfumery. Perhaps he would agree to an interview sometime soon. In the meantime, she'd step back and observe the reactions of the crowd.

She maneuvered around a young couple who were standing too close behind her and walked over to the counter, behind which Clare and Ivy were wisely standing out of the way. At least 8 people had clustered around Guillermo, with another 4 or 5 browsing the shelves conspicuously nearby. The perfumer was spraying blotter after blotter and handing them out.

"Blech," said Ivy, smacking her lips together and sticking out her tongue. "There's so much of it in the air I can taste it."

"Yes," Jasmine agreed, "it's a bit beastmode in here right now. And crowded! I kinda want to leave, but I also want to hang around and people-watch. Hey, do you have a sample for me so I can analyze this stuff at home before I write about it?"

"Hold on, let me make you a decant." Clare took a tester with her into the back room and emerged with a small spray vial in a tiny plastic bag. "He probably should have sent you something in advance. Would have been nice to have a review out before the event to drum up more customers."

“It’s not like he’s done anything like this before. Maybe his head is just so far up his own derriere that there’s not enough room for rational thought in there?” Ivy giggled.

Four

Stephanie Leight stood in Broadway Square across from Good Scents, observing. A warm golden glow emanated from beyond the shop's plate-glass window, and the people inside were waving paper strips under their noses. Most of those gathered were wearing black, several also in heavy dark eyeliner.

Standing out from the sea of black was Clare, the shop owner, wearing a schlubby green cardigan and jeans. To the casual observer, it seemed almost impossible that this blandly dressed individual could be related to the fascinating and vivacious Busia Manya.

To the very end, Mary Buchowski favored patterned dark skirts, long vests adorned with bright floral embroidery, and the occasional lacy blouse, reminiscent of the colorful costumes worn by both male and female Polish krakowiak dancers. Her long pale hair was always braided and wound into a large bun, secured with oversized u-shaped pins. Sometimes, when feeling fancy, she'd tuck in a silk rose. *Busia Manya*—colloquial Polish for "Grandma Mary"—was the perfect name for her. Mary Buchowski was the platonic ideal of a loving grandmother: welcoming, cheerful, and ready with a hug. She somehow always had everyone's favorite homemade cookies on hand, whether oatmeal, chocolate chip, snickerdoodle, or peanut butter. Once, she even conjured up a plate of madeleines for a French visitor.

Word had it she was a witch, but she was also one of the increasingly rare people who truly paid attention to the world around her. She listened eagerly to her customers' tales of woe, and if she didn't have the right remedy on her shelf, she'd craft something special after consulting the thick handwritten book of generations-old folk treatments she kept tucked away in her back room. While the way things smelled had fascinated Billy, Stephanie had always been more interested in how ingredients made people feel. Busia Manya knew the girl would have loved to explore that ancient tome, so she kept it well-hidden.

As Stephanie continued scanning the activity in the shop, her brother Billy came into view. He was standing off to the side, adjusting the cuffs of his somber black suit before sweeping his hand over his raven black hair. Stephanie had the same widow's peak and the same wavy black hair, but that's where the similarities ended. While Billy had also inherited their mother's full mouth and straight nose, Steph looked more like their father. She'd had a rhinoplasty years earlier to remove the hump, but Billy was still more attractive than his sister.

She continued to observe her brother for several minutes. He was tipping his head slightly backward as he spoke, literally looking down his pretty nose at the group crowded around him. Truth be told, Stephanie hadn't seen her little brother in several years, not since their falling out. Before he got the apprenticeship in New York, the siblings had dabbled in perfumery together. Though he considered himself a fragrance genius, it was his sister who had more natural talent. He'd put a formula together, and while it macerated, Stephanie would tinker with the ingredients, making it far better, then swap out the batches. When Billy smelled the mature fragrance, he was always stunned at how much richer and fuller it had become. It was something he chalked up to time. And of course, to his genius. When Billy crowed publicly about his fabulosity as a perfumer, Stephanie got angry. She confessed to him that she had been changing his fragrances all along and was the reason everything smelled so much better. Of course he didn't believe it, so she attempted to prove she was telling the truth by preparing two batches of the same scent—one with his ingredients and measurements, and one that she had changed. Rather than being convinced, Billy accused her of switching the formulas.

There had been no shortage of tension between the siblings, but Stephanie still approached the shop, lingering a moment as if weighing something unspoken. Perhaps she was curious whether Billy's time in New York had changed anything. She crossed the street and pushed open the door to Good Scents.

"Wow, Steph, it's been a long time," Clare said to her latest arrival, noticing how well she fit the zeitgeist of the room in her slim black turtleneck knit dress accessorized with large silver hoop earrings and multiple bracelets. "You look good."

Stephanie looked her hostess up and down and smirked. "And you look...the same."

Clare took that as a compliment, though it was likely not meant that way. There was always something odd about Billy's older sister. She had been interested in Busia Manya's work, and fragrance in general, but didn't seem to take things as seriously as her brother. She also had a mean streak and could be downright insulting. Like when she had the cojones to tell Busia Manya that another ingredient would work better than the one she was currently using. As if the knowledge of a 12-year-old could compare to that of someone who had been preparing homeopathic remedies for 50 years using recipes that were at least 5 generations old. Billy had always seemed somewhat unhappy on the days that Stephanie hung out at the store, and Clare always wondered what the dynamic was at their house.

Though she hadn't seen Stephanie in years, Clare had received an email from her recently. It was a sales pitch for her line of wellness products that included homeopathic remedies and aromatherapy body mists she claimed would be a perfect tie-in between the shop's old and new personas. Clare wasn't convinced and honestly didn't want any ties to the past. Her grandmother had been an amazing person who had helped many people over the years, but that was not Clare's calling. She wanted only to look forward. Besides, this was a perfume store now, and she didn't even sell candles. There was just no room in the small shop to carry additional scented items, which would limit the number of actual perfumes she could offer.

The last time Stephanie had set foot in the store was probably a decade earlier. Clare now watched her take in the many changes she had made since then. Back when it was still her grandmother's shop, Busia Manya opened its doors almost every day for over fifty years, doing everything herself with the barest help from a series of assistants, until she decided she had done enough. Clare had been her most recent assistant and the only family member interested in taking over the business. Her father might have wanted to, but he had died when Clare was young.

During her tenure at Mary's Elixirs, she had convinced her grandmother to modernize the look of the place. Out went decades of clutter, much of it gifts from grateful customers who couldn't always afford to pay in cash, like the various taxidermy animals that had found their way onto shelves. Clare had kept the raven, which she moved to the counter, and the pretty black cat, whom she named Frankincense, that guarded the back room; the tatty old fox and various equally shabby vermin were discarded. Several mismatched small tables had also been retired. While useful for displaying products, they ultimately took up too much space. The long, narrow console that now dominated the center of the room had survived; the rest had been sold at a consignment shop in Hampden. The yellowed cafe curtains in the window were replaced with heavy grey drapes that could be drawn closed on sunny days to protect the stock from the deleterious effects of heat and sunlight. Finally, the walls, which had once been papered in gaudy 60s floral wallpaper, had been stripped and painted in a neutral warm grey. This change created some tension between grandmother and granddaughter, but after it was done, Busia Manya had to admit that the shop looked cleaner and larger with the lighter, albeit boring, color scheme.

Besides the cosmetic changes, Clare had convinced Mary to carry actual perfume. The shelves already held a small selection of homemade fragrance oils and potpourri-style room fresheners for visitors who weren't there for remedies—mostly curious tourists who had read about the shop in guidebooks and local interest publications. Clare wanted a reason for other people to stop by, too. People like her, who cared about smelling good. She had grown interested in perfume in her teens and lamented that Baltimore offered almost no options for non-commercial fragrances. Even well-known brands like Estée Lauder or Calvin Klein were hard to find, let alone niche labels like Le Labo or Ormonde Jayne.

Thanks to Clare's insistence, Mary's Elixirs soon carried interesting independent brands, bringing in a younger, more fragrance-savvy clientele. The final change came after Busia Manya died at the ripe old age of ninety-seven. Clare wanted the shop's name to reflect its evolution from a homey apothecary to a modern perfume boutique. "Good Scents" seemed to make—well, good sense.

A few of the crowd of goth girls that had been sniffing around her brother wandered away when someone pointed out the "cute little raven on the counter," so Stephanie took the opportunity to approach him. "Congratulations," she started. "I wanted to tell you how proud I am of you."

"Stephanie. Really. You proud of me? That's new. I must admit I am very surprised that you showed up here after all that's happened. After your lies and deceit."

"I have always wanted only to help you," his sister replied, "and tried to help you grow and improve yourself."

"Sabotage, dear sister," Guillermo spat out, "is not the same as help. You thought you were better than me, more talented, and you wanted to show off by taking my formulas and changing them. Sure, your tinkering produced delightful scents, but how do you know mine weren't already good? After all, you were just adding to my established base. But we never found out because you destroyed mine before they had time to mature." Guillermo had raised his voice, and those gathered near him were looking at him with curiosity. Realizing this, he looked around the room and flashed a sexy smile. "I'm sorry," he said. "I can get quite passionate when I talk about perfume with others in the business." That explanation, but mostly the smile, seemed to appease those concerned. He turned back to Stephanie and started again, this time in a loud whisper.

"Remember when you tried to teach me how to play chess? You were older and already quite proficient in the game, but I was still a dumb little kid having issues grasping which pieces could move when and where. Rather than encouraging me to move the right pieces in the correct way so I could at least begin to understand the strategies behind the game, you beat me in five or six moves. Every time. Nobody wants to play a game that they can't win, Stephanie. It's not fun. And it's not even a challenge when the other players have unfair advantages. So, I refused to play chess with you ever again. I still have never played the game. To be honest, I've always resented you for not letting me have that. But I vowed you wouldn't beat me in perfumery. You tried to take it away from me when we were younger, but this is my passion, my life. I dream of fragrance. It's all I truly care about. And that's why I don't want to have anything to do with you, because I know that ultimately, all you want in life is to see me miserable. Honestly, I don't understand why anyone would feel that way about their own flesh and blood." Guillermo realized he had been raising his voice again, so he looked around and smiled again. He turned back to his sister.

"Please leave now, Stephanie. And do not come back. I no longer want to have anything to do with you." With that, Guillermo pushed her aside and strode to the other side of the room to schmooze a group of young women who had been looking at him adoringly most of the evening.

"Hello, ladies. I'm sorry I haven't been over here yet. Have you all had a chance to smell my masterpiece, *Lycoctonum?*" Guillermo picked up a tester and a handful of blotters and proceeded to charm the group out of their money.

"Wonder what that was all about?" Ivy elbowed her cousin.

"Will you stop doing that? Your bony elbows are like weapons." Annoyed, Clare rubbed her side. "Those two have always been like that. You're probably too young to remember when they'd be here at the same time, sniping at each other. Stephanie always acted so superior, like she knew more than even Busia Manya, and Billy hated that. He worshipped our grandmother."

"She was a cool lady. I miss her."

"Me too. And though I've made a lot of changes here, I still feel her presence every time I come into the shop."

Stephanie sidled up to the counter, tossing her hair over her shoulder. "Would you believe that my own brother isn't happy to see me? I wanted only to offer my support. Oh, well." She shrugged. "Guess I'll leave now." Clare gave Ivy the side-eye, looking at her face and then her elbow in warning. Stephanie studied the pair for a beat before asking, "Would it be okay if I used your bathroom before I left? Or do I have to buy something for that privilege?" Clare nodded and indicated the back room with a wave of her hand.

After several minutes, Stephanie emerged from the back. "I see you not only modernized the showroom, but it's also quite different back there. It's just shelves and boxes and a couple of chairs. And that awful black cat. Did you keep any more of Busia Manya's things?"

Of course Clare had, but she wasn't going to tell Billy's sister that. Knowing her, she'd probably try to get Clare to give the stuff to her. She strongly suspected that Stephanie would love to get her paws on Busia's book of remedies. That was a family heirloom that Clare planned to pass down to her children someday. If she ever had children. She needed to find a husband first. At least a boyfriend. Just because she wasn't interested in being a healer doesn't mean future generations of Buchowski offspring would feel the same way. In the meantime, the tome was securely ensconced in a safe place.

"Nope. It's all gone. I have no need for any of that stuff."

For a second, Stephanie looked stricken. "Such a pity. I would have been happy to take all of it off your hands."

"Oh, a shame I didn't know that before I took it all to the dump. Sorry, Steph." All lies, but Clare didn't feel any need to be truthful with this woman.

As the event went on, Guillermo's assistant appeared bored. Efraim clearly wasn't into black-clad girls or perfume. He wandered around the shop in a desultory fashion, picking up bottles and putting them down again, absently petting Harbaugh, but mostly looking out the plate-glass window at the activity on Broadway and Thames Streets and sighing audibly. Occasionally he'd look around at Guillermo, determine that he still wasn't needed, and sigh again. Between customers, Ivy watched his progress around the room. Efraim was a little too tall and skinny for her taste. Like one of those East African marathon runners, he was all arms and legs. But kinda cute. She sidled over to him while he was staring out the window.

"Hey," she whispered. Startled, Efraim jumped.

"Sorry, I didn't see you there." He sighed for the umpteenth time.

"What's up with you? You've been acting jumpy all night."

"Sorry. I guess I'm just bored. I'm supposed to be here to help Guillermo if he needs anything at all but look at him. He's surrounded by women and talking about perfume. That's heaven on earth for that guy."

"Do you like perfume?" Ivy was beginning to think that the man was more of a bodyguard than an assistant.

"I love it, actually. I wanted to be a perfumer when I grew up, but the sons of prominent Kenyan physicians don't become perfumers; they become other prominent Kenyan physicians."

Another sigh. "It's a long story, but right now I'm neither what I want to be nor what my father wants me to be. I am, as you say, a 'flunky.' I follow Guillermo, carry stuff for him, open doors, drive him around town. I pick up his dry cleaning every day because everything he wears needs to be dry-cleaned." Efraim paused, checking to see if Guillermo was within earshot. "The job I applied for was lab assistant. I should be helping him make perfume, not running to the post office."

"Why don't you quit if you're so unhappy?"

"I cannot." Efraim looked at Ivy. "And I shouldn't say anything else. Thank you, friend, for listening to my grumblings."

Ivy patted his shoulder and smiled sympathetically. "Hey, if you need to unload, I am here. I'm a good listener."

Clare had just finished ringing up a customer when she noticed a man standing awkwardly by the entrance, as if he was afraid to come inside. Something about him seemed vaguely familiar, though she couldn't quite place him. He was probably in his early 40s, attractive, dark-complexioned with tousled black hair, dressed in a neat slim-fit grey suit, blue tie, and shiny shoes like he thought he might be photographed on a red carpet. She approached him with a smile. "Hi there. I don't think we've met."

The man looked startled for half a second. "Oh. Right. I'm Damarion. Damarion Washington."

Clare blinked. "Are you now?"

He nodded, holding out his hand. "You must be Clare. We've...chatted online."

She took his hand and gave it a quick shake. "Um, yes, we have. We've definitely chatted online." Clare smiled but thought to herself, "Who is this impostor?"

"Well, I'm so glad you could make it. I wasn't sure you'd be able to get away from the museum."

"...The museum?"

"You work in textile restoration, don't you?" she said innocently. "At the Walters?"

A beat of silence. "Uh. Yeah. That's right."

Clare bit the inside of her cheek. "Well, have fun sniffing around...Damarion."

As soon as the man turned away, Clare pulled out her phone and texted the actual Damarion.

Clare: I didn't realize you were going to be at the launch party tonight.

She waited for several seconds before the series of dots that show someone on the other end is responding to her message appeared.

Damarion: Huh? What do you mean? I'm at my brother's birthday party.

Clare: There's a guy here, tall, dark, handsome...

Damarion: sounds like me...

Clare: mid-40s, wearing a nice suit, says he's you.

Clare: I asked him about his job at the Walters. He about choked on his own saliva.

Damarion: Could be Rafael Campos. Perfumer. Nice guy. I told him about the party the other day. Not sure why he's pretending to be me though.

Damarion: Hey, I gotta go. Hope your thing is a success!

There had been a steady stream of people in and out of the shop, with several of them making purchases. Four of the six bottles that Clare had reserved for the Instagram followers were picked up, and she sold three more. Four bottles from other perfumers had found new homes by this point, thanks to Jasmine talking them up. "Thanks for that, Jas." Clare was grateful to the blogger. "You really should hang out here more often."

"No prob. I don't know if you noticed, but I enjoy talking about perfume. If I sell a few more, could I get a discount on my purchase?"

"I will definitely give it some serious consideration."

"Give what serious consideration? I didn't know you had the capacity to be serious." Clare turned around to find a rotund middle-aged man wearing a black kimono decorated with Noh masks over a grey turtleneck, yellow trousers with the cuffs rolled up, and red high-top sneakers.

"Jorge! I didn't think you were going to show up!" Clare walked around the front of the counter to hug her old friend from the *Cognoscented* board. His username had been "IsoEgo," and his persona could be slightly abrasive at times, but Jorge Delgado had been one of Clare's biggest supporters after the accident. He liked to refer to himself as her 'best girlfriend,' which in a way, he was. Clare didn't have many female friends while she was growing up. She had definitely preferred climbing trees and playing softball to putting on a princess dress and playing with dolls. Conversely, Jorge had no problems with playing dress-up, yet the two of them had found common ground in the world of perfume.

"Do you remember the first time we met in real life? I was convinced you were seven feet tall and wore only silk caftans." Jorge moved his hands around his body, acting out the motion of swirling silk.

"I thought the same thing about you!" Jasmine, like Clare, was happy to see their old friend. His presence added a bit of much-needed vivacity to what was fast becoming a somber event.

Jorge looked around the room. "This is weirdly emotional. I didn't expect it to be. I thought I'd just show up, spritz something interesting, tell everyone they're fabulous, and sneak out early."

"You still might."

"Thank you both for being here. I know you guys know you kept me sane in those years." Clare also felt emotional that evening, and she wasn't sure why. Perhaps it was the presence of her youthful crush just across the room. Maybe there was something in the air besides the swirling mist of *Lycoctonum*.

"On that note, you are both fabulous, but I have to run."

"Don't forget to spritz something interesting." Clare handed Jorge one of the *Lycoctonum* testers, which he waved above his head before charging out the door into the evening.

Five

CLARE HEARD THE HIGH-PITCHED female voice with a distinct British accent over the din of the crowd.

"Yoo-hoo, Billy! Over here!"

Guillermo obviously heard it too, for he immediately ducked behind the console table. The voice got louder as its owner pushed her way further into the store.

"There you are my love! What are you doing down there?"

Guillermo knew he was caught and hastily stood up, straightening his suit jacket on the way. "Oh hello, Philomena. I had dropped a blotter and was retrieving it."

The tall blonde woman in the striking midnight blue jacket—Clare was pretty sure it was silk—attempted to get closer to her target. There were too many other people on either side of him to get by, so she simply puckered her lips and made insipid kissy noises in Guillermo's direction. "I have missed you soooo much, my Billy, my love! I didn't know where you had gone off to until I saw the Instagram post about your launch party. My invitation must have gotten lost in the post somewhere, but I wanted to be here to support my dearest darling."

Guillermo's handsome tanned face had turned a few shades paler. "Thank you," he stuttered, clearly uncomfortable. He looked around for an escape route, as if he could feel the panic rising, and that getting a full breath was becoming difficult. It didn't help that the air was a miasma of *Lycoctonum* and the many other fragrances that were being spritzed on blotters for testing. He quickly glanced around the shop without moving his head. Both the entrance to the store and the back room were blocked by browsing customers, and he was on the far end of the room, away from both the front door and the counter, with no place to hide. Thankfully, there were still several people and a console table between him and this woman. Guillermo shut his eyes and took a deep breath, as if trying to ignore Philomena Mcrae. He opened his eyes, but she was still there.

"Ow!" she said, as she was accidentally on purpose elbowed in the breast by the gangly young man pushing his way through the crowd. Efraim.

He found his way to Guillermo's side. "Hey boss, you look stressed. Want to take a break? Let's go get some water." He grabbed Guillermo's arm and steered him through the throng over to the counter and into the back room. While doing so, he announced loudly that they were taking a quick break and would be out in a sec.

Once in the back, Guillermo bent over and put his hands on his knees, as if he was struggling with something or having an anxiety attack. Efraim handed him a glass of water, which he guzzled down. Clare had come into the back to check on the problem. "What's wrong?"

"That woman," Guillermo gasped, holding the glass out to Efraim for a refill. "The one who was leaning on the console."

"Vampirella?" Clare asked. "The tall gal in the cape? You didn't seem to mind looking at her cleavage. Don't think she didn't notice, but I guess that was the whole purpose of the...."

Guillermo interrupted her. "No, not that one. The other woman. The blonde."

Just then, Ivy poked her head into the back. "Guillermo, there's a woman here who wants to talk to you. She says she's your baby mama..."

"What? No!" Guillermo mopped his face with his hand. "I absolutely did not impregnate her."

Everyone stared at him, so Guillermo went on. "I don't have time to explain the whole excruciating story. I will say that we used to work together, but I have no current connection to that woman. In fact, I thought I had gotten rid of her." He shook his head. "Yet here she is." He started looking around the small room, spotted a window behind him, and attempted to open it.

"Sorry, dude, but that's been painted shut for decades. I've been meaning to work on that, but I never expected to have a perfumer attempt to escape his own launch party by climbing out the window. I'll keep that in mind for next time."

"How can you make light of things at a time like this? I need to get out of here. Now!"

There was suddenly a loud crash from the shop and some shouting. Clare and Ivy ran out, leaving Guillermo with Efraim in the back.

Some guests had fled outside; those who remained were trying to pick up the perfume bottles that had fallen off a shelf. The shelf itself, which was glass, was in pieces on the floor.

"Don't touch anything! We'll get this cleaned up." Ivy ran into the back again for a broom and a trash bag. Guillermo appeared to be hyperventilating into one of the shop's signature tote bags, but Efraim seemed to have things under control. In the meantime, Clare demanded to know what had happened.

"I'm so sorry," Philomena seemed upset. "While I was waiting for Billy to come out of the back, I noticed a perfume on that top shelf that I've been trying to find for ages, Maison Linnet *Vérité Sauvage*. It is just the most splendid chypre! I guess I bumped something on the shelf below it, and it all came crashing down. I will pay for any damages. And I definitely want that Linnet. Do you happen to have more?"

Indeed, there was a second bottle of the Maison Linnet fragrance, which Philomena purchased, along with two bottles of *Lycoctonum* and a new incense-forward fragrance by Aurela Parfums called *Solène*. She also agreed to pay $200 in damages.

Ivy couldn't help but notice that the name on her credit card was Philomena Leight.

"Once again, I am sorry for causing the commotion. I assure you it was not my intention. Now please let me see my Billy and I'll be on my way."

"No, ma'am, you'll be leaving now." Philomena turned to see the source of the voice and found a Baltimore City police officer standing behind her, gesturing toward the open door with one arm, his other hand hovering near his service revolver. At this moment, Guillermo peeked around the corner from the back room and was spotted. Philomena pointed at him and said, "I will see you later" before sweeping out the door with the officer right behind her.

Clare looked at the grandfather clock. "I can't believe it's only 7:30! How much more drama will this evening bring?"

A few minutes after Philomena was escorted out, Guillermo was back in the shop proper. Though he looked a bit peaked, he continued to charm his black-clad fans. Efraim was standing guard near the door, just in case another unwanted trouble-maker appeared. Several of the customers who had fled the shop when the shelf fell to the ground had returned after the clean-up, but others had gone for good, no doubt to post the whole thing on social media. Sure enough, within the next hour Ivy found a couple of videos in which both Good Scents and Guillermo had been tagged.

"No such thing as bad publicity, huh?" Jasmine was still hanging around, still observing. She was definitely getting an eyeful tonight.

"Not if it gets people into the shop." Clare suddenly felt itchy and began randomly moving things around on the counter. She was eager for this evening to end.

"Speaking of that," Jasmine pulled the decant of *Lycoctonum* out of her pocket. "Thanks for this. I hope to give it a thorough sniff tomorrow and write it up. I assume it's okay to mention Good Scents on the blog and on Instagram."

"Yes, please and thank you! We always get an uptick in traffic when you give us a shout-out, which I appreciate."

"My pleasure, Clare. Your events are always so...exciting...I look forward to the next one." Jasmine gave the shop owner a quick hug. "Hopefully, I'll see you soon. Will text you when the blog post goes live so you can expect the additional swarm of customers."

Ivy held up crossed fingers, and Clare put her hands together as if in prayer. Even three extra visitors can make a difference in a month's earnings. Not that Good Scents was in any trouble. Busia Manya had purchased the building in the 1960s, so Clare owned it outright. It was just nice to know that she could afford to invest in fresh stock from up-and-coming perfumers and not have to worry that they had to sell it immediately. Who doesn't like a financial cushion?

By the time it was over, there was no doubt the evening had been a success, without champagne, roses, or candelabra and despite the overabundance of drama. Or maybe because of it. Clare sold all twelve bottles that she had stocked for the event, along with six of the bottles that Guillermo had brought with him. Plenty of samples had been given to folks who preferred to test a scent a few times before making the commitment; Clare was sure at least a couple of them would come back to make the purchase. In addition, she was able to move several bottles of scent from other perfumers.

Guillermo seemed pleased.

"Clare and, um, Ivy, thank you both for tonight. I was actually pretty nervous that it wouldn't go well. I know I can be a polarizing character sometimes, but a lot of that is on purpose. I figured I'd seem more like I was functioning at peak elegance that way."

"Functioning at peak... I get it. Some of it." Clare rolled her eyes and paused before continuing, "I couldn't help but notice that you seemed to have multiple personalities tonight. With some people—like Jasmine, whom you thought could be of help to your career—and the various fawning groupies, you were

Charming Guillermo. Imperious Guillermo came out when you spoke to people whom you felt were beneath you. Unfortunately, that seemed to include Efraim, Ivy, and myself..."

"On that note," Efraim said. "Bossman needs me to procure a bottle of bourbon, so I'm off."

Clare exhaled through her nose. "Then we saw Billy, a mostly nice guy who got panicky when Philomena appeared." Clare threw her hands up in frustration. "Can you see why this bothers me? We all showed up for you tonight, and instead of a steady Gracious Guillermo, we got a patchwork. You can't afford that. You can create brilliance in a bottle, but if you can't connect with the people around you, whether they wear it or sell it, it doesn't matter."

"I know. But right now, I'm emotionally exhausted and just want to lock myself in my hotel room with a fifth of something boozy." Guillermo sighed deeply, rolling his head on his neck to ease some of the evening's pent-up tension. "Would it be okay if I left my extra bottles here and picked them up tomorrow morning before you open? I kinda want to get out-of-town ay-sap."

"Sure, no worries. I'll pack them up for you, so they'll be waiting when you get here. We open at 10am, but I'll be here at least an hour earlier to clean up this mess." Clare shook her head at the disheveled state of the room. Ivy was already at work scooping up discarded perfume blotters into a trash bag and straightening bottles that had been knocked askew, as well as checking the floor carefully for any shards of glass that might have escaped the earlier cleanup.

"We'll have to fumigate this place too," Ivy remarked. "No offense, Billy, but that stuff packs a real olfactory wallop."

"None taken." Guillermo went over to Ivy and said quietly, "I am so sorry for misnaming you earlier. I was going with the flow of my perfumer persona and forget sometimes that I'm talking to real people and not other... phonies." He turned to Clare. "I would like to avail myself of your facilities before I leave, if that's okay."

Ten minutes later, he was gone.

Six

THE NEXT MORNING, CLARE finished tidying up the shop and enjoyed an egg sandwich and a coffee before officially opening at 10am. The smell of the egg didn't help with the general perfumy fug in the room, so she propped the front door open for a while. The chilly morning breeze worked like a magic broom as it swept through the shop and neutralized the air.

Because the day seemed to start extra slowly, especially after the hubbub of the previous evening, Clare decided that the free time would be an excellent opportunity to put up a new counter display. A regular customer had the brilliant idea of introducing a suggestion box for things that people wanted to smell like but didn't already occupy shelf space in the store. Clare had found a wooden tissue box cover at a thrift store and put it over an empty box from which she had cut the top. Next to it, she placed a stack of colorful cardboard squares with three questions: name, scent idea, and why? Last was a hand-lettered sign that read, "Have a scent idea? Drop it into the box. If we love it, we'll find it and carry it!" If anything, searching fragrances to fit the suggestions could be a fun diversion during the store's downtime. She pushed Harbaugh, the taxidermy raven, to the far end of the counter, closer to the front wall, and placed the new suggestion box next to the credit card machine.

No customers had come into the shop by 11:30, and Guillermo still hadn't shown up to pick up the rest of his bottles. Clare tried calling and texting him but got no answer. Maybe he was hungover or had skipped town already? Or had Philomena found him? The memory of last night's encounter raised the hairs on her arms. Maybe she should check on him. After all, he was staying just a few blocks away at Ferguson's Wharf, a quick walk. It would be fine to shut the store for half an hour or so.

She toyed with the idea of taking his boxes herself but didn't want to risk tripping on the picturesque yet treacherous cobblestones of Thames Street and dropping something. But why couldn't Efraim just pick the stuff up? Wasn't he Guillermo's assistant?

Clare taped a sign to the door, "back at 12:30pm" and locked it behind her before heading down Thames Street. She took her time walking as it was a beautiful, sunny and pleasantly breezy morning. In Baltimore, the first few weeks of October could be an extension of summer—plenty warm and humid—with the occasional surprise at the end of the month. She could recall wearing a coat on Halloween some years and sweating through her costume on others.

She was still amazed that the enormous building on the water side of Thames Street, between Broadway and Ann Street, was now a fancy hotel. Clare remembered when it had been empty, though it still bore the marks of having served as the police precinct building in the '90s television series *Homicide: Life on the Streets*. Her mom had said that before that, the building had been a recreation center. There had been swing sets on the roof and basketball courts indoors, and Teresa would go there with her brother to play table tennis. These days, the building that was repurposed into the Sagamore Pendry Hotel looked mostly the same on the front, but it had been built out further over the water on a reinforced pier. Clare couldn't afford to eat at the Rec Pier Chop House restaurant there, but she enjoyed walking through the hotel to marvel at the swimming pool that seemed to merge seamlessly with the harbor beyond. Though with much cleaner water.

Clare also had to walk past two bakeries, Pitango and Sacré Sucré, on the way to Ferguson's and wished she hadn't had that egg sandwich for breakfast already. Maybe she could have an almond croissant for lunch though? A few minutes later, she was at the hotel's front desk. The clerk there had her cellphone propped up against a potted plant and was absorbed in that week's episode of *Southern Socialites.*

After being ignored for a few beats, Clare cleared her throat loudly. "Has Guillermo Flares checked out yet?" The clerk, clearly annoyed by the interruption, reluctantly looked up. She clackity clacked on her computer keyboard, then reported, "No, he has not, though he was scheduled to leave today. I'm afraid we're going to have to charge him for an extra day, since it looks like he is going to miss the noon check-out time."

"Do you think you could give me his room number so I could go up and check on him? Maybe his alarm clock didn't go off this morning. He was quite exhausted last night, so he could just be sleeping soundly." The clerk shrugged, as if to say, "Not my problem," and went back to her melodrama.

Clare took a moment to listen to the audio coming from the clerk's phone. It sounded like women arguing. Clare had a thought. "Actually, I know exactly what is going on here. He probably picked up somebody at the bar and took her to his room. I'm going straight up there to give him a piece of my mind."

The clerk looked at her suspiciously. "I'm his, um, girlfriend." Clare hoped she was at least a little convincing. Thankfully, she hadn't chosen to wear the She-Hulk tee that morning. The clerk, seeing an opportunity to witness some real-life drama, grabbed a key and said, "Let me take you up."

Knocking on the door brought no response, so the clerk unlocked it and pushed it open. The room was empty, disturbingly ordinary, and entirely lacking in the drama the clerk had been hoping to witness. With no chance of live drama, the disappointed clerk turned abruptly and went back to her post, leaving Clare alone.

The air reeked of *Lycoctonum*, but also something else that Clare couldn't put her nose on. It was a sensation rather than a smell—a yellow heat, burning, fire. She could see from the doorway that the bed hadn't been slept in. Maybe she was correct in thinking that Guillermo met someone last night, perhaps Vampirella, but they went back to her place. Or did Philomena find him somewhere and make good on her threat to "see him later?" Clare quickly banished the thought and hoped Philomena was cooling her heels in jail somewhere, though that wasn't likely as she hadn't committed a crime. Yet. It made sense that Guillermo had been distracted by last night's activity; perhaps he simply forgot about picking up his leftover fragrance or even checking out of his hotel. But hadn't he said something about drinking some bourbon before going to bed? Clare saw no evidence of bottles or glasses, nor did she see the pink sparkles that, in her mind's nose, suggested the presence of whiskey. Certainly, the yellow heat was something else entirely.

Before she left, Clare checked the bathroom; that door was ajar. As she approached, she noticed something dark on the tile floor. It was a shoe. Unfortunately, there was a foot in that shoe, with a whole body connected to the foot. It belonged to the perfumer, who was splayed face down on the floor.

"Billy!" Clare shouted and hurried to his side. She knelt and was about to touch him when she noticed his eyes were open. "Oh, no, oh no oh no!" She pulled out her phone and called 911. While she waited for the police to show up, she tiptoed around the room trying to piece together what had happened. Nothing appeared particularly out of place. The closet door was not closed all the way, and through the small crack she could see that he had hung up his suit jacket. His toothbrush was in the sink basin along with some frothy greenish stuff; whatever went on had happened while he was brushing his teeth. Clare couldn't see the front of his shirt as he was prone, but the back of it appeared dry, as did his hair. It didn't seem that he had been shot. Also, there was no blood anywhere. Perhaps he had a heart attack?

Eventually, she heard some noise in the hallway. Moving quickly away the body, Clare met a police officer and team of paramedics at the door and led them to the bathroom. They confirmed Billy's death immediately. "He's in full rigor, so he's been gone for hours."

The police officer quickly surveyed the scene and then turned to Clare. After introducing himself as Officer Charles Bacon, he asked, "Ma'am, do you know the deceased? Are you his wife?"

Nervous, Clare stammered, "Yes, the deceased is Guillermo Flares. I'm Clare Buchowski, and I grew up with Mr Flares. He was in town for an event at my shop, Good Scents. He is...was...a perfumer, and I was showcasing his first solo fragrance. He was supposed to be back at the shop this morning to pick up some of the inventory that hadn't sold, and when he didn't show up, I thought I'd come check on him. The desk clerk brought me to his room, where I discovered him on the floor. I didn't touch him or anything else. I was going to check his pulse, but I noticed his eyes were open and realized he was dead." At that, Clare let out a sob.

"Did Mr Flares seem okay when he left your store last night, Ms Buchowski?"

"Yes. I mean, no. It was actually hard to tell. There was quite a bit of drama last night, involving more than one of the people who had attended the event. At one point, it looked like Billy...Guillermo...he was William when we were kids, William Leight was his birth name..." Clare was shaking.

"Perhaps you should sit down, Ms Buchowski."

"No, no. I'm fine. And I wouldn't want to touch anything or disturb any evidence."

"Why would you assume that this was anything but a natural death, Ms Buchowski?"

"Billy was 30 years old. Why would a 30-year-old die while brushing his teeth?"

"It happens. He may have had a history of heart issues. Arrhythmia, the like. People die all the time, Ms Buchowski, at any age. If Mr Flares was from out of town and died suddenly, the medical examiner will probably want an autopsy to determine the cause of death. And if anything suspicious turns up, there will be an investigation. As it stands, the only thing out of place here is you, Ms Buchowski. I suggest you go home and wait to hear from us. But as you seem to think this might be a case of foul play, I'm going to invoke an old cliché, 'don't leave town' as you might be needed for questioning at some point."

Clare frowned. She was attending a perfume show in New York in a couple of weeks.

"I'm kidding, Ms Buchowski. Only TV cops say that sort of thing."

After giving Officer Bacon her details and Billy's parents' address, Clare left the hotel. She felt guilty leaving her former childhood friend all alone on the bathroom floor. "But he's dead," she reminded herself. *Dead.* Not 24 hours ago she'd watched him hyperventilate in her back room and thought it was nothing more than nerves. Now her imagination filled in what she might have overlooked.

As she trudged up Fell Street on her way back to the Good Scents, Clare decided that after what she had just been through she deserved a pastry. Or two. After all, she could be in shock, and sugar was always good for that sort of thing. She stopped at Sacré Sucré and bought a cardamom bun and a monkey bread. After another 200 steps, she realized she had bought nothing with which to wash down her treats, so she stopped at Pitango Bakery for a chai. The spinach feta croissant looked especially good, so she ordered one of those as well, plus a chocolate walnut cookie and a coconut macaroon. Clare couldn't help that she loved baked goods almost as much as she loved perfume. Both made her feel good, and right now she needed that in a bad way.

Seven

Clare was deep in thought when she reached Good Scents and almost tripped over something near the shop's door. She looked down to see two small black teddy bears, heads together as if mourning the dead, clustered with several dark roses and a candle that had been lit briefly but was otherwise brand new. It appeared to be a shrine of some sort. What was going on? How did Ivy find out already?

Ivy had replaced the "back at 12:30" sign that Clare had taped to the window with the one that said "closed." When Clare unlocked the door, she found Ivy hunched on a chair in the back room, knees in her face, feet on the seat.

"Hey, don't yell at me. I didn't feel like working today, so I closed the shop. I am exhausted from yesterday."

"How did you know about Billy?" Clare put her purchases down on a shelf and took off her jacket.

"Yeah, what happened there? I see his stuff is still in the shop."

Clare told her cousin that he hadn't shown up, so she went to his hotel to find him. "I found him all right. Dead on the bathroom floor."

"Good one, Cuz. Are you sure he wasn't just passed out drunk? Why would he be dead? We just saw him here, being a somewhat charming jerk. He seemed fine when he left last night, didn't he?"

"You didn't think he looked a bit pale? A little off?"

"Well, he had a couple of scares last night, between that Philomena woman and his sister. I figured he just needed a good night's sleep. A good stiff drink or three. Okay, stiff might be an awful choice of words." Ivy paused. Sipping her coffee, she realized by the look on Clare's face that she wasn't kidding. "Billy's dead..." The sentence hung there, quiet and unfinished, like it had surprised her to say it aloud.

"Unfortunately. And I found the body."

"Mother of pearl.... And you found him? He's like, *dead*, dead?" Ivy jumped off her perch on the chair and pushed her cousin down in her place. "Maybe you should sit."

"He was as dead as one can get." Clare opened a bag and attempted to extract a pastry. "I'm actually glad you didn't open the shop. I can't imagine dealing with customers today. I'm shaking so badly I can't get this thing out of the bag." After a bit more struggle, Clare finally wrestled the monkey bread out of its container, pulled off one of its croissant-like protuberances and stuffed it in her mouth.

"Ew. How can you eat after finding a dead body?"

"I'm eating my feelings," Clare mumbled with her mouth full. "What about that shrine though? When did that show up?"

"What shrine?" Ivy loped into the shop and peeked out the window. "Yup. Looks like a shrine. Kinda creepy." She grabbed the chocolate muffin she had been eating and picked off a piece of crust. "Musta just happened. I've been here for like 45 minutes, and there was nothing out there when I arrived." Ivy ate the crust and pulled off another bite. "So, what do you think happened? Are you absolutely, positively sure that..."

"I believe the paramedic. And the cop. He said there was a good chance that the medical examiner would request an autopsy, so we'll find out then." She was going to add that she felt Guillermo had been poisoned but thought better of speculating right now. She wasn't in the mood to answer any more of Ivy's questions.

"You're awfully quiet all of a sudden, Clare. What are you thinking?"

Clare shook her head. "I think we should put the rest of the bottles of *Lycoctonum* on the shelf. Nobody's going to be picking them up now, and once this gets out, it might be in demand. It's sad that there's not enough inventory to make a significant amount of money, but perhaps we'll make enough to help pay for the funeral. Oh, his poor parents! The police are probably there right now giving them the bad news."

Just then, someone rapped on the front door, which gave both ladies a start. "Maybe it's the police?" Clare went into the shop, pulled back the window shade, and saw her mother standing there with a look of concern on her face. She quickly opened the door.

"Oh my gosh, Mom, I totally forgot about Vetiver. C'mere, boy." Clare bent over to greet her scruffy mutt, then stood up to kiss her mother on the cheek.

"I see. Vetiver gets a kiss first, then your mother."

"Hi, Aunt Terri. Sorry we forgot about the mutt. It's been...a morning." Ivy came out of the back room with one of the many white bakery bags in her hand. "Want a cookie?" She offered the bag to her aunt.

Teresa Buchowski sniffed the air. "Hm. I think you need to fumigate this place. It smells of fried eggs and death."

"Funny you should say that..." said Ivy at the same time that Clare exclaimed, "How did you know?"

"Know what? I have some errands to run and figured, since I hadn't heard from you, that you were probably hungover from last night's festivities. Thought I'd wake you up and return my granddog." Terri looked around the shop and spotted the missing shelf. "What happened here? Oh, and what is that pile of stuff outside? You know the trash men won't pick up unless everything is in a can."

Clare opened the door and looked at the ground in front of her shop. When she had returned from the hotel, there had been just a few flowers and candles, but now there were ten times as many. She didn't realize black teddy bears and roses were so easy to procure on a random Friday in October, but when she looked closely, she saw that some of them had been spray-painted.

"Mom," she said as she went back into the shop and closed and locked the door behind her. "That's not garbage. That's a shrine. Billy Leight is dead."

"Oh, heavens!" Teresa put a hand over her mouth. "His poor mother. What happened?"

"I really don't know. All I can tell you is that he was supposed to come over this morning to pick up the rest of his bottles," Clare pointed to the cartons on the floor, "and when he didn't, I went to his hotel to see if he was ok. And he wasn't—he was dead on the bathroom floor."

Teresa slowly blew a stream of air through her lips, as if to calm herself. "I'm so sorry, love. I remember you guys were close when you were young. And you had such a thing for him."

"Mom, I was a kid."

"Yes, but you were so serious. You had to be here at your grandmother's to see him when he came to visit and threw a tantrum when anything changed your plans. Like homework, or dance class, or a trip down the ocean. It didn't last long, but it was pretty intense while it did."

"I honestly don't remember any of that. I remember thinking he was cute, but I don't remember being obsessed like that. Besides, he was my BFF, so we didn't like each other that way. At any rate, he grew up and went away, became a perfumer. And he changed. He didn't seem like the same nice kid we knew. He was mean to Ivy and treated us like staff. And now he's dead."

Ivy interrupted, "He wasn't entirely mean. He did apologize to me for calling me by my deadname. He said it was just part of the new persona he had adopted, along with the new name."

Just then, a text came in from Jasmine.

`Jasmine: Post is up! Here's to new customers! I sent a text to Guillermo, but he hasn't responded.`

```
Clare: Because he's dead
Jasmine: Ha ha!
Clare: I'm serious, Jas. I found him...
Jasmine: Holy...
```

Jasmine quickly edited her post just moments before Ivy pulled it up on her phone.

Black Narcisse

Fragrance Review: *Lycoctonum* by Guillermo Flares

Availability: Currently only at Good Scents in Fells Point, Baltimore

Scent Type: Gothic floral

Wear Time: Long

Projection: Extreme

Vibe: "Poison garden at twilight"

I've smelled a lot of perfumes that want to be dark, mysterious, and a little dangerous. Most of them just come out smelling like a mall witch with a Sephora gift card. But *Lycoctonum*, Guillermo Flares' first and final release, is the real thing. This scent doesn't flirt with darkness. It blooms in it.

Let's talk composition. You won't find "wolfsbane" listed anywhere on the label, but the name says it all. *Lycoctonum*, the scientific name for that infamous poisonous flower, hangs over the scent like a velvet shroud. There's no loud top note shouting for attention. Instead, it opens in a hush: bitter green blackcurrant buds, a curl of absinthe, a thread of clary sage that smells like something dry and sharp tucked between the pages of a grimoire.

The floral heart is ghostly. Violet leaf and what I swear is a ghost of hellebore—bitter, white, not quite real. A dark rose that doesn't bloom so much as bleed into the rest. It doesn't smell fresh. It smells remembered.

But it's in the base where the magic happens. This is where the whole thing collapses like a ruined cathedral into damp oakmoss, leather-bound secrets, black amber, and this inky, iron-laced finish that made me pause. It's not pretty. But it is beautiful. You feel me?

Like cool velvet on skin. Like dusk in an old forest. Like the last word in a letter you were never meant to read.

Final Thoughts: Wearing *Lycoctonum* feels like keeping a secret. Or confessing one. It's not for everyone—but if you wear it, it will wear you back.

4.8/5 stars

Would I buy it again? If I could. But the batch is limited.

ETA: And Guillermo is dead.

Clare finished reading and was quiet for a few minutes, trying to decide if they should open Good Scents after all, since the post mentioned the shop. People had been coming around to add things to the shrine. Perhaps they wanted to come inside? Wait! The shrine!

"I have a question. Can someone tell me how a shrine was erected within minutes of my discovering Billy was dead? As far as I know, the only people who are aware of this fact are the police, the paramedics, and the three of us."

"And Jasmine."

"Right, and Jasmine. Who I told just minutes ago. Someone else had to know."

"Maybe one of the paramedics had loose lips?" Teresa offered.

"That's a problem. But also, it's not like Guillermo was real-world famous. Just Instagram-famous."

"I think that counts as famous enough," Ivy countered. "There are lots of people the general public don't know but still have millions of followers on social media."

"Right. So that is a possibility. Or it could be one of the hotel workers. The person who took me up to the room, the front desk clerk, didn't hang around with me long enough to see the body, but she might have come back up with the paramedics? But then again, she didn't seem to recognize his name when I initially asked if he had checked out."

"Maybe someone from housekeeping? They all have keys, right? Maybe someone found the body before you did, could identify it, and then blabbed on social media?"

"Whoever it was, I still don't feel right about opening the shop today. Besides, it's already 3. No use opening for a handful of hours. Let's call it a day and head home."

"Three already! I need to get going." Teresa kissed her daughter and hugged her niece before opening the door. "It's looking like a funeral parlor out here," she muttered to herself as she closed the door behind her.

Eight

THE NEXT MORNING, CLARE climbed out of bed and clipped Vetiver into his harness. It was grey and drizzly outside, which somehow felt right. She put a raincoat over her sweatshirt and jeans and slipped out the door onto Broadway. The wet cobblestones shone slickly in the feeble morning light as the woman and her dog made their way west toward Caroline Street.

Clare hadn't been able to sleep for most of the night, her mind too busy trying to figure out how Billy had died. She replayed the scene over and over again, but nothing seemed especially suspicious. The best she could tell was that Billy made it back to the room, removed his jacket and hung it in the closet, then went to the bathroom to brush his teeth. And then what happened? Had he had a heart attack? Had he fainted, hit his head on the edge of the sink basin and fallen to the ground? He had been prone, with his face slightly turned toward the sink. She could see only one eye and half of his face. Might he have had a head injury on the hidden side? She wished she had tried to turn him over, but she knew she had been right not to. Besides, she heard the paramedic say that he was in full rigor mortis, which would have made him too stiff for her to move.

She thought about the scene a bit more as she watched Vetiver do his business. What was she missing? There had been an overnight bag on the bed, but it was zipped shut so she couldn't see what was inside. His shoes were still on his feet. And where was Efraim? He had left the shop a few minutes before Billy in order to pick up the bottle of bourbon he had requested. Demanded, even. Clare was pretty sure she had not seen a bottle anywhere in the room, nor had she seen Efraim. What had happened to him? She wished she knew more about the man. Did Billy know him from New York, or had they met in Baltimore?

And then there was the mysterious smell. Rather, not a smell but a sensation. She noticed it just around Billy's body. He positively reeked of *Lycoctonum*, but there was also this peculiar yellow flame-like heat emanating from him. It wasn't an element of his perfume creation; she had smelled enough of it during the event that she would never forget it. It was something else that didn't belong. What was it?

When she got back to the shop, Clare realized she didn't want to think about the events of the day before, so she picked a fragrance that was both light and soothing. Winter's Tale *Skin Memory*, with its combination of white tea, orris, linden, rice steam, and white musk was the kind of scent that you wear when you don't want to be asked how you're doing but need something to remind you that you'll make it through the day. It's like a favorite sweater, worn thin and familiar.

As she opened Good Scents, she couldn't help but look at the ever-growing heap of remembrances that were being left in front of the shop. The teddy bears were soggy with rain, yet the blackness of every item in the pile made it look like it had been charred in a fire.

Ivy grabbed the phone on the second ring; calls had been coming in non-stop. She was tired of answering, but a few of them had been requests to put bottles of *Lycoctonum* on hold. There had even been an international call requesting that two bottles of the scent be mailed to the UK. Between the calls and the influx of customers, they'd be sold out in another couple of days. "Good Scents, may I help you?"

"This is Detective Ayanna Briscoe for Clare Buchowski."

"Hold on please," Ivy put the phone on the counter and poked her head into the back room where Clare was packing up the bottles for the UK requester. "There's a detective on the phone for you. Ayanna Briscoe."

Clare went into the front of the store and picked up the receiver. "Hello? This is Clare Buchowski." She felt nervous. Was the detective calling to tell her that Billy had been murdered? That she was a suspect? She knew that the person who found the body was always a suspect, at least in her favorite crime procedurals. Sometimes they were the actual killer.

"Ms Buchowski, this is Detective Ayanna Briscoe from the Baltimore City Police Department. I was wondering if I could speak to you about Guillermo Flares."

"Of course, Detective. What would you like to know?"

"I would rather meet in person, Ms Buchowski. Would that be possible? I could come to you if that's convenient. I wouldn't mind seeing the place Mr Flares had been before his unfortunate end."

"Are you saying that he was murdered?" Ivy, who had been standing practically on Clare's feet, eavesdropping, opened her eyes wide.

"I would rather not discuss that on the phone. Is there a time that is most convenient for you to meet today? Would you possibly be available in an hour or so?"

Just before 2pm, Detective Briscoe opened the shop door. She closed her umbrella with one hand and shook off the excess rain before stepping inside and depositing it in the receptacle just within the doorway. In her other hand, she held a large hot beverage cup and a somewhat soggy white paper bag. "Can I put these down somewhere so I can get out of this wet jacket?"

Clare, who had been waiting for the detective, took the cup and bag from her hand and put them on the counter. She then helped Detective Briscoe out of her jacket. "Let me hang this up in the back room for you."

The detective looked around the room and, seeing two customers whispering in the corner, said, "Is there somewhere more private we could talk?"

"Of course. Follow me."

Ivy indicated that she had the shop, and Clare led Detective Briscoe through the doorway into the back room. She then opened another door that revealed a somewhat steep staircase to her second-floor apartment. "I hope you don't mind dogs, Detective. I have a terrier mix, and he might be a little curious about you."

Briscoe followed Clare upstairs into the cozy kitchen area. Vetiver padded in from the next room and gave a sharp bark before carefully sniffing the detective's pants legs. Once satisfied that their visitor was okay, he went over to his bed in the corner and curled up in it.

"Now, what can I do for you, Detective?"

Ayanna Briscoe took out her notebook and pen. "I know you told the officer at the crime scene, but I'd like you to tell me again how you knew Mr Flares and how you came to find his body."

Clare told Detective Briscoe about knowing Guillermo as children, about his spending time in the shop with her grandmother, and that they didn't have much contact after grade school. She had heard snippets about his life now and again over the years, but until he came to see her the previous month, she hadn't spoken to him in at least a decade. She related the events of the party, how he had words with his sister Stephanie and a woman who claimed to be the mother of the children he insisted he didn't have. Otherwise, the evening had been a success in every way. She told the detective about worrying when he hadn't shown up the next morning and her decision to visit him at the hotel. Clare then described the crime scene to the best of her ability.

"Is it true that since he was a visitor to Baltimore and died alone in a hotel room, the Medical Examiner will require an autopsy?"

"Yes. That should happen sometime later today." Detective Briscoe glanced at her shirt while taking a sip of her matcha latte and was dismayed to see it coated with a dusting of powdered sugar from her almond croissant. She flicked at it with her hand before realizing it was now all over Clare's tablecloth.

"When do you expect the results? Tomorrow or the next day?"

"Ms Buchowski, this is not considered a suspicious death, so the timeline for results won't be as expedient as you would like."

"If it's not a suspicious death, Detective, then why are you here questioning me?"

"Standard procedure. We need to rule out foul play. And if the autopsy finds something suspicious, we've already got a jump on getting information from any witnesses that might have been on the scene."

"I see." Clare thought for a moment. "If the autopsy shows nothing conclusive, no heart attack or stroke, will there be a toxicology report done? Would that be available in the next week or so?"

"This is the real world, not television," Detective Briscoe advised. "It could be months before the results of the toxicology report are available. The best we can do in the short term is get an idea of the contents of Mr. Flare's stomach at the time of death. Other than that, we won't know for a while.'"

"I believe Mr Flares was poisoned."

"Sure, I suppose that is possible. Or a drug overdose. But let's not get ahead of ourselves. According to the paramedics' report, his death does not seem to result from a gunshot wound or blunt force, nor did he seem to be stabbed, but it could be anything at this point. Again, it's possible this was a completely natural death."

Clare paced for a minute, then stopped. "I don't think so. I know this will seem strange to you, but I sensed the poison. I just don't know what it is yet. It's a substance I haven't encountered before."

"You 'sensed' it? Hmm. Interesting. Please, tell me about this sensation." Detective Briscoe's tone was patient, probing but not dismissive. Clare ran a perfume shop—certainly eccentric—but she didn't seem unmoored from reality. Ayanna uncrossed her legs, then recrossed them in the opposite direction as she waited for the shop owner to continue. She brushed a light dusting of powdered sugar from her dark pants.

After taking a deep breath, Clare related the story of her long-ago car accident and the subsequent changes to her olfactory abilities.

"I smelled *Lycoctonum* for the first time when Guillermo brought me a lab sample—about 8 milliliters of the scent in a small generic bottle. After the usual spritz on a paper blotter and giving it a good sniff, I tried it on my skin. I could detect the tang of the blackcurrant, a prominent dark rose note, a vanilla-y warmth from the amber and the tolu balsam, and the leather. I felt rather than smelled the 'hellebore accord,' which gave the sensation of both large spikes and tiny pellets in multiple shades of green, with just a hint of metallic cucumber from the violet leaf and the earthiness of angelica. Overall, the fragrance was eerie and beautiful. Not as strange as it might have been, but definitely far from commercial."

Detective Briscoe continued to listen patiently before mumbling, "It just smelled like perfume to me, but then I don't wear the stuff...." Clare noticed the slight hesitation in the detective's voice and the way her eyes drifted briefly, as if recalling something distant. "My mom wore *Shalimar*, and I get nostalgic any time I smell it. I even have a small bottle of it to sniff when I miss her the most," the detective admitted, a bit sheepishly.

"There is hope for you yet, Detective," Clare smiled. "We'll make a perfume lover out of you before you know it."

"Yes, yes," Detective Briscoe took another sip of her matcha. "Continue with the smell you didn't smell, Ms. Buchowski."

"It's not that I smelled nothing. I smelled everything that I just described to you, the blackcurrant, rose, amber, and leather, and I still detected the green spikes and pellets. However, I felt an additional sensation when I sniffed the body."

"You actually sniffed the body?" Briscoe ended her musing about fragrances and put her cup down. This was taking the love of smells maybe a tad too far.

"The air around the body. I didn't know Bil... Guillermo was dead at the time. I saw him on the floor, thought he might have fallen and hurt himself, or fainted, so I knelt beside him to check his pulse. But that wasn't necessary. His eyes were open, but he wasn't seeing anything." Clare paused and took a breath. "I could smell the strong fragrance of *Lycoctonum* on his person, which made sense as he had sprayed it so many times at the event. It was on his clothes and in his hair. At that point, I was extremely familiar with the perfume and all the feelings it gave me. But as I said, I could feel something extra. There was a burning sensation in the air. Not a smell, just a sharp yellow heat, like a flame, and it emanated from somewhere on his person. At that point, I refrained from touching the body. I've watched enough television procedurals that I know better than to potentially tamper with evidence."

"The Baltimore City Police Department appreciates that."

"So, what happens next? Have the next-of-kin been informed? Will there be a press conference?"

"Ms Buchowski, you watch entirely too much television." Clare couldn't disagree with that assessment. "Yes, his parents have been called. Thank you for providing the contact information. As for the press conference...no. There are so far no signs of foul play. And Mr Flares wasn't a local politician or celebrity.

He wasn't famous at all. There is no need to speak to the press about any of this."

"But he was Instagram-famous! Didn't you notice the growing pile of teddy bears and roses in front of the building?"

"You mean the pile of burnt trash? You know it won't be picked up unless it's in the proper receptacle..."

Clare interrupted the detective. "It's a shrine! To Guillermo Flares! Take a look on your way out. Almost everything in it is black, which is a color associated with him on his Instagram. Most of the attendees at the launch party last night were dressed head-to-toe in black. You know... like Goths."

"Goths?"

"Yes, people who listen to a particular genre of music. They wear black or dark clothing, sometimes pale makeup, but not always. I know I'm oversimplifying, and not everyone who dresses this way is necessarily 'goth.' They could be 'emo,' or maybe they just like watching *The Addams Family* and wearing black."

"You seem to know a lot about this topic, Ms. Buchowski."

"Actually, I don't. But the PR material for Mr. Flares' fragrance called it a 'gothic floral,' so I did some research to understand the concept. And honestly, I still don't fully get it. Some insist that goths must like goth music; others don't. The music fans consider non-fans posers. Really, the term is mostly a catch-all for anyone who looks a certain way—black clothes, dark hair, pale skin, an embrace of darkness or even death—but mostly, it's just a stereotype."

"I see." Detective Briscoe didn't, but she also didn't think music or fashion mattered much in this case. "And this Instagram thing... Mr. Flares was popular there?"

Clare spent a few minutes outlining the social media connections for the detective and suggested that news of Guillermo's death must have spread that way. "I know Jasmine Reed's blog post reviewing *Lycoctonum* went viral through her Instagram account. What I don't know is who first posted about Guillermo's death before that. From what I can piece together, the timeline looks like this: I found the body, then returned to the shop to find the shrine already started. After that, Jasmine posted her review, and the shrine's popularity exploded. I'm assuming the shrine expanded because of her post, which revealed that Guillermo Flares had died. The question is, who learned about Guillermo's death in that roughly ninety-minute window between when I discovered his body and when I returned to the shop?"

Detective Briscoe thought for a few moments.

"Perhaps you posted on Instagram when you found the body? After all, wouldn't a dead perfumer be good for sales? Especially if the scent is marketed toward a population who, as you say, 'embrace darkness and perhaps even death'?"

"There it is," Clare thought. She found the body, so she was a suspect.

"I did not post about his death. You can check my account." She continued, "Detective, according to Mr Flares, there were only 40 bottles produced. Once those were sold, there would be no more. That's such a small number it wouldn't be any problem at all to sell them whether the perfumer was alive or dead. They might sell faster if the perfumer were dead, but once they were sold, they were gone. A live perfumer is always going to be more valuable because they could bring out a second edition of a discontinued fragrance or even create more fragrances."

Detective Briscoe considered this and had to agree that by this logic, a dead perfumer isn't particularly valuable to the owner of a perfume shop. "If you didn't post about his death, then who did? As you seem to be full of theories, I'm sure you have one in this case as well."

Clare shook her head. "No, not really. Ivy—my assistant, whom you met when you came in—and I had been going over the possibilities. There were two paramedics and Officer Bacon, who for sure knew that Guillermo was dead, but not that he was anyone worth talking about. It's likely someone from the hotel staff found out if they had been nosy enough to follow the paramedics upstairs and listen outside the door. Other than that, I do not know. Unless," she paused, screwing up her face in thought, "someone found him before I did. Like a housekeeper or anyone else with a key to the room. The paramedic said that Guillermo was in full rigor mortis, so he had been dead for hours. Someone could have entered his room at any time during the night and into the morning."

"Housekeeping would only attempt to clean a room after 8 or 9am. And I would hope that one would alert hotel management upon finding a dead body on the premises."

Clare shrugged. She could think of only one other person who might have had access to the room key.

"I think that's all I have for you right now, Ms Buchowski." Detective Briscoe closed her notebook, stood, and brushed off any additional powdered sugar on her clothes. As she headed down the stairs to the shop, she said, "If you think of anything else that could be useful to us, should this turn out to be anything other than a natural death, please call me." After handing a business card to both Clare and Ivy, the detective put on her raincoat, took her umbrella, and went out into the downpour. She stopped and looked at the shrine. It still appeared to be a pile of burnt garbage, but when she looked closer, she recognized that there were soggy black plushies and bunches of black spray-painted flowers in the heap. She took a photo with her phone and headed through the rain back to her car.

"What was that all about?" Ivy looked alarmed as Clare came back into the shop. "Does she think you killed Billy?"

"Possibly." Clare then quickly added, "But I didn't."

"Of course you didn't, Cuz. Why would you? The question is: Who did?"

Clare thought about it for a long moment, considering all the visitors to the shop the night before, plus the legions of people that Billy had probably ticked off in the last few years.

"I feel like there are at least three people who could have done it, just by what I saw last night. Clare raised her index finger. "That Philomena person, who scared the bejeezus out of him. He made her sound like a stalker." She raised her middle finger. “His sister, Stephanie, who bullied him practically from birth.” Then, her ring finger went up. “And Efraim, his assistant, who Billy didn’t treat particularly well.”

“He’s a perfumer, too.” Ivy added. “He told me he was originally hired as a lab assistant.”

“Interesting. So all three of them potentially have experience with poisonous substances.” Clare paced the room. “Then there’s our mystery guest.”

“Which one? There were lots of people here we didn’t know.”

“One in particular, a good-looking guy in a suit. Said his name was Damarion Washington.”

“That’s a coincidence! You have a friend with that name.”

“Not a coincidence, Ivy. He was pretending to be Damarion. I texted the real deal, and he said it could have been a perfumer called Rafael Campos. The guy barely left the doorway. It’s like he was just here to watch Billy.”

“Seems sketch, Cuz. I think we should add him to the suspect list.”

“But does he have a motive for murder?”

“I have a feeling you’re going to try to find out.”

Nine

IVY ALWAYS HAD BOUNDLESS energy, fueled in no small part by all the caffeine she consumed daily, and she liked to keep busy. To prevent her from bouncing off the walls, Clare suggested she regularly dust the shelves with the long-handled feather duster that had once belonged to their grandmother. And because it was such an old-fashioned cleaning tool, Ivy insisted on wearing a frilly white apron while she worked. Today, she wore a snug black t-shirt with a long black tutu—a combination that, along with her long arms and legs, gave her serious French-maid-ostrich vibes.

After an hour of flitting about, Ivy dusted her hands off and surveyed her work. "It must be the chill in the air, but I'm always hungry these days. I could murder some tempura broccoli from Ekiben. Interested?"

"Unfortunate word choice. But now that you mention it, I could eat some tofu nuggets—or shrimp snacks. Your choice."

Once Ivy headed out on her snack run, Clare returned to scrolling through the accounts following Guillermo Flares on Instagram. She wasn't sure what she hoped to find, but poking around couldn't hurt. He had a ridiculous 32k followers, impressive for someone who hadn't yet released any of his own fragrances. Most accounts were private, likely fans of his pretty face, but there were several belonging to people in the perfume industry. Perhaps she'd spot Philomena this way, though it was possible Guillermo had blocked her. Searches for "Philomena Mccrae" turned up nothing, so maybe she didn't have an account at all. Clare considered using the phone number from Philomena's Good Scents customer account, though she much preferred sending a DM over dealing with her in person.

The bell over the door jingled, pulling Clare from her phone. A young woman entered, her dyed-black hair tipped with purple in a shaggy wolf-cut that highlighted her high cheekbones and long neck. Winged eyeliner and dark lipstick to match the purple tips of her hair gave her an effortlessly precise look. Under her classic trench coat, Clare glimpsed a smart black wide-leg pantsuit paired with a deep purple blouse.

"Excuse me," the woman said as she approached the counter. "I'm Parker Strong. I worked with William Leight at LuxeOne. You might say we were... lab partners. He told me years ago that if anything ever happened to him, I needed to find you and give you this."

She handed Clare a worn black Moleskine notebook. Flipping it open, Clare saw pages filled with notes and formulas for dozens of fragrances. "He carried this everywhere," Parker added, "always scribbling something. He said you'd know what to do with it."

Clare was puzzled. Why would she know what to do with it, and why was she the one entrusted with this information? "Thank you, but I'm not sure why he thought I should have this."

Parker stroked Harbaugh's feathers and cooed at the store's resident taxidermy raven as if it were alive. She looked at Clare. "I don't know what kind of relationship you had with him, but he talked about you all the time. Said you were the only person he trusted. Well, other than me, I guess."

Clare was stunned. She explained to Parker that while she and Billy had been childhood friends, they hadn't spoken in years. Not until the launch party, really.

"Your grandmother was probably Billy's biggest single influence." Parker was wandering around Good Scents, as if she were trying to imagine the old homeopath's shop within the more modern space. "I used to joke with him that his mantra when creating a fragrance was 'WWBMD' as in 'What Would Busia Manya Do?' He laughed, but that was the way he thought. Sure, he learned stuff at perfumery school and could apply those skills at LuxeOne, but he always went back to what she had taught him in his youth." She ran her finger along the shelf holding the last of the *Lycoctonum*. "It was cute, actually. In those moments, he was a little boy again." Parker picked up one of the elegantly packaged bottles and took it to the counter. "I should probably buy one of these. It's not my cup of tea, but it'll be a collector's item someday."

Clare was surprised. "You don't like it?"

"Don't judge a book by its cover, Clare. Despite my propensity to wear black, I like girly florals with lots of orange blossom and musk, like L'Alouette *Neroli Glacé*. It was the PR description that sold me on that one: 'This scent is for the customer who always stops to smell the flowers but also buys the pastry.'"

At that moment, Ivy barged in the door with her arms loaded. She dropped her bags on the counter. "I got both the tofu and the shrimp snacks, and since I had to pass by Kilwin's, I bought some sea-salt caramel fudge for dessert."

"You actually didn't need to get anywhere near Kilwin's."

"I do when I take a detour."

"A woman after my own heart," said Parker, who was still standing by the counter.

"Ivy, this is Parker Strong, a friend of Billy's. She came in to give me a very unusual gift." Clare held up the Moleskine. "She was about to invest in a bottle of *Lycoctonum* when you arrived."

Ivy looked Parker up and down. "Well, any friend of Billy's is...someone I'm not sure about trusting. I've met some of his so-called friends, and they were alarming." She started pulling the food containers out of the bag but thought better of it. "Should I just put this in the back? The onions and fried smells will probably stink up the shop." Clare nodded, and Parker took this as her signal to leave.

"Nice shop you have here. If I find myself in Baltimore again, I'll definitely be back." Before picking up the bag with her purchase and strolling out the door, Parker took the time to fill out a suggestion card and drop it in the box.

The shop was empty for the time being, so Clare walked into the back room to partake of the Ekiben goodness. As she used chopsticks to shovel a piece of tempura-fried broccoli into her mouth, Ivy asked through the shrimp she was chewing, "What was that all about?"

Clare showed her cousin the Moleskine notebook. "Parker said I was the only person he trusted, and he told her to bring this to me if, and I quote, 'anything bad happened to him.'"

"Wow," Ivy replied as she speared a cube of crispy tofu on a single chopstick. "That brings up all sorts of questions. 1. How did she get the notebook? 2. If Billy gave it to her before he came here, did he know something was going to happen? And C. How on earth were you the only person he trusted when he trusted Parker to get the notebook to you?"

Clare added, "Roman numeral IV. What does any of this mean?" Ivy stabbed her cousin in the arm with a dirty chopstick. "Oops. Accidentally got some broccoli schmutz on your sweater. So sorry." After a brief chopstick sword fight, they heard the shop door open again. As she tucked the Moleskine next to a bottle of hand sanitizer and a box of pens within a cubbyhole under the front counter, Clare mused, "I need to put this in a safer place, but where?"

Two people had come into the shop but were not together. The first was a quite elderly gentleman who looked around the shop before shuffling toward Clare. "Hello, young lady, I need your help with something."

"Happy to help, Sir. What do you need?"

"I'm looking for a perfume that I read about in The New York Times recently. It was a very interesting article about a perfumer who has some sort of condition where her senses get crossed."

"That would probably be synesthesia," Clare supplied helpfully.

"Yes, I believe that was it. She has just created a new perfume that is named after a kind of leather." Clare had no idea. She had let her subscription to the Times expire. Fortunately, the person who had come in at the same time and was now browsing on the other side of the room knew exactly what he was talking about.

"Ah! I read that myself the other day! The perfumer was Christine Nagel, and the fragrance was Hermes *Barenia*."

"That's it! Thank you, Miss!" The gentleman turned back to Clare. "Do you have this fragrance? I would love to smell it."

Clare regretfully admitted that their shop did not sell designer fragrances, and sadly the closest place that would carry a luxury brand like Hermes was probably not even in the Baltimore area. The man seemed sad.

The other customer interrupted again. "Sir, I have a bottle of *Barenia* at home. If I made a sample of it and brought it here to the shop, you could return on another day to smell it."

"Ohhh, that would be wonderful! *Barenia* sounds like something my late wife would have enjoyed. It has lily in it. Her name was Lily, and she was quite fond of perfume. I used to buy her a new bottle every Christmas. Her very favorite was Yves Saint Laurent *Paris*." The man's voice became a little shaky at the memory. "I miss her."

Clare wiped away a tear. "Do you live in the neighborhood, Mr..."

"Barnard. Walter Barnard. Yes, I live over on Ann Street. I like to walk through the neighborhood on nice days and have passed by here many times. I remember when it was a shop that sold folk remedies, but that was some time ago now."

"That was my grandmother's shop. She dabbled a little in perfumery, too, but her primary focus was healing." Clare had grabbed a pad and pen and was writing down the man's name.

"If you want to give me your phone number, I can call you when the sample of *Barenia* is here."

"Thank you, Miss..."

"Clare. Clare Buchowski. I'm happy to do it." Clare looked gratefully at her other customer, who smiled and nodded.

After the elderly gentleman left, Clare went over to the woman who was browsing Good Scents' selection of wintertime fragrances.

"That's so nice of you, Lina. Thank you."

"No prob. I love being in the right place at the right time." Lina was a friend from Clare's time at Catholic High. They hadn't been close in those days, but they had recently made a connection thanks to their mutual love of fragrance. "I just stopped by to see how you were doing. Hanging in there?"

"Well, sure. It was a tremendous loss, but Billy and I weren't close anymore. It doesn't really affect my day-to-day life." That was a lie. Clare couldn't stop thinking about Billy and trying to figure out who would poison him.

"That's good to hear. I heard you had a thing going with him at one time..."

"Ha! That was almost 20 years ago, back in grade school!" Clare wasn't sure why people thought they had been a couple. They had been children. Must be that the Baltimore rumor mill—run by her mom—was still cranking out stories.

"No need to get defensive about it!" Lina laughed and smacked Clare on the arm with the back of her hand. "As an adult, he was a hottie. Hey, I watched his Instagram reels." Clare had raised her eyebrow. "I guess he was a cute kid, too. I totally get the attraction."

Clare folded her arms and pretended to be annoyed. "Is there anything else I can do for you, Lina?"

"Actually, yes. I was looking for something super sexy but also cozy to wear in a couple of weeks when I go to my sister's for Thanksgiving. She's invited her hot boyfriend's even hotter brother. I've had my eye on him for years, and now he'll be a captive audience. I want something that makes me feel like dessert...but also the main course."

"Girl, have I got the perfect fragrance for you!" Clare took Lina over to a shelf labeled "cozy," and pulled down a bottle of *Chestnut Suede*, by a Virginia-based perfumery called Belle Tower. She spritzed it onto a blotter and handed it to her friend. "This one opens with roasted chestnuts glazed in brown sugar with a hint of saffron. It's rich and sweet but not cloying. As it settles, a velvety suede wraps around smoky vanilla and the honeyed scent of dried fig. A whisper of labdanum and skin musk grounds it all in cozy intimacy."

"Oohh, it smells divine! And your description gave me goosebumps! I think I need this." As Clare spritzed it on Lina's wrist to see how it worked with her body chemistry, her friend took a look at the price. "Do you do layaway?" She chuckled and then fished out her credit card. "This one is too good to pass up."

"Are you going to be okay here in the shop by yourself for three days?" Clare desperately wanted to go to this fragrance festival in New York, but she didn't want to leave Ivy alone. Business had been booming in the two weeks since the death of Guillermo Flares. Halloween weekend had been positively bonkers, sales-wise. Another 5 bottles of *Lycoctonum* had been purchased, which was no surprise. Several seasonal scents that Ivy had insisted on stocking were also big sellers.

On Halloween afternoon, a young man had bounded into the store in full scarecrow costume, complete with face paint, fake straw sticking out of his cuffs and collar, and autumn leaves glued to his overalls. He smelled faintly of Elmer's Glue. "I need something that screams October. Not like 'Target Fall Decor.' I want a full-on witch's pantry." Clare offered a blotter spritzed with one of Ivy's favorites, Juniper & Rue *Pumpkin Séance*.

"This one is a gourmand for a witch who collects old cookbooks. It's sweet but also has a dusty bookshelf finish. The notes include pumpkin, candied ginger, spiced rum, and cloves, but also patchouli and an antique paper accord." The young man sniffed, nodded, and bought it immediately without trying it on.

"Would you like to try it on your skin before making the purchase?" Clare hated returns, which often happened when a fragrance was purchased in haste.

"Oh, I'm a scarecrow. I don't have skin," he said as he dug a credit card out of the straw peeking out between the buttons on his plaid shirt.

Another big seller on Halloween was the tooth-achingly sweet *Tricks & Treats*, by Zip! Parfums. Its candy corn accord and caramel popcorn note smelled like a pillowcase stuffed with a child's Halloween loot. "I don't know how anyone can wear this stuff," Clare said to Ivy as its latest purchaser skipped out the door. "It's just too much for me."

"You're just too old to appreciate it," her younger cousin retorted as she unwrapped a piece of Bit-O-Honey from the pumpkin-shaped candy jar on the counter and shoved it in her mouth.

"I'm surprised we haven't sold more atmospheric stuff, like Thorn & Briar *Mare Tenebris*. Such a strange aquatic chypre that makes me think of moonlight reflecting off the absolute stillness of deep water. It's melancholy and oddly romantic."

Her cousin shrugged. "Yeah, no. I'd rather smell like candy."

It was no surprise that the shrine outside Good Scents had doubled in size on Halloween. More than one customer had tripped over a stuffie or candle on their way into the shop, but none had complained. Clare thought of putting a fence around the shrine but figured the City would fine her for erecting a structure on public property. It was a bit of an eyesore, clashing with the brick rowhouses and cobblestone streets of the historic Fells Point neighborhood. So far, nobody had reported the shrine itself, but it was definitely getting out of control. Besides the legion of black teddy bears, a few people had added stuffed vampires, which Ivy had recognized as being one character on every child's favorite educational program. Clare once heard her muttering in a bad Bela Lugosi accent, “One! Ah ah ah! Two! Ah ah ah!” as she counted the perfume bottles on a shelf.

After the surprise popularity of Halloween as a perfume-buying holiday, Good Scents desperately needed more stock. The Scented Affair at the Greenpoint Terminal Warehouse would be the perfect event to connect with other independent fragrance creators and pick up some more inventory.

“Go! I’ll be fine. If I get into a bind, I can always get Aunt Terri in here to lend a hand.” Clare’s mom had worked in the shop from time to time, especially if she had her nose on a new fragrance, which she’d take as payment for her help. “Just bring me something fun from the Big Apple. I’ve still never been, so I’m desperately jealous.” Ivy had been moving bottles around on the shelves to make it look like they had more stock than they actually had. “You really need to make some more connections there. I was going to call June Chapel and North of Autumn and order a few more bottles of their fumes. We’re totally out of *Lethis Water*, and we’re down to the last bottle of *Equinox Drift*.”

Clare was on the computer, poring over recent customer sales. “A-ha! Found it.”

“Found what?” Ivy then said, sotto voce, “A-ha! Ah ah ah!”

“I thought that since I was going to be in NY, I might look up Billy’s so-called stalker, Philomena. I see you created an account for her during the event, or did she already have one? Did you notice that her credit card said ‘Philomena Leight’?”

Ivy shrugged. “I think so, yeah. Now that you mention it. It was just so bonkers in here, I guess I forgot.”

“Do credit card companies issue cards with pseudonyms? The charge for $1247.74 went through fine, so the card is probably legit. But the name.... I feel like we didn’t get the complete story from Billy.” She scribbled down a phone number and stuck it in her wallet.

“Be careful! We know nothing about his life in New York other than what he told you and what we learned from his Instagram account.” Since Billy’s death, both Ivy and Clare had watched every one of the reels posted to the @theguillermoflares, as if they'd find a clue as to who killed him. "Plus," Ivy continued, "I know you're convinced, but we won't actually know that he was murdered until that toxicology report comes in. As busy as the M.E. is in Baltimore City, it might be months yet."

"I know! I'll be careful. I want to see if I can find anyone who worked with him at the lab, hopefully someone who worked there when Philomena was there—assuming she left at some point. Billy painted her as scary and maybe crazy, but honestly, she didn't seem that way when she was here in the store. Sure, she knocked down a shelf, but she legitimately wanted that discontinued scent. And she apologized and paid for damages. That doesn't seem like out-of-the-ordinary behavior for a perfume fiend."

"What about the warning she left for Billy though? 'I will see you later.' Didn't you find that at all threatening?"

"Maybe she just meant she would see him later. I aim to find out."

Ten

CLARE HAD BROUGHT HER e-book reader on the train, loaded with cozy mysteries by her favorite authors, but she couldn't focus. She was thrilled to be headed to her second-favorite city on earth and excited to meet new indie perfumers. That was, after all, the ostensible purpose of her trip.

But the city was also where Billy had lived and worked, and where, perhaps, someone had wanted him dead. Shouldn't she poke around and see what she could uncover? The thought made her stomach twist. Clare had never been one for danger. She hadn't even learned to ride a bike, wary of the cobblestones in her old neighborhood. Skateboarding? Forget it. And now... she was actively searching for a murderer?

"Clare Buchowski," she thought, "are you out of your gourd?"

That Billy had trusted her so completely made it feel like her responsibility. She just didn't know where to start. Questions needed asking, but of whom? She wished she had grilled Parker more thoroughly while the woman was still in the shop, instead of getting lost in the heady notion that Billy had confided in her.

The Greenpoint Terminal Warehouse was located alongside the East River and a block away from the original location of Paulie Gee's. Clare was sad that the Baltimore outpost of one of her favorite pizza joints had closed, so she had promised herself that she'd visit the Greenpoint location while she was in the area. In the meantime, she needed to stop thinking about food and concentrate on perfume, perfumers, and murder, perhaps not in that order.

The warehouse was already packed with fragrance industry people. Not only were there dozens of independent perfumers from all over the country and abroad but also perfume store owners looking for the next big seller, PR companies hustling for clients, and the usual bloggers, influencers, and frag-heads hoping to promote themselves as much as any fragrances and creators that they might discover. Clare wasn't sure where to begin, though she had started a list of fragrance houses that seemed promising. Perhaps she would just wander down the closest aisle and wend her way up and down, visiting each booth as she came to it. She hadn't been in Brooklyn more than an hour before she felt the urge to see how the shop was faring without her. She texted her cousin.

Clare: Hey, what's going on? How's my baby?

Ivy: Vetiver? Your mom has him. I'm sure he's being spoiled rotten(er) as we speak

Clare: I meant the shop. Is everything OK there?

Ivy: You just left a few hours ago. We've barely opened. No customers yet. Go have fun. I guess. If you know how to have fun.

Clare: pbbbbbblttttt!

The warehouse smelled of too many things at once. Bergamot, gasoline, suede, cumin, and cloves all jostled for space in Clare's sinuses. She paused just inside the exhibit floor, letting her eyes adjust to the lighting. The booths unfurled in rows, each one a world unto itself: linen-draped tables, flickering LED votives, blotter strips in tiny urns, cloth-draped displays, ornate wooden boxes, the occasional glass bell jar.

Clare exhaled and chose a direction.

Word had gotten around about the death of Guillermo Flares, so Clare wasn't surprised to receive the murmured condolences from several vendors at the show. Clare crossed each of them off her mental list of companies that would want to have any sort of launch party at Good Scents. That sort of thing—death—could put a damper on things, and she would likely have to wait a while before hosting another perfumer.

The first booth she visited at The Scented Affair was heavy with incense. The words "Nocturnal Veil" were written in elaborate black script on a theatrical swath of deep purple velvet that had been draped over the back wall of the booth. Julien Artaud, a rail-thin Frenchman with ink-stained fingers, looked up from polishing a bottle and offered a smile that didn't quite reach his eyes. "Would you like to smell *Black Stem*, my new cherry fragrance?" He spritzed a blotter before she responded and handed it to her.

Clare had yet to smell a cherry fragrance that she liked. Most smelled like the idea of cherry, like cough drops or a children's drink. The closest thing to realism they achieved was mimicking the scent of bright-red maraschino cherries, the jarred kind with long stems that she sometimes would practice tying in knots with her tongue. She sniffed the blotter. *Black Stem* opened with the bite of sour cherry and the bloom of crushed rose petals, lush, but not syrupy. The heart deepened into tannic plum skin and black tea, both dry and faintly smoky. She could sense something dark and brittle underneath, with hints of vetiver and labdanum. This perfume was not about sweetness, but about depth. Clare took a card and a sample to test again later. She liked the fragrance, but there was something vaguely sinister about the perfumer. She'd had enough of that recently.

The next booth couldn't have been more different. Bitter Leaf Studio's plain arrangement of wood crates and hand-labeled bottles allowed the fragrances to speak for themselves. A woman in loose linen sipping something from a thermos introduced herself as Reyna. She held out a blotter; "This is my latest, *Groundskeeper*." Clare sniffed and swooned. This was a coffee fragrance as it should be: black, roasted, bitter, with just the edge of something green, like the inside of a roastery at 5AM. There was cardamom with its citrus edge and something both nutty and woody, which Reyna identified as toasted hazelnut shells. The base was like raw earth, with a whisper of patchouli like a forest after rain.

As Clare placed an order for the shop, she noticed that the liquid in Reyna's thermos cup was pale and watery, not coffee at all. "It's chamomile tea," Reyna confirmed. "I hate coffee."

Clare had to elbow her way down much of the first aisle to get past the humanity clogging it: influencers taking selfies in front of a booth so overloaded with pink cuteness that she at first mistook it for a Sanrio ad; people standing in the middle of everything, fiddling with their phones; and others having loud conversations smack in front of a booth, oblivious to the vendors or anyone who might want to speak to them. More than once she narrowly avoided being spritzed in the face by an atomizer pointing in the wrong direction. Why are so many of them solid black so it's impossible to see the hole where the fragrance comes out? Also, why are some people so rude? Clare often thought that the world would be a much nicer place if there were no people at all. Just dogs.

Her next stop was the booth belonging to L'Atelier d'Hécate, a tiny house that specialized in fragrances that evoked magickal potions. The perfumer, Rowan Firth, had followed Guillermo Flares on Instagram, and his creations were similar in emotion to *Lycoctonum*, at least as far as Clare could tell. She definitely wanted to smell the one called *Pluvial Veil*. As Clare picked up the tester, Firth, who had just finished with another customer, walked over to her. After glancing at her nametag, the perfumer said, "Ms Buchowski. Please accept my condolences over the death of Guillermo Flares. I knew him a little when he was still William Leight. Our time at LuxeOne overlapped, and we occasionally had lunch. He spoke fondly of a woman who I believe was your grandmother? He claimed to have learned more from her than he had in perfume school."

Clare felt a pang of sadness. She wished she had known Billy as an adult. Before Guillermo.

"Thank you. My grandmother was special. It's nice to hear that he still thought about her."

Firth held out his hand for the tester. "Let me spray this for you and get your opinion. I'm pretty sure our mutual friend would have appreciated it."

Clare inhaled. Rain on stone, juniper crushed underfoot, a wisp of smoke threading through damp birch. It felt like someone had left a fire behind to walk deeper into the woods. It was melancholy but oddly comforting. The drydown wrapped her in vetiver and soft resin, like pulling on a wool coat that still remembered the forest. "It's lovely. Could I get a sample, please?"

Eventually, Clare was able to make her way completely up and down both sides of two aisles, placing a large order with Lys & Fern because she still felt bad about their spoiled summer event, but also she loved their scents, and so did her customers. Surprisingly, she also found something for the store at Shocking Pink, the cartoonish booth that seemed to attract more selfies than orders. While their decor screamed "insipid fruity florals inspired by cartoon cats," the company made very nice scents that were both playful and sophisticated. There she found a cherry scent that she could live with. Correction, she actually loved it. *Glass Orchard* was bright and mouthwatering, combining tart red cherry with redcurrant and the sparkle of pink pepper over a base of white tea, suede, and an amber accord that was both rich and transparent at the same time.

By 2pm, Clare was suffering from olfactory fatigue and decided it was a fine time for pizza. The original Paulie Gee's wasn't yet open, so she strolled a couple blocks further to his Slice Shop for a piece of pepperoni pizza drizzled with hot honey. November was having an unseasonably bitter start, and she briefly considered buying two more slices to put in her pockets as hand warmers. As she headed back to the Greenpoint Terminal Warehouse, she decided she would hang out for only an hour or so longer before finding her hotel and checking in for a well-deserved nap. After that, maybe she'd wander into Manhattan and loiter around LuxeOne for a while.

As she approached the venue, she noticed several people outside listening to the preachings of a man who was handing a flyer to anyone who was willing to take one. Dr Lavender, as he called himself, had theories about the metaphysical side of scent, specifically things he called "olfactory alchemy" and "psychic fragrance resonance." Clare took a flyer that advertised a lecture he was giving that evening in a church basement in Manhattan. Though she had become comfortable with her own olfactory issues, her psychosomatic sensory substitution, as it were, she was intrigued by the ideas Dr Lavender was presenting and thought it could be worth her while attending his talk. Perhaps it would lead to her understanding of herself and her abilities (or lack thereof) more fully. Also, the flyer advertised that absinthe would be served, and she had always been curious about that particular flavor. It wasn't a fragrance note she could smell accurately, instead, Clare heard delicate glass wind chimes, tinkling gently in a minor key. There was also something low and secret in the background, like someone whispering a spell just out of earshot; it made her spine prickle every time. It was one of the many sensations she felt when she smelled *Lycoctonum*. She knew absinthe was there without knowing it was there.

Eleven

CLARE HADN'T COUNTED ON how tired fighting the crowds would make her feel and decided to pack it in before her hour was up. She took a bus back to the hotel, musing about how public transportation was so much better in New York than it was in Baltimore. It was well after 3pm when she reached the hotel, so she thought better of taking a nap. Dr Lavender's talk was scheduled for 7pm in SoHo, so she would have some time to hang out around LuxeOne in Chelsea beforehand. Clare felt grubby and a bit stinky after walking through fragrance residue for hours, so she took a quick shower before heading out.

A short while later, as she emerged from the subway a few blocks from her destination, Clare congratulated herself on picking such a convenient hotel. It was just a few blocks' walk to the L train into Manhattan, and she only needed to transfer once, to the C train, to get to Chelsea, where LuxeOne was housed in a nondescript highrise on 8th Avenue. Unfortunately, the sun was setting, and it was getting chillier. She spotted a coffee shop and ordered a cup of chai to drink while she loitered near the highrise entrance. Clare didn't really have a plan; she just hoped that she would recognize LuxeOne employees by the way they smelled. Hopefully, some folks would wear badges, which could be even more helpful. After about fifteen minutes, she was feeling stupid and obvious as people began to emerge from the building in clusters. Eavesdropping could help, but getting closer to the door might make her stand out even more. She edged closer anyway.

Clare wasn't even sure what or whom she hoped to find while hanging out on the sidewalk, but she was desperate. She knew how these things went: the person who found the body was usually a suspect. If she found the killer before the case even became a case, then she could avoid that messy bit. She knew she hadn't killed Guillermo, of course, and after thinking about it for five minutes, decided that it couldn't have been Ivy. Certainly, it wasn't her cousin! She embarrassed herself even contemplating that prospect. Ivy had gone through a lot in her brief life and wasn't about to do anything stupid like killing a person just because they thought it was amusing to call an obvious woman by a man's name. There'd be a lot more dead people if folks gave in to their momentary anger. There were already too many dead people because of that sort of thing.

As she stood in front of what she had started referring to in her head as "the LuxeOne building," Clare realized she was hungry. The various food smells that hung in the air didn't help. There was the acrid scent of roasting chestnuts, which, while not exactly pleasant, was a harbinger of the holiday season and always brought a fierce sense of nostalgia. It was also one of the things that smelled the same to Clare today as it had before her accident. She had adored coming to New York with her parents. They mostly did touristy things, like taking a walk through Times Square or visiting the Empire State Building. During one holiday-time trip, they saw the Rockettes at Radio City, after which they grabbed a snack of chestnuts to nibble on while they walked up Fifth Avenue to see the decorated windows of department stores like Saks and Bergdorf's. Her mother had put a couple of chestnuts in each of Clare's coat pockets to help keep her little hands warm. She had kept those chestnuts for months afterward, to remind her of the wonderful time they had together on that trip. And then they got moldy and had to be thrown away. She chuckled to herself at the memory of her mom discovering them in her pockets when she readied the coats for their annual trip to the dry cleaner.

After her brief olfactory visit down memory lane, Clare decided that mentally naming all the scents that were wafting by might be a good game to play while waiting for... whatever it was she was waiting to smell. The sugary smell of caramelized nuts was particularly intoxicating, but right now it was mingling with the fragrance of halal cart chicken with white sauce and the peculiar smell of hot iceberg lettuce.

Many people in New York wear perfume regularly, so the breezes often carry the powerful scents of saffron and ambroxan, sandalwood and leather, and orange blossom and vanilla, in pairs and combined with other notes. Occasionally she'd get a whiff of the velvety musk of Iso E Super, one of her favorite synthetic aroma chemicals. And then she smelled it. *Lycoctonum.* But how? As far as she knew, there had only been 40 bottles made. Thirty-six of them had been brought to the shop to sell, plus two testers. And the last two bottles were in Guillermo's personal collection. Or so he had told her.

"This is a very limited edition, Clare. So we cannot waste a drop of this precious fluid." She hadn't been sure if Guillermo had been serious or was just doing what she understood to be his normal posturing. She played along. "Oh yes, so rare that people will kill for a bottle." Had that been true? She didn't believe it at the time, for it was only perfume. Unless the fragrance had been made with the last bit of a substance no longer in existence, the formula could be rebatched repeatedly to make more and more bottles. Clare dismissed the thought. Nobody would kill over a bottle of perfume. But why else would a perfumer have to die?

Clare woke herself from her reverie and attempted to find the smell of *Lycoctonum* in the air again. There it was! Stronger now, as if someone wearing it was within reach. She looked at the group of people who were gathered just outside the building's entrance. Wasn't one of them Parker Strong, Billy's friend who dropped off the Moleskine? She had purchased a bottle of his fragrance when she was in the shop, which explained how Clare could smell it currently.

Clare turned to leave, or at least hide, but it was too late. She was spotted.

"Clare! Hi! Parker. Remember me?"

Clare turned around, trying to act cool. "Oh yes, Parker. Billy's friend. Nice to see you again." She leaned in and said, "I thought you said *Lycoctonum* wasn't your kind of fragrance, but I notice you're wearing it."

"I realize I said that, but the more I smell it, the more I am intrigued. I've been trying to reverse-engineer it to no avail. There are parts I just can't figure out." Parker paused thoughtfully. "I know this isn't a nice thing to say, but I have a feeling that Billy didn't work alone on this scent. It seems too complex for his skillset."

Clare thought, darn right that's not nice.

"By any chance, have you had time to look through that Moleskine I gave you? Did you notice anything about this scent in it?" Truthfully, Clare admitted she had not had time to go through the notebook. Something always came up.

"Hmm, I don't know what you've figured out so far, but I feel like there's probably some absinthe in there."

"Interesting! I'll have to try that." Parker looked at her watch. "I gotta dash. Nice running into you, Clare. Enjoy your time in New York." With that, she headed off in the opposite direction.

Clare was taken aback by Parker's revelation about Billy's inability to create a scent like *Lycoctonum* on his own. Part of her wanted to chase the woman down and talk to her, but the rest of her was tired and cold and had somewhere else to be. Clare was pleased, however, that she had found something out, however small, and hadn't wasted her time hanging out in Chelsea. Time now to find out what she could do to repair her damaged sense of smell. Her fingers were crossed in her mittens as she walked back to the subway entrance.

The salon was packed tighter than she'd expected, with people on velvet chairs sitting shoulder-to-shoulder, the air already thick with conflicting perfumes. Clare sat somewhere near the middle, wedged between a woman in patchouli and pencil shavings and a man who smelled unmistakably of jasmine tea and a lack of sleep. Once seated, she took the opportunity to study the rest of the audience. It seemed to comprise a mix of scent devotees, artists, skeptics, and one or two people who just came for the absinthe. Beyond the flimsy wooden lectern in the front of the room was a blank wall upon which was projected the title of the lecture.

"Soul in the Bottle: An Introduction to Olfactory Alchemy and Psychic Fragrance Resonance," by Dr. Norbert Lavender

Just as Clare finished reading the title, Dr Lavender appeared, wearing a sweeping coat the color of dusk and a slightly askew cravat. He adjusted the microphone and began.

"Good evening, fragrant members of the scentological literati. First, we will examine Olfactory Alchemy, or The Sacred Geometry of Scent. We speak of perfume as if it were an accessory. Ornament. Vanity. I am here to remind you: it is none of those things. It is ritual. Communion. A Portal."

Clare heard a chuckle and found it disrespectful. Dr Lavender continued unfazed.

"In ancient alchemy, three stages marked the transformation of matter: nigredo, albedo, and rubedo. These are not merely symbolic; they are the exact phases a fragrance follows as it unfurls on skin. Top notes? That is nigredo, the blackening. Chaos, unfamiliarity, the moment the soul is cracked open. The heart? Albedo, the whitening. Cleansing, reflection, memory. The base? Rubedo, the reddening. Integration, the truest version of you, revealed in scent."

Clare listened intently, but much of it seemed like jibber-jabber to her. Perhaps she wasn't deep enough to understand this stuff. Or maybe he was just a charlatan? A man a few rows over raised his hand to speak. When Dr Lavender acknowledged him, he stood.

"What about citrinitas, the yellowing? There are actually four stages of transformation, with citronitas being the third. It represents the awakening of consciousness. You've skipped that one entirely."

Dr Lavender thought for a moment before giving a dismissive wave of the hand. "Citrinitas is a phantom phase. It was buried because it doesn't produce gold. It produces vision. And that's more dangerous. That stage has importance to only one person here." He seemed to look at Clare when he said that, but she could have been mistaken. "I've also skipped cauda pavonis for many reasons. Now who is giving the lecture here?" His critic sat and Dr Lavender continued. Clare was intrigued by the stage the man in the audience referred to as "the yellowing" and that Dr Lavender had referred to as "producing vision." The mysterious note that Clare had sensed near Guillermo's dead body had been yellow.

"Now, we will discuss Psychic Fragrance Resonance. Smell as Soul Mirror. Each of you sitting here emits a scent, whether or not you wear perfume. Your aura hums at a certain pitch. And the right fragrance doesn't just match it. It harmonizes, like a tuning fork to the soul. Some perfumes act like shields. Galbanum, vetiver, labdanum—they are protection. They keep memory from flooding you too quickly. Others are keys. Orris, mimosa, cardamom—they unlock what you've forgotten to remember."

Clare raised her hand. She wanted to go back to that citrinitas thing. Dr Lavender ignored her.

"A client once came to me, claiming she dreamed in monochrome. I gave her a perfume I designed, *Rose Narcosis*, with rose de mai, cinnamon, and patchouli. She called me the next morning. She'd dreamed not only in color, but also in scent. Her childhood, her lost sister, a garden that no longer existed that was full of roses that she swore matched the perfume exactly."

Dr Lavender paused for effect. The room was quiet now. Someone lit a clove cigarette in the back, which he pretended not to notice. However, the face he made revealed that he was not happy with that person's aura.

"You may not believe me. You may say this is all poetry and perfume, myth and musing. But the next time a stranger walks by, and you are stopped cold by their scent, ask yourself: What did it remind me of? Or more frighteningly, what did it awaken in me?"

"Thank you for your attention. I'll be available for aura-sniffing consultations in the antechamber."

Was that it? Clare looked around the room. Several of the attendees seemed to have fallen asleep. Others were getting up to leave. "I can't believe I wasted my time like this," she thought. "This was a real nothingburger." She had sincerely hoped to learn something tonight, but perhaps it had seemed too good to be true. Was there anything in the area worth exploring at this time of night? Clare had come all the way from Brooklyn, and she might as well do something interesting before she took the train back to her hotel in Williamsburg. As she stood to leave, Dr. Lavender approached her. He had beelined through the dispersing crowd, like he'd meant to talk to her all along. Lavender closed his eyes and took a long, calm breath through his nose. He let it out slowly, reopened his eyes and observed her for a few moments. This entire process felt to Clare like it took hours but had only been several seconds. Finally, the man spoke.

"Your aura is fragrant with questions for which I may have answers."

Clare indeed had questions, and several of them involved her current location to the door, how fast she could get to it, and what she was going to do when she escaped the building. Instead of fleeing, she thought there couldn't be too much harm in playing along. Maybe Dr Lavender could help her, but she had a feeling that if a Magic 8 ball would suddenly appear, it would tell her, "Outlook not so good."

"I do have questions. Many of them. The reason I came here tonight was to see if you could offer an explanation, scientific or metaphysical, about the way my sense of smell works. But I am also looking for people who might help me find out who killed a... friend of mine." Clare hesitated to call Guillermo a friend, but Billy had been a good friend at one time, hadn't he?

"Your sense of smell... how do I put this..." He tapped the side of his nose and leaned in close yet not close enough to touch. "Like memory. Not a memory. The absence of one. A room that used to have something in it."

Clare stared. "Excuse me?"

"You're anosmic. But only in one direction. You smell the past. But not the present."

She narrowed her eyes. Was he guessing? Was this performance?

"You've had trauma," he continued softly, "but something else happened. Your sense of smell is tethered to something other than scent. You're... redirecting."

"Redirecting what?"

"Your perception. You smell what matters to your mind, not your nose."

She didn't reply. Clare thought about how lately she's been smelling sounds. Emotions. Ghosts of things no one else noticed. She thought they were part of the whole "other senses taking the place of the missing sense" thing that she's been experiencing for years. But he was right. She had been smelling things that had no smell. Like the man seated next to her, who smelled sleepy. Clare suddenly recalled that Guillermo had smelled of guilt when he had come into her shop the first time.

"You have a rare gift," Dr Lavender continued. "Or perhaps it is a curse. It depends on how you use it." Then, as if he hadn't just dropped a psychic bomb on her, he slipped her a business card. On the back, he scribbled a single word: "Wolfsbane." She was still staring at the card when he disappeared into the crowd like vapor.

Her time with Dr Lavender left Clare with more questions than answers. It felt very late, but it was only 9pm. Clare had had nothing to eat since her slice of pizza at 2, and she was hungry. She realized she had been spoiled living and working in a restaurant-dense neighborhood like Fells Point, where pretty much any cuisine she desired—except Chinese, as there was still a dearth of great Chinese restaurants in Baltimore—was within walking distance. Luckily, her visit with Dr Lavender had taken her to an area of Manhattan similarly crowded with places to eat. She decided on Thai Diner.

To combat the chill she was feeling from the frosty November air, she ordered a Thai Toddy, a teapot full of rooibos tea and rye whisky seasoned with honey, lemon, and fragrant star anise. Everything on the food menu sounded so good, Clare had trouble choosing, finally settling on the cozy-sounding stuffed cabbage *tom khaa.* She had always been a fan of Polish stuffed cabbage, especially Busia Manya's *gołąbki*, and was curious to taste a Thai-flavored version. As she savored the delicious makrut-lime scented dish, Clare pondered the events of the day. She'd made several good connections at The Scented Affair, and she hoped to make a few more tomorrow. She felt somewhat bamboozled by Dr Lavender—who, to be totally honest, wore so many competing fragrances he smelled like he had recently run the gauntlet through Macy's perfume department and said "yes" to every SA who offered to spray him with the newest release. That he could sense anyone else's aura through his own Pigpen-style cloud was up for debate. Yet, the insight he offered almost seemed like he knew her.

All the food and thinking made Clare sleepy. It was fortunate that the restaurant was a straight shot to the Williamsburg Bridge, so she could skip the combination subway trip and blocks-long walk that would be necessary to reach her hotel and get a rideshare to do the dirty work.

Twelve

While Clare hadn't had a particularly satisfying night of sleep, she was determined to have a good day. Her thoughts had been occupied by the events of the previous 24 hours, and she found herself dreaming about the color yellow. She went through the bag of perfume samples she had brought with her and applied one of her new favorites, *Patchouli Dreams* by Salon de Mireilles. It was a fragrant mélange of pink pepper, black tea, vanilla, and lots of chocolatey patchouli that was the next best thing to curling up by the fireplace with a cup of hot cocoa. Just one spritz at the base of her throat, so she'd be the only person to sense it. It would also make her scarf smell lovely all day.

Before she left the hotel, Clare received a text from Ivy.

Ivy: I found him.

Ivy: Efraim. Found him on Instagram. We had dinner last night.

Guillermo's former assistant had been a ghost since the launch party. Ivy, bless her internet-stalking soul, must have gone through hundreds of profiles.

```
Clare: Wait, what?
Ivy: You will not believe the Philomena story.
Clare: Call me.
```

A moment later, Clare's phone rang. "I hope you're sitting down," Ivy said. "Because this is bananas." Ivy was buzzing with energy from the thrill of discovery. "Ok, so, according to Efraim, Guillermo—he was still Billy then—met Philomena when he was working as an apprentice perfumer at LuxeOne. She was a laboratory assistant who kept the labs tidy, stocked supplies, calibrated equipment, that sort of thing. She musta had a thing for him, because she hung around Billy, flirting, but also encouraging him." Ivy stopped to take a breath. "Then she asked him out, and he said yes."

"He'd been hoping for a casual thing near the office, but she wanted to go to this boujee party at Buddha Bar. She went home and put on this eyepopping sexy dress, and Billy was feeling good about the evening. I guess, 'cause, boo…"

Clare broke in. "Slow down, Ivy. You're talking a mile-a-minute."

Ivy laughed. "Sorry, Cuz. Anyway, so they get to this party and Philomena is hanging from Billy like, and Efraim couldn't stop laughing at this description, 'like a monkey in a coconut tree.' She's drinking all the champagne and introducing him as her boyfriend. Poor guy just wanted to go home at this point, but she made them hang out until the wee hours. Efraim said he should have just left her there, but Billy wasn't a jerk. Well, back then he wasn't. When he couldn't take it anymore, he poured her into a cab. She was all sitcom-drunk, rubber arms and wobbly legs, and he had to carry-drag her up the stairs to her apartment. He put her to bed with her clothes on, left some aspirin and water on the bedside table, and left."

Ivy stopped talking momentarily, and Clare could hear her drinking something.

"On Monday, Philomena told everyone that he was a perfect gentleman, and she couldn't wait to go out with him again.

Meanwhile, Billy's like, 'nope.' She asked him out again and again and wouldn't give up. They weren't going out, but she was telling people they were, and, get this: she told them they were married. He found this out when his coworkers started congratulating him."

"Wow! She sounds like a lot to handle."

"Yeah, so much so that he skipped town and changed his name and stuff."

Clare couldn't stop pacing as Ivy recounted it all.

"God, Clare, can you imagine? You're trying to be polite on a first date, and suddenly people think you're married."

Clare pinched the bridge of her nose. "So that's why he changed his name. Not just rebranding. He was in hiding."

Ivy continued in an almost giddy way. "Efraim's cute. His hands are ridiculous. Like... long-fingered, artist hands. He should be making perfume instead of hiding out."

"Oh, honey."

After a few minutes, they ended their call. Clare thought she might need a drink after hearing all that but would settle for a nice cup of coffee. And definitely a pastry. The night before, while mapping out the route to the Greenpoint Terminal Warehouse from her hotel in Williamsburg, Clare noticed that the area was positively lousy with bakeries. Within a block of her hotel there were three: giant-cookie king Levain, Martha's Country Bakery, and La Bicyclette. Clare had scrolled through their positively mouthwatering Instagram feeds while she was brushing her teeth and decided on La Bicyclette, as it offered several pastries she had never tried. Once there, she was overwhelmed by the selection but limited herself to just two items: a savory kugelhopf and an apricot oreillon, to go. Before she had even put her wallet away, Clare had sampled each of them. As she munched on the laminated fruit pastry, she mused that they probably meant to call it an oreille, an ear, and not an oreillon, which meant mumps, but singular. She absently mused if it was possible for a person to have one mump as she made her way toward Greenpoint.

As usual, while making the tough choices about which pastries to try, Clare neglected to order a beverage. She needed coffee far more than she needed sugar, though her sweet teeth had argued more persuasively than her lack of sleep. Nine blocks later, she stopped at Bakeri for a café au lait and a slice of banana date walnut bread that she planned to save as a snack. The cinnamon rolls had also been mighty tempting, but she knew she wouldn't have been able to resist eating it right away. As it was, the banana bread didn't make it to Greenpoint.

Eventually Clare arrived at the venue, warmed by the coffee and good cheer generated by all the sugar and butter she had just consumed. Once inside, she peeled off her hat and scarf, and after shaking off the pastry crumbs, shoved them into the large silver tote bag she carried on every trip to New York. The bag was the only thing she owned that was even slightly stylish. It had been a gift with purchase at Saks some years ago, her reward for spending entirely too much money on high-end skin products that in the long run only exacerbated her rosacea.

Her friends at June Chapel Perfumery were next on her rather long agenda. Their delicately evocative scents had all been good sellers for her, and they had two new ones for her to try. *Moonwake* seemed luminous and wistful, like warm summer air, drowsy with tea and pear blossom, dew-dappled linden, and mimosa, on a base of cashmere musk and ambrette. *Silvered Sliver* started out like an early morning after rain, with the scent of storm-washed stone and tender greenery, moving into the dreamy vintage sweetness of orange blossom and iris, with a bit of resin and incense in the base. Clare ordered both, and a few more bottles of the scents she had sold out of recently.

As she wandered through the warehouse, chatting with perfumers, picking up samples, and placing orders, Clare thought about Philomena and what the chances might be of meeting with her while she was visiting New York. She had only one more day, and while she had a phone number for the woman, she wasn't sure if she should call out of the blue. Nor did she know if Philomena was even in the city. It had been two weeks since Billy's death; surely his stalker had heard about it by now. But that was giving her the benefit of the doubt. Philomena was at the top of Clare's list of suspects because she seemed to have the most motive.

According to Efraim, Billy had spurned her advances. Yet Philomena not only pretended they were in a relationship, but she also told their co-workers that they were married. That seemed more than a little delusional. Would someone who thought Billy was her husband do something as shocking as kill him? Until the autopsy results came back from the Medical Examiner's office, it was still being considered a natural death. Clare was certain he had been poisoned, which likely made it a premeditated murder. It was probably foolhardy to attempt to talk to someone who might be a murderess, but she didn't have confidence that the police would question the right people. She shuddered as she reminded herself that she could well be a suspect.

If she was going to get to Philomena somehow, Clare needed a plan. She ran through potential scenarios in her mind.

Scenario 1: Clare calls Philomena. Philomena hangs up on her.

Scenario 2: Clare calls Philomena and arranges a lunch meeting. She says to her suspect, "Billy is dead." Philomena replies, "I know. I killed him." Police are called, the killer makes a complete confession, the end.

That was never going to happen. It was too easy, like a bad episode of any 70s crime drama.

Scenario 3: Philomena calls Clare. Wait, what?

"Clare? Clare Buchowski, is that you?"

Clare looked around the crowded warehouse, trying to find the source of the voice. It was familiar, but not. She spotted a well-dressed woman with long blonde hair walking toward her, waving an arm heaped with jangly bracelets. When she got closer, Clare's heart caught. This woman looked exactly like Philomena.

"It's good to see you again, my dear!" Philomena exclaimed as she grabbed Clare in a crushing hug. Had she conjured this woman up simply by thinking about her? It hadn't been good to see this woman the first time, Clare thought, but she found herself returning the embrace. Why was Philomena being so friendly? It's not like their initial meeting had been under the best of circumstances, unless she had enjoyed being escorted from the premises by a police officer. "How are things in Baltimore? How's business? I want to apologize again for the trouble I caused that evening. I hope you've forgiven me. I would like to continue being a customer of yours."

"Your rather large purchase made up for the hubbub." It was almost the truth. She had offloaded two bottles of a fragrance that had been hanging around for a while and made a tiny profit on the cost to fix the broken shelf. Of course, she couldn't put a price on the loss of her childhood friend Billy Leight and the impact he might have had on the fragrance world as perfumer Guillermo Flares.

Philomena had her hand on Clare's forearm, as if they were the chummiest of chums. "Good, good. How's Billy? Or do you call him Guillermo now? I haven't been able to reach the dear for weeks now."

Clare couldn't tell if Philomena was playing dumb or really didn't know. She decided to be forthright with the woman whom the perfumer had referred to as his stalker. "I call him Billy. Called him." She corrected. "He's dead."

"Oh, ha ha! I know he enjoys playing hard to get sometimes, but this seems to be a more permanent tack than usual. Has he left Baltimore and gone back to Rome yet?"

"Ahhh...I think he's become a permanent resident of Baltimore. Philomena, I'm serious. Billy died the night of the launch party." As Philomena was suspect number one in her book, Clare stretched the truth a bit. "The death was deemed suspicious and is still under investigation. I'm surprised that you hadn't heard about it."

All the blood left Philomena's face, and she wobbled a bit in her platform boots. She dropped her bags and put shaking hands to her face. "Oh, she's good," thought Clare. "She seems genuinely upset." Suddenly, Philomena sat down hard on the ground and began crying great, heaving sobs. A few people around them stood back in alarm, but another woman charged out of the crowd and knelt beside the distraught woman.

"What did you do to her?" she asked Clare angrily.

Philomena clutched at the other woman. "My husband is dead! My sweet, sweet Billy."

The other woman made soothing noises to the woman on the ground while looking questioningly at Clare. She nodded and repeated that Guillermo Flares had died the night of his fragrance launch and that the situation was under investigation.

"Oh, my darling! Here, let me help you up. Let's get some water and sit somewhere. You can't just cry on the floor in the middle of everything." She looked at Clare and cocked her head at her bawling friend. "Grab an arm and help me get her up." Once Philomena was on her feet, they slowly walked her to a bench against the far wall. Two people had been sitting there spraying each other with fragrance samples but quickly jumped out of the way when the trio of women approached. "Sit, Philly, sit. Let me get you some water."

"I'd prefer gin, Mags. Please."

"Not sure they have any of that here, but I'll check." She looked at Clare. "Stay with her. I'll be right back."

True to her word, within a couple of beats Mags returned with bottled water, which she handed to Philomena, along with a handful of tissues. "Blow, darling. And have some water."

Clare's day had suddenly gone sideways, and she wasn't sure what she could do about it. She still had several fragrance companies that she wanted to visit before she left for the day. It was only coming up on noon, and she hoped she'd be able to salvage at least a few hours, though she suspected that this whole "Billy's dead" thing was going to take some time to work out. As she was about to check her watch, Clare admonished herself, "Stop being so selfish! The woman is in pain. You wanted to talk to her, and this is your chance." She took a seat next to Philomena.

"I'm sorry. I didn't realize that you didn't know. From what I could tell, word spread fast on social media."

"I don't use social media." Philomena sniffed.

Another one! Clare thought. Good for them. That's probably smart. It's often not worth the trouble, even if there are lots of cute dogs on Instagram.

Philomena blew her nose and looked at Clare with red eyes. "How did it happen?"

Clare related to Philomena how she had found the body at the hotel, and that's all she knew. There was an autopsy, and she presumes a toxicology report if the autopsy showed nothing, but as of today, she hadn't heard either way. Clare was hesitant to tell Philomena that she thought it could have been poison that killed him. In her mind, the woman was a suspect; if Philomena had killed Guillermo, she'd know exactly how she did it.

"I'd really like to talk to you more about this," Philomena said in between sniffles. "But I have had a terrible shock and just want to go home."

"I understand. I'm so sorry that I had to be the one to tell you."

"Are you free for lunch tomorrow? Perhaps we can talk a bit if you are available. I think you should know the entire story."

Clare's train home didn't leave until 4pm. She had planned to hit up the expensive department stores to sniff designer and prestige brands, but that could wait until another trip. Instead, she made plans to meet Philomena for lunch. Until then, she had plenty more vendors to visit while she was at The Scented Affair.

The next morning, Clare awoke, feeling that she had accomplished a lot during her brief trip to New York. She had placed orders with ten perfume companies, both new and familiar, and had a pocket full of samples from other perfumers that she believed had potential. She just wanted to get Ivy's take on them first. They had fairly different fragrance sensibilities; her 22-year-old cousin understood what young people seemed to prefer, while Clare did better with more mature palates. What Ivy referred to as "the olds."

Not only that, but she had also made contact with her number one suspect and was having lunch with her. But before that, Clare needed to get coffee and breakfast. She decided to go to La Bicyclette for a latte and an almond croissant, this time remembering to order the caffeine first.

Before she left Brooklyn, Clare needed to find a fun and quirky souvenir for Ivy. "What to get the gal who has nothing, apart from jealousy over my trip to New York without her?" She poked around in a couple of shops and found a vintage zine with an article titled "The Scent of Revolution: Olfactory Propaganda & Urban Rebellion" that was a contender, but it didn't scream New York. Another possibility was a little enamel pin shaped like a coffee cup that said, "Anxious but Articulate." Clare liked that one so much, she bought it for herself. Finally, in a used bookstore, she spotted a bowl of hand-stitched patches. The one of a cartoon rat dragging a slice of pizza up a flight of stairs was perfect. What was more New York than "Pizza Rat?"

Thirteen

AROUND NOON, CLARE MET Philomena at Buvette, since it was near Philomena's home in the West Village. She said it would be an easy walk for her, and in her current state of mind she needed easy. It was a bit out of the way for Clare, especially as she had her luggage with her, but she was desperate to get the whole story from this woman. Plus, it was a public place, and that made Clare feel a little better about the situation, especially if it turned out that Philomena was the murderer.

Philomena Leight was impeccably turned-out in a navy-blue military-style jacket over a crisp white shirt, and wide-legged trousers over short boots with kitten heels. Her long blonde hair was tucked into a chignon, and she wore large pearl earrings and a pale-yellow silk scarf tied in a knot at her throat. Clare felt like a schlub in her usual uniform of graphic tee, pilly cardigan, and skinny jeans with sneakers. She had run a comb through her hair but hadn't bothered to put on makeup.

After they were seated and had ordered drinks, Clare asked how Philomena had met Billy. The story that she heard was similar to the one Efraim related to Ivy.

"I met darling Billy when we worked together at LuxeOne. He was so... well—you know this—good-looking. And I've always been a sucker for a pretty face." Philomena chuckled. "He was so focused on his work I don't think he realized I was flirting with him, and when I asked him out, he said no the first, oh, three times. Finally, he agreed." She reached her hand back to pat her hair before continuing. "I think he wanted to do something dreadfully boring and American, like get a hot dog and sit on a curb somewhere to chat. But I had been invited to this fabulous fête downtown, and I thought he would make perfect arm candy." Philomena smiled at the memory and took a long drink of her gin & tonic.

"The champagne flowed that night, and I had a great time. But I must admit that I drank too much. I was a party girl in my youth, and sometimes I forget my age. Honestly, I don't remember what went on for most of the evening, only that Billy took me to my apartment, tucked me into bed, and kissed me on the forehead. I think I fell in love with him at that moment."

"Did you ever go out with him again?" While hearing Philomena's side of the story was interesting, Clare wanted to get to the meat of the matter.

"Darling, we not only went out again, we got married!"

Clare had seen the name Philomena Leight on the purchase receipt from the launch party, and the woman had referred to Billy as her husband just yesterday—which matched the story Efraim had told Ivy—yet she was still taken aback. Clare wanted Billy's side of the story to be the truth. Instead, she found herself believing Philomena.

"You look stunned, my dear. Why? What did Billy tell you about me?"

"He said he had known you, but there was no current connection, and he thought he had gotten rid of you."

"Oh, my." Philomena made a moue of disappointment. "It's unfortunate that he felt that way." She looked Clare directly in her eyes. "I loved him. So much. I would have done anything for the man. And I did." Philomena chugged down the rest of her drink before continuing.

"I don't know if you were aware of this..." Philomena leaned forward to whisper, "Billy wasn't a particularly talented perfumer."

Clare had just heard something similar from Parker Strong, but it seemed more shocking coming from Billy's wife.

Philomena sat back again and went on, "But he was so beautiful, and he tried so hard. He had this desire, no, it was a need, to be famous. I did what I could to make him feel admired, loved, but I wasn't enough."

"After about six months of marriage, he started to pull away from me..."

Clare interrupted, "So you never had children? You introduced yourself to my cousin Ivy as his 'baby-mama.'"

"No, we never had children. I suppose I said that because I was feeling ornery, and it would get attention. Now where was I?" Philomena did not seem to appreciate being interrupted in the middle of telling a story. "Ah yes. Billy had heard about this society of perfumers in Rome, and he flew out a few times to meet with them. After his last visit, he came home declaring he was a 'new man,' nay, a 'different man.' He started calling himself Guillermo and expected me to do the same. He tried on a few ridiculous accents but could never keep them up for more than a few words at a time. So, he gave up and used his own voice, but in a raspy whisper. It was as if he'd joined some fragrance cult. He called it a 'transmutation of the self.' I called it nonsense. Guillermo dressed differently, ate different things than Billy had. He said Guillermo had better taste, better instincts. He stopped responding to his real name. If I called him Billy by accident, he looked at me like I had used a slur."

Philomena stopped talking long enough to wave down the server for a second gin and tonic. "Would you like anything stronger than iced tea, Clare?"

"No, thank you. I'm good." Clare played with her fork. "And then what happened?"

"The whole time I knew him, Billy had been obsessed with some old book. Claimed it contained formulas no one should have access to, that it was important and mystical."

The server returned with her drink, which Philomena gratefully accepted. She took a long sip of her G&T. "I know this is a summer drink, but it's my favorite. The bitterness of the tonic water matches my personality perfectly. Anyway, what was I saying?" Philomena looked up as if to find the answer on the ceiling. "Ah yes. My husband had always stayed up most nights, tinkering with ingredients and scribbling notes, muttering about 'perfecting the accord.' It got worse after he had been to Rome. After that, he barely touched me. It was like he was married to this mysterious book." Philomena took a sip of her drink. "I don't know if the thing even existed, because he didn't seem to have it with him. Just that old Moleskine notebook of his." Philomena abruptly picked up her menu. "Should we order some food?"

Clare was ravenous and couldn't wait to eat. She had been perusing the menu surreptitiously, not wanting to upset Philomena as she spun her tale, and had settled on the Croque Madame some minutes ago. Clare was practically salivating at the thought of a hot ham and cheese sandwich topped with a sunny side up egg. She imagined pricking the yolk with her fork and felt a little warmth in her nether regions. Man, it had been way too long.

Once the server had taken their order, Philomena continued.

"Where was I? After several weeks of feeling like I no longer existed, Billy came to me and announced that he had quit his job at LuxeOne and was moving to Rome temporarily."

Clare thought for a few beats, then asked, "How was he able to afford to live in Rome if he had quit his job here?"

"He claimed to have received a 'prestigious apprenticeship' to a supposedly famous fragrance house that I had never heard of. Circolo dei Profumieri. But he never had to worry about money. I have more than enough for both of us. I don't know if you can tell, but I'm a few years older," Philomena paused, waiting for the compliment.

Clare dutifully responded, "I thought you were in your late 20s."

Philomena smiled. "Thank you. I have the Mcrae genes to thank for that. Plus, a fabulous plastic surgeon." She paused to sip her drink. "In any case, Billy said he'd be back."

Clare leaned forward, wanting to hear more of this part of the story. "Did he ever return?"

"No. I heard from him only sporadically over the last three years, usually requesting that I deposit more money into his account. I couldn't tell you whether he had been in Europe the whole time or not."

"So you never met his assistant, Efraim?"

"He had an assistant? No, this is the first I've heard of him. They must have met in Rome, or wherever he was."

"He was the one who took Billy to the back room after you arrived at the party."

"Ah. The rude young man who poked me in the chest." Philomena absently rubbed the side of her left breast almost sensually. A man at the next table stared.

Clare asked one of the questions for which she sought an answer—one which may or may not further incriminate Philomena. At this point, she believed the woman, but there was still something not quite right about things.

"What did you mean by 'I will see you later'?"

"When did I say that?" Their food had arrived, and Philomena was examining her salad Niçoise with a critical eye. "Didn't I say no anchovies?"

"Sorry, ma'am, I'll have the kitchen make you a new one." The server reached to remove her plate, but Philomena stopped him. "Never mind that. Just bring me a side plate and I'll pick these devils out myself."

"Yes, ma'am."

Clare had not heard her dining companion request that the anchovies be left off her salad, but then she had been fantasizing about oozy egg yolks. She cut into her fancy French ham and cheese sandwich and sighed at the sound of the crispy bread crackling under her knife. She skewered a piece of sandwich onto her fork and used it to puncture the egg yolk, sighing again as it ran onto the plate.

"Where were we?" Philomena broke her reverie. "Ah, yes. You wanted to know what I meant when I said, 'I will see you later.' Is that what I said? I'm sure I meant merely that I would see him later. As in, at a point in the future. Why?"

Through a mouthful of cheese and bread, Clare said, "It seemed like a warning more than a promise."

"I don't know. Maybe it was. Look, when you spend 3 years waiting for your wayward husband to return from some potentially dodgy apprenticeship with a mysterious cult-like group he says is temporary and then you find him in another state acting like he's god's gift to goths, no matter how much you love the chap, you might say stuff that you don't mean. Out of anger and frustration." She had removed the last of the anchovies from her salad and waved the server over to remove the plate of offensive fish parts from the table. "Don't forget, Clare," she pointed at her with her fork, "at the time, I was being escorted from the premises by one of your local gendarmes."

Philomena dropped her fork and put her well-groomed head in her hands. "And now I'll never see my Billy again." She stood suddenly and said, "Please excuse me."

For a minute, Clare wondered if Philomena was going to leave the restaurant and stick her with the check. Those gin and tonics cost $16 each, and Clare couldn't help but calculate the number of pastries she could buy back home with that money. She gave the woman the benefit of the doubt and enjoyed the rest of her croque madame without having to listen to her conspiracy theories about what Billy had been up to in Rome, or wherever he had been.

After a short time, Philomena returned with dry eyes and a fresh coat of lipstick. "I'm sorry to have run out like that. I made myself upset. I hope I have answered all of your questions. Can we talk about perfume now without mentioning my late husband?"

After lunch, Philomena insisted they stop at Bigelow Chemists for a sniff, but Clare was drained simply from being in the woman's presence and lied about needing to catch an earlier train. Part of her could understand why Billy left her—no matter the reason, that's exactly what he did—his wife was exhausting. She felt like she had mostly gotten the truth out of Mrs William Leight, but the woman hadn't exonerated herself completely. Clare thought if her own husband spent three years in a European cult, she wouldn't have understood it, either. It might be grounds for divorce... but murder?

Fourteen

Clare hung out at the station for a while before boarding her train with a large coffee, two snacks she didn't want, and the vague hope that she might achieve something like rest.

That hope died around Metropark.

The train had filled up quickly, and Clare settled into her seat, tucking her tote bag at her feet. An hour into the ride, the coffee she'd sipped earlier made her need the restroom. On her way through the car, she noticed a man two rows up open a full-size sheet cake on his tray table. On the way back, she saw him and his seatmate—a woman in business attire—attacking the cake with plastic forks. It was red velvet. Clare could smell the cream cheese frosting from her seat, which triggered something primal. She rummaged through her tote bag and pulled out the two snacks she had purchased for herself at the train station: a plain bagel with butter and a granola bar. She still didn't want either, but she ate half the bagel, wishing she had ordered cream cheese. Without coffee to wash it down, it was a little dry and starchy. And because it wasn't cake, Clare didn't feel satisfied.

She pulled out the banana pudding she had purchased for Ivy from Magnolia Bakery in Moynihan Train Hall and examined it. She popped off the lid and scraped up a little of the cream.

"Mmmm," she sighed as she sunk her spoon further down into the container to get bits of all the strata—the cream, the cookies, the pudding, and the banana. After two more spoonfuls, Clare looked into the container. There was no mistaking that some of it was no longer there. She contemplated smoothing out the rest so the missing part wouldn't seem so...missing. But if she put her spoon back in, it would only come out with more pudding on it, and before she knew it, it would be gone.

Like Billy.

It hadn't escaped her that the pudding was yellow, which seemed to be the color of the moment. Clare had promised herself that she wouldn't think about the case on her way home. She had devoted entirely too much time to it already. She closed her eyes and brought her fist to her forehead, forgetting that there was still a spoon in it. "Ow!"

The ride home was supposed to be a bit of quiet time for her noisy mind, but it had been anything but. Perhaps if she put in her earbuds and queued up a calming ambient playlist? Instead of music, she heard a man's voice with a British accent calmly narrating a story about a small bear who wore a raincoat. She spent a full five minutes wondering if this was an ad before realizing her earbuds had accidentally paired with someone else's phone. Across the aisle, a little boy was smiling, nodding along like it was gospel.

Clare continued to listen. She unwrapped the granola bar and stared out the window, nibbling contentedly. By the time she reached Baltimore, Clare felt oddly soothed. Not well-rested, not relaxed, but gently reminded that much of life unfolded beyond her influence.

Good Scents had already closed for the day, so Clare was surprised to find her cousin waiting for her. "Where's my pressie?" Ivy jumped up and down like a child whose parent had just returned from a business trip. Clare rummaged through her shoulder bag for the embroidered patch. Ivy was confused by it at first. She turned it over in her hand like it was a puzzle she was trying to solve, frowned slightly, then raised an eyebrow and said: "A rat. With a slice of pizza." Realization hit a second later. "Wow! Possibly the most quintessential New York thing! I love it!" She jumped off the seat behind the counter and charged at Clare, who braced herself for her cousin's customary boa constrictor-like hug.

"Oof! You're welcome." As Clare disentangled herself from Ivy's long limbs, she remembered something. "One more thing." She reached back into her tote bag and pulled out the cup of banana pudding, which she handed to Ivy.

"Some of it appears to be missing," Ivy said as she pointed out the obvious spoonfuls that had been removed.

"Sorry. I couldn't help myself."

"I would have done the same thing. Tell me all about your trip while I eat this." Ivy looked into the bag and pulled out a plastic spoon. "Did you use this?"

"No, I scooped out the pudding with my fingers."

"Ew either way. Let me grab a clean spoon from the back. Oh, by the way, Jorge came in yesterday to see you. Said you should call."

Clare gave Ivy a couple of days off to repay her for minding the shop, so for the moment, all was serene at Good Scents. Ivy hadn't sold much while her cousin was out of town, but Clare was sure it wasn't from lack of trying. As she emptied the trash, Clare noticed folded pieces of cardstock with writing on them. She pulled out pieces labeled, "Traumatic Gourmands," "Haunted Candles," and "Forest, but Sad," and knew immediately that her cousin had rearranged the fragrances in her own weird way at least once while she had been in New York. As she wondered what else Ivy had gotten up to, the bell above the door jangled hard enough to make her flinch. It was 11am, and Clare was already over-caffeinated.

"Good morn, milady." Jorge pretended to tip his hat, then curtseyed. Clare laughed.

"I was going to give you a call today. Ivy said you had stopped in."

"Yes, and she was up to all sorts of mischief."

Clare waved one of the pieces of cardstock in the air. "I saw."

"So how was the show? Will your shelves soon be teeming with new fragrances?"

"That's the plan. The show was crowded and chaotic. But I placed a bunch of orders I'm excited to receive."

"Give me the highlights. I want all the gossip, regrets, everything."

"Well, I met a perfumer who believed that fragrance was a 'temporal architecture of self-expression.' I said I just like things that smell like grass and soap. He looked at me as if I had three heads."

"God, I love niche perfumery. Such fragile egos. Such lofty copy." Jorge placed his chubby elbows on the counter and leaned forward. "Did you bring me anything?"

"What is it with you people? I go away and everyone wants a souvenir."

"Heck, I'll take your used blotters, if that's all you have. I'm bored, jealous, and need a vacation."

Clare handed him a pile of blotters, some with names scribbled on them, others without. "These are all probably going to smell the same, since they've been living together in the bottom of my tote bag for a few days."

Jorge pulled one out of the pile and ran it under his nose. He made a face, then read the name written on it. "*Rat Hotel*? Is this for real?"

"Yep. By a Brooklyn perfumer called, shockingly enough, Brooklyn Fumery. It has notes of concrete dust, tomato leaf, saffron, and a 'hot pipe accord.'"

As he continued to sniff *Rat Hotel*, Jorge spoke, "Okay, real talk. You've been back for a day and a half. Did you do any investigating while you were in the big city?"

Clare revealed she had bumped into Billy's wife, and that she was the one to break the tragic news about her husband.

Also, they had a somewhat strange lunch involving unwanted anchovies and runny egg yolks.

"She said that they hadn't spoken in three years. Not since he ran off to Rome for some highbrow internship with something called the Circolo dei Profumieri."

Jorge finally put the Rat Hotel blotter down. "I need a palate cleanser now." He made a face. "Circolo dei Profumieri. Sounds like either a very expensive perfume house or a cult."

Clare nodded. "Philomena thinks it's a cult. I'm not sure she's wrong." She showed him the discarded blotters. "Are you done with these?" Jorge waved his hand to indicate that yes, he was indeed finished sniffing them. "And apart from a brief crying jag, she otherwise seemed weirdly detached. Like she's already mourned him once and doesn't have the energy to do it again. She gave me the impression that he had just disappeared one day and never looked back."

"And now he's dead."

"And now he's dead." Clare gathered her thoughts. "Did I tell you what I smelled when I found Billy?"

"No, do I want to know?"

"It wasn't an aroma, actually; it was that weird sense-switching thing that happens when I can't really smell a smell. He reeked of *Lycoctonum*, of course, we all did that night, but I sensed something hot, fiery. Yellow. It felt like a warning. Or a signal. I don't know what it meant, but it wasn't natural."

Jorge had been wandering around the shop while Clare was talking. He picked up random bottles and sniffed their atomizers. He moved some other bottles so they were precisely aligned with the edge of the shelf. Clare knew this meant he was thinking.

"I want to go back to this Circolo dei Profumieri thing. Do you have your laptop handy?"

Clare ducked into the back and emerged with her laptop. Jorge powered it up "Okay. Circolo dei Profumieri. Let's see what the internet gods tell us." He squinted at the screen. "Hmm. Vibes already questionable. Their website is minimalist.

Just a black screen with a Latin quote and a flickering candle animation. Very Dan Brown meets Byredo."

"What's the Latin?"

"Per fumum ad veritatem. Through smoke to truth. Very cult-y." Jorge continues clicking around the site. "They don't list their members. They refer to them as 'Acolytes of the Nose.' Weird. But there's a mention of chapters in Rome, Grasse, Marrakesh, and 'off-site sanctuaries.' That sounds... ominous."

"Guillermo went to Rome. Or at least that's what Philomena thinks."

After a few minutes, Jorge said, "Okay, I found a blog post from a perfumer who claims they were invited to a retreat but ghosted when they asked too many questions. They said it felt less like a mentorship and more like an initiation."

"Initiation into what?" Clare was pretty sure she really didn't want to know.

"Well, according to this blog, the Circolo believes perfume is an ancient sacred art descended from temple rituals, and that certain scent combinations can alter consciousness. There's a whole sidebar about olfactory ascension. They sound very into secrecy, symbolism, and bespoke leather notebooks. Oh, and get this, there's a rumored internal classification system. Levels of the Nose. Apprentice. Disciple. Ascendant. And then the final tier is called Profumus."

"Hm. Well, here's something for you, Jorge. Philomena said that Guillermo wasn't a talented perfumer. The former friend who gave me his notebook said something similar. So he'd never get to Profumus. This doesn't sound like a simple perfumery organization that offers internships to eager young noses."

"Then what was he doing in Rome?"

"If he had actually been in Rome. I think I need to talk to Efraim. I have a feeling he knows something about all of this."

Fifteen

After Jorge left, Clare decided she really wasn't cut out for this sleuthing business. While she was a fan of crime procedurals, those took only 43 minutes plus commercials to solve. The time it took to finish a bag of cookies and a coffee. But so far, in real life, she had downed at least 50 coffees and consumed the equivalent of a bakery full of sweet treats and still didn't know who had killed her childhood friend Billy Leight, aka perfumer Guillermo Flares. And she only had three suspects, but there could be dozens more. Anybody who had met him during his time in Baltimore could have slipped him the poison.

As she pondered the burden she had taken upon herself, her mother called.

"Hi Clare. Are you home yet?"

"Yes, I got in yesterday. What's up?"

"Good, because I'm on my way."

Fifteen minutes later, the shop door opened, and Vetiver bounded inside, followed by Terri. "Vetiver was starting to think I was his mommy, right, boy?" Terri bent over to scratch behind the ears of the scruffy terrier.

"Ma, I was only gone for three days. Please don't give me the old 'if you're going to have a pet, you need to be responsible for it' argument. I know that, and I am. It's just sometimes I need to do things that Vetiver can't participate in."

"I know, honey. I was just yanking your chain. How was New York? Solve any mysteries while you were there?"

"Actually, no. The more questions I asked, the more mysterious the mystery became. But I ordered a bunch of new stock for Good Scents. We should be set for the holiday madness."

"Speaking of the holidays, I was thinking. Should we invite the Leights over for Thanksgiving? This will be their first big holiday without Billy, and they don't have much family left in town."

"I don't know, Mom. Considering that he died after an event in my store, they probably won't want to see my charming, dimpled face." Clare grimaced for effect. "And if Stephanie is going to be in attendance, I will have to give you my regrets now."

"Is she that bad? You always talked about her as if she were Satan's spawn, but I don't remember her being such an awful child."

"Oh, Mother. You were never there to see the trouble she caused. Grandma couldn't stand her." Clare reached out for Vetiver, who stubbornly stood behind Terri's legs like a naughty toddler.

"Busia Manya loved everyone! I never heard her say a bad thing about anybody. She was the most generous soul I have ever met. She didn't even complain when you turned her charming little shop into something boring and grey." Terri looked around the shop as she said that.

"Again, you weren't there. Grandma and I had some words in multiple languages about that paint color. If Budeke's paint shop hadn't already burned down, I know she would have stomped up Broadway herself to cancel the order. Probably would have brought back more of that awful floral wallpaper she adored." Clare frowned. "I miss her so much."

"I know you do, sweetheart." Terri bent over to pet her granddog once more. "Then it's settled. I'll invite the Leights over for Thanksgiving."

It had been quiet, and a quiet shop was boring without Ivy to liven things up. To pass the time, Clare had rifled through the suggestion box. Several people thought it was a cute idea and had slipped their ideas through the slot. Clare had pulled out two of her favorites and thought up fragrances for them. She might not be able to physically create perfumes, but not even her wonky sense of smell could prevent her from fantasizing about it.

Name: Judy Cutler

Scent Idea: "A clean scent that smells like money, but not new money. Old money. Think of winter in Gstaad, but for under $50."

Why?: "I'm manifesting my second husband."

Clare couldn't help smirking. She imagined cool, dry iris for that silk-scarf elegance, a little oakmoss to suggest family trust funds, and a whiff of aldehydes like expensive dry cleaning. Maybe vetiver for backbone and a thread of ambergris, or at least Ambroxan pretending to be ambergris. Judy would want compliments. Lots of them. And she could get it for under $50... if she bought a travel spray.

Then there was this one:

Name: Brittany

Scent Idea: "I want to smell like the meanest girl at your middle school sleepover."

Why?: "Because she had power. And amazing hair."

Clare could see it: synthetic strawberry, pink hairspray aldehydes, a hit of white musk, and something plasticky and nostalgic. Maybe ethyl maltol, like the edge of cotton candy. Add a powdery floral note, just a whisper. Teen spirit and cruelty.

Clare blew out a breath. She missed playing with aroma-chemicals, creating miniature worlds in scent. She knew exactly why Billy had been so obsessed with it. Clare probably wouldn't have joined a fragrance cult, but she understood the appeal. There was something addictive about turning a feeling—heart-break, awe, the first sip of coffee on a cold morning—into a bottled story. She still dreamt about it sometimes.

Vetiver kept his human company in the shop for a couple of hours before Clare closed up for the day. They went for a quick walk around the block before heading up to her apartment to scrounge up some dinner.

Clare settled on her comfy plaid couch with a bowl of buttered pasta with a hot dog chopped up on top of it and started a grocery list on her phone. As she was typing "frozen spinach," the phone rang, startling her.

"Soooo…whatcha gonna do for your birthday, Cuz? You're going to be over the hill tomorrow. Should be special."

"I'm going to be 30, Ivy. Still a long way from dead."

Ivy cleared her throat.

"You know what I mean. Thirty isn't old. And I have no plans to do anything. I'll probably just hang out with Vetiver and watch *The Princess Bride* for the umpteenth time while eating an entire chocolate layer cake with a spoon."

"Sounds amazing. How about coming over to my place to do that? We'll have dinner. And I'll bake the cake."

Clare raised an eyebrow. "You're going to cook?"

"Maybe. Or, to be on the safe side, I can order in. But I'm going to bake you a cake."

"No gifts, okay? I don't want you to buy me anything."

"No promises. Come over at 7. Bring the mutt."

The next evening, after a fairly busy day at the shop, Clare only wanted to stay home with the cake she had purchased on her early morning grocery run. But she had promised Ivy she'd come over, so she snapped Vetiver's harness on and grabbed her Blu-ray of The Princess Bride before heading out the door. She honestly had not wanted to make a fuss of her birthday this year. It seemed selfish to celebrate anything right now, but she supposed that having dinner with a friend was better than staying home and trying to figure out who had poisoned Billy. Or even worse, staying home, trying to figure out who had poisoned Billy, and feeling sorry for herself.

Clare and Vetiver walked up Thames Street and took a left on Wolfe. This part of the neighborhood was a visual history of Fells Point. Buildings from the 18th and 19th centuries stood alongside a few more recent ones. Some homes were tall and narrow, while others were short and squat. She always puzzled over the tiny twin houses with rickety wooden siding and wood-shingled roofs that resembled something from the story of the three pigs. Other buildings had storefronts, and several of the brick facades had been covered by the faux stone architectural facing known as Formstone. She once read that Baltimore native John Waters had described it as "the polyester of brick." Clare felt that was an insult to polyester.

Ivy's small apartment was above a law office on Fleet Street. Clare couldn't figure out how she lived so close and yet was constantly late for work. After climbing the narrow stairs, Clare rapped on Ivy's door. It creaked open, and she was immediately hit with a waft of cardamom, fried onions, and vanilla.

"Surprise, Scorpio!" Jorge shouted, flinging a handful of confetti directly at her face. "Before you yell at me, this is biodegradable."

Clare blinked and coughed. "I think I inhaled some of it. Will it still biodegrade in my lungs? Also, if this is that confetti with the wildflower seeds in it, Ivy will have to invest in a lawnmower. I don't think she's ever vacuumed this carpet."

"No time for science!" Jorge said, grabbing her hand and spinning her into the room. "It's your birthday, and we are celebrating the fact that you've made it to thirty without being murdered, arrested, or becoming a true crime podcast subject. That deserves champagne."

"I told you I didn't want a party," Clare muttered, but she was already smiling. Ivy's apartment was small, but she had strung fairy lights across the bookshelves, and there was a table overflowing with mismatched candles and snacks. A tiered cake—not chocolate, Clare noted, and a bit off-kilter—sat next to a silver tray of Polish poppy seed cookies, courtesy of Clare's mother, who was holding a glass of wine and talking to Jasmine about synesthesia.

Ivy emerged from the kitchen in an apron that said, "Don't Ask." "We're having tandoori chicken." She had wisely ordered dinner from their favorite Indian restaurant, so they feasted on the chicken, along with samosas, biryani, and lamb saag. Afterwards, Ivy stuck a few candles in the top of her wonky cake, which she announced was Earl Grey olive oil cake with lemon buttercream, candied thyme, and blackberries. It was surprisingly delicious. Clare was touched that she had gone to so much trouble and amazed that her cousin had such mad baking skills.

After dinner, Jorge made an announcement. "I have a surprise for you, Clare." He rubbed his hands together.

"I tried to stop him," Ivy said, "but Jorge made a slideshow."

"I'm a weirdo, but I love a slideshow," Jorge said, opening his laptop with a flourish. "It's called Thirty Notes to Clare. Don't worry, it's only mildly embarrassing, and at least five of them are real perfume ingredients. But first, a toast." Jorge raised a glass filled with something vaguely pink and bubbly. "To Clare. Thirty, thriving, and still smelling better than anyone in this room."

Everyone joined in, and Clare let herself feel the warmth, the absurdity, the scent of joy: cookies, spices, and basmati rice. It was the first time in weeks she hadn't been haunted by the smell and vision of imagined poison.

Ivy dimmed the lights, and everyone gathered around the laptop.

The slideshow began.

"Note #1: Galbanum," Jorge announced, as a grainy photo of Clare in a windbreaker standing in front of a mountain of laundry appeared on screen. "Because you're sharp, green, and slightly bitter when people talk to you before coffee."

Laughter filled the room. Jorge continued.

"Note #2: Orris. Elegant. Complex. Slightly melancholic. Smells like you have secrets, which, let's be honest, you do."

Clare let herself relax and enjoy the show. Image after image of her life danced across the screen. Blurry selfies from *Cognoscented* meetups. Ivy trying to steal Clare's fries while wearing a perfume blotter behind her ear. Clare holding puppy Vetiver and crying. Clare on her first day at Catholic High. Clare as a little girl with her beloved daddy. By the end, Clare's cheeks were wet and hurt from smiling. Her champagne glass was empty, and someone had placed a plastic tiara on her head without her noticing.

They sat in silence for a beat, then Clare raised her glass.

"To thirty," she said. "And no corpses tonight."

Everyone clinked glasses. This evening was just what she needed. Family, good friends, and excellent food. No one mentioned Guillermo. For one night, Clare was just Clare. Still breathing. Still smelling. Still here.

Sixteen

THE NEXT MORNING, AFTER moving some bottles around to make room for the new stock that would arrive any day, Clare decided it was time to flip through Billy's Moleskine. The notebook was crammed with handwriting in tight loops and hurried scrawls, some of it scribbled sideways up the margins, as if the writer had been desperate to capture every thought before it slipped away. There were also some random folded pages from other notebooks and sticky notes tucked here and there, making the book bulge slightly. Before she had a chance to examine any of the entries more closely, someone entered the store. She was surprised to see it was Detective Briscoe. "Uh oh," Clare thought. "Something must be up." She shoved the Moleskine back into its hiding place and slipped out from behind the counter.

"Detective Briscoe, what can I do for you today?"

"Please call me Ayanna," the detective said as she shook Clare's hand. "I'm off duty. I thought I'd, um, take up your challenge to make a perfume lover out of me."

"I know I can." Clare held out her arms and spokesmodeled the array of fragrances around them. "Pretty sure there are at least two, if not more, perfumes here that you will love. But before we sniff, I need to learn a little more about you. Your hobbies, things you enjoy doing besides being a kick-ass detective for the Baltimore City Police Department..."

"No need for flattery, Clare." Ayanna chuckled. "Let me think. What do I like besides being a kick-ass detective? That is a big part of my life, for sure." She paused. "Hm...you've put me on the spot, and my mind is totally blank. I know I must have some hobbies." Ayanna laughed again, this time uncomfortably. After a few seconds, she said, "Okay, I enjoy snowboarding, believe it or not, though I don't get to do it as much as I'd like."

Ayanna shrugged off her coat, which Clare took into the back room. When she returned, Ayanna stood with her eyes tightly shut, as if to conjure up images of more things she enjoyed. "Let me give you some other info. I'm the middle child of five, four boys and me. I had to grow up tough to deal with the teasing of all the pesky males I had to be around all the time. Which continues to this day." She made a face. "I grew up here in the city, in Upton, just below Druid Hill Park."

"You mean 'Droodle' Park," Clare mock-corrected. "Pretty sure you're the only person who pronounces it 'Droo-id Hill.'"

"Oh, the Balmer accent!" Ayanna laughed. "I've tried hard not to pick it up, but my first beat was in East Baltimore, and it was hard not to tawk dat way affer hearing it aww day. Hon."

"So, what else can you tell me about yourself? I can see you're a fairly conservative dresser, even when you're not on the job." Clare eyed Ayanna's finely woven cream-colored sweater worn with a silk scarf in a blue and orange geometric pattern and navy trousers.

"Don't get me wrong, I enjoy being girly sometimes, wearing high heels and lace and all that fine stuff. But there's just no time for that in my life right now. I'll tell you what I really enjoy. A good matcha latte. Do you have anything that smells like that?"

Clare smiled and nodded in affirmation. "You've given me something to work with. Wait right there, and I'll be back with a few things for you to smell." With that, Clare knew that the shop needed a tiny café table and chairs for what she would start calling "personal consultations." She had helped many people find a signature scent or three, but she rarely did it an armful at a time. Yes. That would be a great new service to bring in customers who might otherwise be intimidated by fragrance because the selection was too vast.

Arms laden with tester bottles, Clare returned to Ayanna. She placed the bottles one by one on the console at the center of the room, arranging them carefully so the labels faced out. "Okay, I've picked a few scents I think you'll like. Let's start with *Matcha Ceremony* by Kindred of Laurel." Clare sprayed a blotter and ran it under her nostrils. "This one is all matcha latte. It has the green bitterness of the tea tempered by creamy milk, rice powder, and tonka, with a hint of vanilla. Underneath is a base of calming hinoki wood." She handed the blotter to Ayanna, who sniffed it.

"Wow! This smells exactly like a matcha latte!" Ayanna seemed astonished that this delicious substance was perfume. Clare recalled that the fragrances the detective knew from the past had been flowery and girly and powdery. Not anything she ever thought she could get into. But when introduced to fragrances that smelled like her favorite beverage, suddenly she was all in.

"Can I put this on my skin?"

"Of course. Why don't you roll up your sleeves? You might want to try more than one." Clare spritzed a bit of *Matcha Ceremony* on the inside of Ayanna's right wrist and picked up a second bottle. "This one is for the snowboarder in you. It's called *Whiteout*, by Half Moon Atelier. It's meant to feel like the cold air of a mountaintop in the winter. There's frozen pine, also birch bark—which can smell like wintergreen—a bit of peppermint, and a substance called aldehydes. In this fragrance, aldehydes are meant to mimic the sun sparkling on snow. There's some musk in the drydown as well." Clare handed the second blotter to Ayanna, who was still sniffing her wrist. Ayanna took the second blotter.

"I don't think anything can top the matcha one, Clare." She put the blotter to her nose. She opened her eyes wide and exclaimed, "This is the scent of Mount Sunapee in New

Hampshire, where I learned to snowboard. I can feel the cold air slicing through my adrenaline. It smells like snow and breathless speed." Ayanna started shaking her head like she couldn't believe her nose.

"Do you want to try this one on skin?"

"Not just yet. Let's put that aside for now. It's incredible, but I don't know if I want to smell like that all day."

"Gotcha. Now how about this one?" Clare handed a third blotter to Ayanna. "This is called *Reserve*, and it's by an indie perfumer called Elaine Goldfinch. These are all from independent perfumers, by the way. Small companies that work on a small scale. In many cases, the perfumer not only creates the fragrances but also runs the company. I think *Reserve* is something you could wear to work, but also at any time. It smells of soft suede gloves with hints of crisp vetiver and sparkling pink pepper. There's also some iris and violet leaf in here, which give it the tiniest lipstick vibe. It's businesslike but also feminine."

Ayanna took the third blotter and sniffed it. "I'm getting a bit overwhelmed here."

"We can take a break if you'd like. You're not used to this, and an untrained nose can get tired easily." Clare knew from experience that olfactory fatigue can happen when one's nose temporarily stops registering smells that it's been exposed to for a while. It's the brain's way of tuning out background stimuli so it can focus on new information. Like when one stops noticing a repetitive sound, like a loud fan. When smelling several perfumes in a row, the olfactory receptors and brain can become overwhelmed and stop distinguishing between scents accurately. It's especially common when scents are strong, complex, or very different from each other, or if one doesn't take frequent breaks between fragrances.

"No, it's not that. It's all the images and feelings that are flooding my head. As a cop, I really try not to do so much feeling. It can be an occupational hazard."

Clare nodded. "I get that. We'll take a break from sniffing, though I have two more that I want to share with you when you're ready. Why don't you reset your nose in the meantime. Some places put out little glasses of coffee beans, but I feel like that only adds another smell for your brain to process. The best thing is to sniff something totally neutral, like your own shoulder." Clare demonstrated by turning her head to the side while lifting that shoulder to meet her nose. "Take a deep breath, smell the nothingness."

"That sounds like some sort of Buddhist koan. 'Smell the nothingness.'"

"Working here all day, it's a state of mind that I can never achieve. Fragrance is my life."

Ayanna seemed to consider this for a moment. "Do you 'feel' any of the notes in these fragrances, rather than smell them?"

Clare picked up the bottle of *Matcha Ceremony* and sniffed the cap. "Yes. Most of them I do smell. I especially get the matcha and vanilla in this one and the pine and aldehydes in *Whiteout*. But I can't smell the birch bark in that one, which is fine because I could never stand wintergreen. Sadly, because the sense of smell is so closely linked to the sense of taste, some things I can't smell I also can't taste. A glass of birch beer just tastes like sweet fizzy water."

"You had said that sometimes if you can't smell a fragrance, you sense it in other ways. Can you sense the birch bark?"

"No, actually, that note just doesn't exist for me." Clare walks a few steps away and takes a bottle off the shelf. "Sometimes I can't smell the dominant note in a fragrance. For instance, this one is primarily about gardenia. But natural gardenia is one of those ingredients that's far too expensive to use in perfumery, so it's either a synthetic note, or a combination of other floral notes that approximate the smell of gardenia. This one here has synthetic gardenia, which I know because when I smell it, a big chunk of it is replaced by the sensation of what I think of as mossy blue spirals. I can see the shape and color and feel the slightly fuzzy texture in my mind." She pulls another bottle off a shelf. "Now, this one has a combination of white floral notes to mimic gardenia. When I smell it, I do smell it. There are no weird sensations with this one."

Ayanna is fascinated. "I've never heard anything like that. It's so strange, but so interesting. Have you studied your condition?"

"Yes, a little. It's clearly not common, as I haven't been able to find anything on people who have a similar issue with their sense of smell. Some doctors have called it 'psychosomatic sensory substitution.' They explain it as multiple senses stepping in to replace the one that is lost. I don't know what it is, but I've adapted to it completely. The issue has been part of my life for a decade now. Sometimes, though, I wish I could smell like normal people. I even attended a lecture by a guy who calls himself 'Dr Lavender' when I was in New York. I thought maybe he would understand my issues, but it turned out he's just a charlatan."

Clare wasn't sure she believed that entirely, but she said it anyway.

"I know I said I was off duty," Ayanna began, "but I am so fascinated by your 'issue,' as you call it, and how it pertains to the death of Guillermo Flares. Can you explain that again to me?"

"Sure. His fragrance, *Lycoctonum*, is something I can smell pretty much in its entirety. It mostly registers in what is called the 'olfactory bulb,' a part of the brain that is just below the frontal lobe and above the nasal cavity. I can smell the tart blackcurrant opening, the rose, the amber, oakmoss, etc. There's also something in it he called a 'hellebore accord.' An accord is a combination of notes that are meant to evoke the smell of something else, in this case the plant hellebore, which doesn't have much of a smell on its own. He chose to interpret this scent as something dark and green." Clare waved her hand as if to erase those words from the air. "The smell green, not the color. Once you get into perfumery, you'll understand that there are notes that smell green, like tomato leaves or basil. Recognizing the distinct notes is a brain-training thing that I'd be delighted to help you with if you are ever interested. The only thing in *Lycoctonum* that didn't register as a smell to me is the absinthe he used in that hellebore accord. I can smell it a little, but it mostly registers in my brain as the tinkling of delicate glass wind chimes."

Ayanna nodded, occasionally sniffing the *Matcha Ceremony* on her wrist.

Clare continued. "Because it had been sprayed so much in here that evening, the smell of *Lycoctonum* was imprinted on my psyche. Ivy even remarked that it could be tasted because the concentration in the air was so strong. We had it in our hair and on our clothes, as did Guillermo. But when I found his body, that wasn't the only smell I smelled. Or rather, sensed. There wasn't much scent left in the bedroom, as he had apparently not passed through there in a while, but the bathroom was still fragrant. *Lycoctonum* was there in all its mysterious beauty, but I could also feel that odd heat. The sensation of flames, yellow flames. And when I bent down near his body, the feeling only got stronger. But of course, I could also smell the *Lycoctonum*. I don't know why that additional sensation would float around him. I just knew it didn't belong."

"Perhaps it was the smell of death?"

"Oh, no. I've been around dead people before. The whole family was with my grandmother when she passed, and her smell didn't change. And there are always dead rats in this neighborhood. They just smell bad. No yellow flames."

"Poison though? It couldn't be anything else? The smell of the fabric softener they use at the hotel, the carpet cleaner, his toothpaste?"

Clare shook her head. "I suppose it could be something like that. I could go to Ferguson's Wharf and ask them to smell their towels and stuff, to rule those out. They'll think I'm a weirdo, but I guess that's nothing new." She chuckled bitterly. "It's not like I've ever been Miss Popularity."

Ayanna smelled the other perfumes that Clare had pulled for her, plus a couple more she found on her own after reading the shelf cards listing the notes for each scent in the shop.

"I think I've probably done enough for one day. I need to go home and detox or something." They both laughed.

"It can be a lot, for sure. But you seem like you're getting the hang of it."

"I hate to admit it, Clare, but you were absolutely right. I can feel myself getting into fragrance in a big way now. Now that I know it's not all flowery, girly, powdery stuff. And I'm going to make my first purchase. I'll take a bottle of that delicious matcha scent, please. And I might come back for more later."

"Baby steps!" Clare said as she picked up a new bottle of *Matcha Ceremony* off the shelf and took it to the counter. "I'll include some samples of the other fragrances you tried. How would you like to pay for this?"

As Clare rang up the transaction, Ayanna filled out a suggestion card and dropped it in the box. "Thanks, Clare. This was fun. See you soon."

Clare wasn't sure how to take that. Did she mean professionally in a police manner, or as a customer?

Seventeen

THIS TIME OF YEAR was always hard on Clare. It was her birth month, which should be somewhat joyous, but November was also the anniversary of her father's passing. He had died 21 years earlier on a chilly, grey day, much like the one Clare was currently viewing through her windshield. She totally understood why her mother wanted to invite the Leights and their grief over for the holiday. Teresa Buchowski firmly believed in the adage, "the more the merrier." As if it had any truth to it. But she was a fan of distraction, even if it wasn't a good one.

The family had dwindled down over the years until it was just Clare and Terri. If it were up to Clare, they'd leave town for a few days, do something fun. Maybe go out west. Vegas would definitely be a distraction, possibly even a fun one. But her mother wouldn't hear of it. Especially now that Clare had the shop. "Think about all the Black Friday sales you'd lose."

For the past several years, they had Ivy celebrating with them, and her cheery personality was a welcome addition. But Clare was pretty sure her cousin would jump at the chance to spend the holiday in Sin City, or anywhere other than Baltimore. Maybe next year.

She turned her trusty old Toyota Corolla into the driveway of Saint Stanislaus Cemetery and continued up the winding trail to the Buchowski family plot. Clare put the car in park and got out with a handful of mums and a can of her dad's favorite beer. It seemed like the thing to do, to visit the cemetery, to be one with her grief.

"Hi Daddy." Clare was certain that her father couldn't hear her, and she wasn't sure she believed in an afterlife, but she could appreciate the ceremony of it all. She bent over to pull the few weeds that had grown over her father's bronze plaque, despite the best efforts of the groundskeepers, and placed the mums on top.

"I miss you so much." She sniffled, rifled in her coat pocket for a tissue. Not finding one, she wiped her nose on the sleeve of her hoodie. Clare then cracked open the beer and poured it on the grave.

Just beyond her father's grave was that of Busia Manya. Unlike the rest of the family's more modest headstones or plaques, Mary Buchowski's resting place was marked with a tall, custom-made memorial of red granite decorated with a carved red poppy—the national flower of Poland—and the phrase "*Na zawsze w naszych sercach.*"

"Forever in our hearts, indeed, Busia." Clare bowed her head as if in prayer, squeezed back a few tears, and turned toward her vehicle.

Just a few rows over from the Buchowski family plot, Clare saw her.

Stephanie Leight.

Billy's sister stood by his grave with her hands in her coat pockets, back stiff, breath fogging in the cold. She brought no candles or flowers. It was just her alone, staring down at the plain grey stone. Clare hesitated, then approached slowly across the grass. Fallen leaves crackled underfoot.

"Stephanie."

Stephanie turned. Her eyes were unreadable behind dark sunglasses, the kind with thick square frames that looked more like armor than fashion. "Clare."

Clare pulled her sleeves over her hands, wishing she had brought gloves. “I didn’t know he was buried here.”

“Yeah. Mom and Dad didn’t ask for input.” Stephanie’s voice was flat. “I’m actually surprised they didn’t have him cremated, so they could keep their darling little boy on their mantel forever.” She shifted her weight and glanced back at the headstone, as if it had interrupted her thoughts.

Clare tried for civility. “I was just over visiting my dad. I didn’t expect to...”

“See me here?” Stephanie cut in. “Don’t worry. I don’t come here often.”

Clare nodded. “Still. I’m sorry.”

Stephanie let out a faint, bitter laugh. “For what?”

“I don’t know,” Clare said. “Everything?”

Stephanie looked down. She toed the fresh dirt on her brother’s grave. “He always said you understood him. The way his mind worked. The way he talked about scent like it meant something cosmic.”

Clare tilted her head. “It did. To him. To me, too.”

“Yeah. Well. To me, it smelled like ego.” Stephanie’s jaw tensed. “He was always trying to prove something. And I made sure he couldn’t.”

It was the first honest thing she’d said. Clare’s voice softened. “He looked up to you, you know.”

Stephanie’s mouth twitched. There was silence. A train horn sounded in the distance.

Clare stepped closer. “Why were you always so hard on him?”

“You wouldn’t understand.”

Clare didn’t answer. She didn’t understand. She would have loved to have a younger sibling who worshipped her. That’s probably why she loved Ivy so much.

Stephanie spoke again, this time almost absently. “I still have one of his bottles. Something he mailed me a few months ago. Said it was his ‘breakthrough.’ I never opened it.”

“Why not?”

Stephanie blinked behind her sunglasses. "I didn't think it would be good enough." Then she turned, pulled her coat tighter, and walked back to her car.

Clare stood alone in silence, watching her go before walking back to her car, the chill biting harder now that the conversation was over. Stephanie's words replayed in her mind: "I didn't think it would be good enough." Clare had heard cruelty dressed as pragmatism before. But this was different. Not overt malice. Not grief, either. Did Stephanie hate her brother? She'd belittled him. Undermined him. Treated him like a child playing dress-up while she was busy being serious. But hate? Clare didn't know. And that was the problem. "I didn't think it would be good enough." Not good enough to open. Not good enough to grieve. Not good enough to keep alive? Clare felt a cold dread: had Stephanie taken her brother's life, or had she just been indifferent to it?

The next morning, Clare was still feeling some of the melancholy she had felt at the cemetery. "Hey, can you stop that, please?"

"What, this?" Ivy squeezed a handful of bubble wrap, which made an absurdly loud popping noise. She was wrapping a bottle for shipment and could never resist popping the wrap as she worked.

"Yes, that. I've got a headache. And I'm still trying to process yesterday's trip to the cemetery."

"Hey, I told you I'd go with you if you needed me to. I know it's hard."

"I know, and I appreciate it. But it's something I needed to do on my own." Clare took a sip of her coffee. "I saw Stephanie at the cemetery."

"What, Billy's sister? Was she gathering bones to powder for one of her 'healing potions'?"

Clare gave a humorless smile. "No. She just stood there at his grave. Said she didn't think what he made was good enough."

Ivy wrinkled her nose. "Wow. That's a hell of a eulogy."

Clare stared into her mug. "She kept talking as if he were a failure. Like she made sure he stayed one."

"She used to bully him," Ivy said. "Remember the chess stories? Three moves and done? That's not sibling rivalry. That's a psychological experiment."

Clare didn't laugh. She shifted. "But would she kill him?"

Ivy paused, hands still. "Like... *kill*-kill?"

Clare nodded, eyes serious.

Ivy leaned back against the counter. "Okay. Look. She sounds as if she still thinks she's smarter than everyone else. And yeah, she's got that quietly terrible big-sister energy. But poison? That's deliberate. That's personal. You think she's got that in her?"

"I don't know," Clare murmured. "That's the worst part."

Ivy's voice softened. "Do you think she feels guilty?"

Clare hesitated. "Yes... but not exactly about his death. About what she let happen, or didn't. About who she was when she was with him, or who she wished she could have been."

Ivy exhaled slowly. "That's not nothing."

"No," Clare agreed. "But it's not proof of innocence, either."

Later that afternoon, Clare decided to dispose of the ramshackle mess of a shrine in front of the store. The sun was shining, which made her realize what an eyesore it had become. She was also tired of people reminding her that she needed to put her trash in a receptacle if she expected the Department of Public Works to haul it away. Clare had left the small mountain of plushies and silk roses through Halloween, but creepy time was long over. She pulled on rubber gloves and grabbed a couple of trash bags from the back room and got to work out front. As she shoved the various mangy items into a bag, recoiling from the smell of dog urine that soaked parts of the shrine, she thought about the people who had left these things. It seemed impossible that so many people had passed through the doors of Good Scents on the night of the launch party. The turnout had been good, but the size of the shrine seemed to indicate that far more were in mourning than had been interested in purchasing the dead perfumer's final fragrance. Clare thought of something she had not yet considered: had one of Guillermo's fans killed him? Did he have a relationship with one of them that went sour? Were there rival perfumers among them, perhaps ones that had knowledge of poisonous ingredients? And, just as important, how had they, or anyone, gotten Guillermo to take poison? There were far too many questions, and she hated that she couldn't answer any of them.

When she got back into the shop, Ivy told her that Detective Briscoe had called.

"Why didn't you grab me? You know I wanted to hear from her.

"You were up to your elbows in dog pee and rotten roses. You'd have wanted to wash up before touching your phone."

"Yeah, you're right." Clare sniffed herself. "I reek! Damn dogs." She looked up at the ceiling as if Vetiver were upstairs listening. "Not you, baby. Other dogs." She peeled off the rubber gloves and shoved them into the trash bag. "I'm going to get rid of this and go upstairs to change. I'll call Briscoe while I'm up there."

Hands and face washed and clad in a fresh t-shirt and cardigan, Clare returned Ayanna Briscoe's call.

"I'm sorry this has taken so long, Ms Buchowski...Clare, but we've finally opened an investigation into the death of Guillermo Flares. We've had the ME's report for a little while, but it's Baltimore. We're busy." The detective paused before continuing. "Look, I shouldn't be telling you any of this, but the report noted that there had been some cardiac activity, ventricular fibrillation, which should not happen to a healthy young man with no other signs of heart disease. There was nothing unusual about the contents of his stomach. Looks like his last meal had been a pastry of some sort and possibly coffee. But we are still waiting for the tox report, and I hope that we'll get something in before the holiday."

"Thanksgiving or Christmas?" Clare was stupefied that it took so long to get anything done. But as the detective said, it was Baltimore, and they were busy.

"Either would be good, actually." Briscoe lowered her voice. "I think you might be right about poisoning, but you didn't hear that from me."

Clare knew she was right, but she hadn't expected to hear this from the police. "What makes you say that?"

"Like you, I have a hunch. I know I shouldn't even think that way. But there were no outward physical signs that the deceased habitually used drugs, no organ damage. And there were no markings anywhere to show something had been injected. However, there were small vesicles—blisters—on his wrists, which showed that he had been in contact with something poisonous. And of course, the ventricular fibrillation, which can happen as a result of poisoning."

Clare found herself excited. "I knew it! Now I just have to figure out what the poison was."

"What's this 'I' business? I'm just keeping you informed of the situation, though I shouldn't get you more involved than you already are. Under no circumstances are you to attempt to figure this out on your own. If Mr Flares was poisoned, he was murdered. This could be a very dangerous situation that you should stay far away from."

"Can I ask a question though? You're treating me as if I'm not a suspect. Is that true?"

"As I said, I'm going by a hunch. A murderer doesn't just offer the means of death to a police detective. And you have no motive."

"I also have no alibi. I was home alone after the event. My dog wasn't even here with me."

"Understood. I just don't think you did it."

"I didn't do it. I would never do something like that."

"While I have you on the phone," Detective Briscoe changed her tone to one that was more casual. "Do you still have a bottle of that *Reserve* fragrance in stock?"

After ending her call with Ayanna and going back down to the shop, Clare allowed herself to feel some relief. Part of the reason she had been working so hard to figure out who had poisoned Billy was to exonerate herself. And now that she knew the detective had believed her, she could breathe a little easier. She had never been on her own list of suspects, of course, so she still had some work to do. Clare was still playing over in her mind all the things that had happened while she was in New York. The weird Dr Lavender and his card with the scribbled word "wolfsbane." How had he known about that? What did he know about it? Clare knew she should contact him to ask questions, but she wasn't sure what questions needed to be asked. And what about Philomena? She had seemed like a nice woman who was more than a little eccentric. Clare was inclined to believe her story. But why had Billy changed like that? The more she thought about it, the more she realized the signs had been there for a long time. The Baltimore rumor mill had been telling various stories about Billy for years, about where he had gone to school or not, about his different personality. Maybe he just needed to meet the right people—or the wrong ones—to bring about a complete change. In a way, it was a bit like alchemy.

Billy had been sweet. He'd come to her grandmother's shop after school, sniffing fragrance oils, scribbling in a marble composition book about top notes and basenotes and dreams. But somewhere along the way, that sweetness curdled. He left Baltimore as if he were escaping something. And maybe he was. The fear that he'd never become who he wanted to be. This was Nigredo, the death of the self, the burning away of who he was. He shed the name Billy like an old skin.

Then came Guillermo. He told Philomena he was a "different man." He put on a new suit, ate different things, and said he had better taste and instincts. This was Albedo: purification, refinement. He polished the soot off himself and presented something gleaming and mysterious.

But Clare saw it now. It wasn't clarity. It was control.

Despite that, he wasn't satisfied. The pomp didn't satisfy the ache. Guillermo began chasing something else, something older. He became obsessed with her grandmother's multilingual book of remedies. He believed there were answers in it. This was Citrinitas, the illumination. The light of understanding.

Right now, he should be in the final stage. Completion. Enlightenment. Guillermo Flares, full-fledged perfumer, philosopher of scent, unburdened by the past. But it didn't take. He died with secrets. With unfinished formulas and unopened vials. With his body still caught between who he was and who he was meant to be. That would have been Rubedo: the union of all things. The philosopher's stone. But he never reached it. He didn't transmute. He just... disappeared.

"He never reached Rubedo," Clare said out loud.

Ivy, mouth full of poppyseed cookie, said, "Rubedo? That sounds like a luxury foot cream."

Clare, lost in thought, blinked. "It's the final stage of spiritual transformation."

Ivy chewed, nodded, and wiggled a little. "Ah. Soul glow-up. Check."

Clare gave a faint shake of her head, amused.

Ivy finished her cookie, bounced on the balls of her feet, and said, "Clare... I have something I need to tell you."

Eighteen

"I WAS THINKING THAT I'd like to go out with Efraim again." Ivy folded her long arms around herself as if to stop herself from bouncing around. "I like him."

"Oh, honey."

Clare was pretty sure that Ivy wasn't Efraim's type. But as a cisgender heterosexual woman, she didn't feel it was right to speculate where he fell within the LGBTQIA+ spectrum. And that was his business, and possibly Ivy's, depending on their relationship.

"I'm sorry I forgot to ask all the questions when we went out to dinner, but I was just having a good time. I got the dirt on Philomena, but you got it from the who..."

Clare knew exactly what Ivy was going to say. "Horse's mouth. Horse, as in the animal. The phrase is 'straight from the horse's mouth.'"

"That's just weird. I like my way better."

Clare and Ivy compared Philomena stories. Efraim's matched Guillermo's in that he had gone to Rome to escape Philomena, whom he did not marry.

"But according to the horse, they married, and he ran away to join a cult?"

Clare wondered if Ivy cut off some of the long wild curls that hung down past her ears, she might hear better. "He claimed to have won a prestigious internship. Philomena thought it was a cult because after he had flown to Rome a few times to meet with this group, he started acting like a different person and insisted on being called by a new name."

"But is it a cult?"

"Call Efraim and let's find out."

Ivy stuck her lip out in a childish pout. "I think he's ghosting me. He hasn't returned any of my texts or calls."

"Give me his number. I'll call him."

Clare punched in his number.

"Efraim? This is Clare from Good Scents. I was wondering if you wouldn't mind coming to the shop so I can ask you a few questions about Guillermo. Mostly stuff I'm curious about." Clare stopped, listened. "Oh, come on. I'm not above begging. Pretty please?" Clare paused to listen again. "I just met Philomena and got her side of the story. Yes, I know you told Ivy, but I wanted to hear it from you myself. And I'll tell you what she said."

Ivy was leaning into her so hard, listening in, Clare thought they were both going to fall over. She put the phone on speaker. "I can make it worth your while by buying you dinner."

"Well, I haven't eaten yet..." Efraim sounded unsure.

"So you're in? Great! How about tonight if you're not doing anything?"

He hesitated. "Sure. Ok. Tonight is fine."

Clare picked up the phone and turned off the speaker. "Fabulous. See you around 7. The shop will be closed, so knock on the door and I'll let you in. Ok. Bye."

"Why was that so easy for you?" Ivy frowned.

"I wouldn't call that easy. But maybe because I'm non-threatening."

"Are you saying that I am?"

"Where do you want to eat tonight, Ivy? Someplace close. I don't feel like traveling."

"How about The Point? We haven't been there for a while."

There was a rap on the door a couple of minutes before 7pm. Clare opened it for her guest. "Efraim, come on in."

"Hi Clare." He smiled and gave an awkward little wave. "Hi Ivy. How are you?"

"Hi, Efraim. We're going to a restaurant just up the street, if that's okay with you."

Efraim looked like he might change his mind. Then he smiled. "I'm actually glad you called. I've been replaying the night of the launch party repeatedly in my head, trying to figure things out. It might be good to talk to someone about it."

Clare and Ivy grabbed their coats, and the three headed to the restaurant on the corner of Thames and Ann Streets. Once seated, Clare got straight to it. "The thing I am most curious about is the missing bottle of bourbon. When you left here that night, you were on a mission to buy a bottle for Guillermo. But when I found him the next day, there was no evidence that you had done so. There were no bottles or glass in his room."

"Oh, that one is easy. I'm not from here, so I didn't know where the closest liquor store was."

"There are, like, three of them, a block from here." Ivy had her arms folded. She was still annoyed that Efraim hadn't responded to her texts from the previous week. Just then, a server came by to take their drink orders.

"I think I'm going to need something strong to get through this evening. Can I get an old-fashioned with extra cherries, please?" Ivy looked at her dining companions. "Since we're talking bourbon. It sounds good right now."

"Make that two," Clare agreed. She might need something strong, even if she wouldn't be able to taste the whiskey.

Efraim chuckled. "Can't argue with that. I'll have one as well." After the server left, Guillermo's former assistant continued his answer to Clare's question. "Like I said, I didn't know. So, I headed in the wrong direction. I think Guillermo had wanted me to have the bourbon in his room waiting for him when he got there, but that didn't happen. He got there before me and shot me a text. He said he wasn't feeling well and was just going to go straight to bed. That I didn't have to bring him any alcohol. So, I said goodnight and went to my room without stopping by his."

"But what about the next morning? You seem to have disappeared."

"Ah, well, Guillermo had planned to go back to Rome right away, but I hadn't ever been to Washington DC. We had agreed that he wouldn't need me for a few days after the launch party. He'd go back to Europe, and I'd explore DC, and then I'd meet up with him in a week. I checked out of the hotel early, like 8am, and took a train to DC."

"And you didn't stop by his room on the way out?"

"Clare, he was my employer, not my friend. He didn't pay all that well, and he didn't treat me great. When he said he didn't need me, I was happy to be free for a time. I wasn't going to stop by and have him suddenly remember he needed me to do something for him."

"Makes sense." Ivy looked at Clare.

"Hey, I pay you a living wage." Clare stuck out her tongue.

Ivy smiled. "And you are my best friend."

After a beat, Efraim cleared his throat. "So, Clare, tell me about your meeting with Philomena."

Clare related what she had been told, which matched Efraim's version pretty well. Except for the part about getting married.

Efraim rubbed his chin. "Wow. He swore up and down that she had become a stalker and he had to leave the country to get rid of her."

"Philomena said he had joined some sort of perfumery organization in Rome, where he started acting strangely and changed his name."

"Yes, that's sorta what happened." Efraim screwed his mouth and narrowed his eyes as if he was thinking especially hard about it.

"So… he really joined the Circolo dei Profumieri?"

"What? Oh, my god. Is that what she told you?" Efraim slapped his hand on the tabletop. "HA!"

"Yes, that's what she said."

"No, absolutely not. Guillermo wouldn't last five minutes in that crowd. Too many rules. No, we met at a studio called Compagnia Aromatica Internazionale. Sounds fancy, right? But it was basically a co-op of weirdos in a moldy building near Campo de' Fiori."

"Wait. So it wasn't a secret society?"

"Not unless you count their Wi-Fi password. I'm sorry, but I can't seem to stop laughing." Efraim's shoulders shook with his mirth.

"Then what was he doing there?"

"Trying to figure out how to be taken seriously. Making things. Learning. Failing. Starting over. That place gave him space to screw up in five languages."

"But Philomena thought…"

"Philomena. Of course. She heard 'Italy' and 'perfumery' and googled her way to the most dramatic conclusion. Which, to be fair, seems to be on-brand for her. Guillermo told me she was a bit of a drama queen." Efraim started laughing again. "I know, look who's talking, right?"

"Okay, so not a cult. Tell us about how you met at this Aromatica place."

"We were both studying with a perfumer called Balordo Laddro. This guy was totally fascinated by Guillermo's constant chatter about some old book that he once had. He spoke about it as if it held all the secrets of the world. He described it as a relic, a life's work passed down and added onto until it stopped belonging to one person. And that some entries were written like spells. Or prayers."

"Ah, that would be our family's book of folk remedies. It was essentially a cookbook for our grandmother. It held recipes for the various tinctures and salves she made for her customers."

"Exactly. Guillermo was obsessed with that book. He had copied down several things from it over the years he had access to it, and he recopied them into a Moleskine he carried everywhere with him. His life's work was in that notebook. I suppose it's lost now."

The server had brought their drinks, and Clare sipped hers thoughtfully. "Actually," she said, "I have it. One of Billy's friends brought it to me a while ago. She said she worked with him at LuxeOne. You said he had it in Rome. I have it now in Baltimore. How is that possible?"

"Perhaps he had gone through several of them over the years? You may have an older book, while the one I saw him with could have been volume six. Or he could have taken it to her in New York before he came here for the launch party. Who knows?"

"But why take it to her to give to me when he could have given it directly to me?"

"Clare, judging from the stories you've heard from me and his... wife, do you think the man was the same person you knew as a child? He changed so much over the years, it's hard to say exactly what his reasons were for doing anything. Also, pretty sure he didn't know he was going to die that night."

Ivy interrupted them. "Can we get crabby tots to eat while you guys are yakking? I am starving." She patted her belly, which grumbled audibly.

Clare flagged their server, and they ordered food. There were just too many mysteries involved in the Billy Leight/Guillermo Flares saga. Perhaps these minor details weren't the important ones. What she really needed to do was figure out who had killed him.

Nineteen

THE SHOP HAD BEEN doing steady business all day. Just after lunchtime, a pair of 40-something women came in. After greeting them, Ivy offered her assistance. "Can I help you find anything in particular?"

"No, we're just browsing right now. Thanks," said the shorter of the two. She had dark curly hair and was wearing a denim jacket embroidered with the logo of an easy listening band from the 70s. The other woman had already made a beeline to the shelf on which the last few bottles of *Lycoctonum* were displayed.

"Here it is!" she whispered loudly to her short friend. "This is the one I've been reading about!" She picked up the tester from the shelf and examined it, then cautiously sniffed the atomizer. "It smells strong. I don't know if I'm going to like this one."

"Gimme that, Heather." The short one snatched the tester from her friend's hand and grabbed a blotter from the cup on the shelf. She gave it a good dousing in scent and shook it a bit before putting it to her nose. "Ooh," she murmured, "this is different. But nice." She took another long sniff, closed her eyes, then fell to the ground.

"Emily! Oh my!" Heather immediately squatted down to her friend, who was now unconscious. Ivy rushed over. She had been scrolling through Instagram, but she jumped into action when the woman shouted.

"What happened?" Ivy asked.

"She took a sniff of this stuff, this Lycock...lycock...Guillermo Flares thing, and she went down. Emily! Wake up!" Heather was patting her friend's hand more and more rapidly, then started shoving at her shoulder. "Wake. Up!" she commanded.

Emily lay there. Ivy slapped at the distraught Heather's hand and said, "Quit it! That's not helping." She then took Emily's pulse, which was feeble but there. Ivy let out a sigh.

Clare came out of the back room at that moment.

"What's going on here?"

"She fainted. I think. What do you do when someone faints? Is there such a thing as smelling salts, or did I just make that up?" Ivy looked afraid.

Clare scanned the shop for something that could smell like those salts. What exactly did they smell like, anyway? She took it literally and grabbed something salty, a bottle of Flavigny Fragrances *Sel Noir*, which featured top notes of black salt and pink pepper that should be pungent enough to pull this woman out of her faint. Just then, another customer came in and announced his presence as he unwound his scarf. "Harlan Bixby." Clare cringed internally and handed the bottle of *Sel Noir* to her cousin.

While Clare went to deal with Mr Bixby, Ivy spritzed a blotter and held it under Emily's nose; her immediate reaction was to sputter and sneeze. Emily opened her eyes in a panic, then rubbed them. After a few moments, Emily took a deep breath and rolled over onto her side, then attempted to sit up.

"Slowly now," Heather helped her friend into a seated position as Emily grabbed the blotter from Ivy's hand. "What is that stuff? It's amazing!" Emily sniffed deeply, noticing the rosy white floral heart and the strong base of amber, patchouli, and black musk.

"Are you okay? What happened?" Though the woman seemed fine now, perhaps a little dizzy, Ivy was concerned. Stuff like this could be harmful to a business, especially one that was involved with the recent death of a perfumer. The perfumer of the scent that had made Emily pass out.

"I don't know, really. I pass out sometimes. My blood pressure plummets, and so do I. It's something called vaso-vagal syncope. It's not serious, but it can be scary. The last thing I remember was sniffing the *Lycoctonum* and thinking it was interesting stuff." Emily shook her head. "That poor perfumer. He created something great and then, just like that, he died."

Heather volunteered, "Actually, we came here specifically to smell that perfume. We read about it online and had to experience it before it was all sold out." She continued, "We're from Pittsburgh and decided to take a road trip, maybe get some Christmas shopping done while we're here. There are some cute shops on Thames Street. And we'll have some crab cakes."

Emily chuckled at that. "Pittsburgh isn't known for its crab cakes." Heather whispered something in her ear as Emily tried to stand up. "Honestly, I feel much better. Would love a glass of water though, and maybe a place to sit that wasn't the floor."

Clare was busy on the opposite side of the room with Mr Bixby and his story of the tragic reformulation of his favorite fragrance, so Ivy scurried into the back room for a bottle of water and a chair. When she returned, both women were gone, as was the tester of *Lycoctonum*. Meanwhile, Clare was spraying yet another blotter with a classic fougère-style fragrance and had missed their escape.

"Burnt biscuits!" Ivy ran her fingers haphazardly through her wild curly hair and cracked her neck. She had worked at the shop for a few years but had never been there during a shoplifting. Clare had experienced a few incidents, but, in general, people don't tend to steal niche perfumes. Not random thieves, at least. Their stock was on the expensive side, so there was always a possibility that something would walk out the door, but so far Good Scents had been lucky. "Good thing we have that other tester."

Clare was still dealing with Bixby. "You're the only one who has taken this seriously. That's why I enjoy coming to your shop so much. I prefer the shops in New York, of course, but Good Scents does in a pinch." Clare nodded because she had nothing to say. Bixby went on. "Let's go back to the second one. I think it had potential. Something woody. Was it vetiver?"

"Yes, sir. Haitian vetiver. Dry, grassy, a little earthy."

He set the blotter down with a sigh. "I must let these ferment in my thoughts. There are no quick answers in perfumery, Ms Buchowski. Only questions and the courage to live with them." Clare smiled with her mouth but not her eyes. Bixby rearranged his scarf around his neck, signaling he was ready to leave, and started toward the door. "Until next time, Ms Buchowski."

Once Bixby was out the door, Clare let out an exaggerated sigh, hoping that Ivy would laugh. Harlan Bixby was a semi-regular thorn in their collective side, who took up a lot of time and had, to this point, never purchased a thing. He never even asked for a decant. But Ivy wasn't laughing.

"We've been robbed."

"What? But we've both been standing here for the last hour."

"Yeah, and that's when it happened. That *Sel Noir* worked like a charm in reviving the chick who passed out. Then she wanted to sit on something that wasn't the floor, so I went into the back to grab a chair. When I returned, both of them were gone, and so was the tester of *Lycoctonum*."

"Is that all they took?"

"I think so."

"Whew, Ivy. You scared me. I thought someone had come in and taken money or something more important than a half-full tester."

"I'm sorry. It's just that I've never been involved in a situation like that. I can't believe I fell for their histrionics. Dang, I am gullible."

"No, Ivy. You are a good person. That's different."

"Well, I'm going to think twice about being nice to random people who pass out in our store from now on."

Twenty

REACHING INTO HER POCKET for her keys with her right hand, Clare placed her left hand on the doorknob; it turned smoothly, and the door creaked open. Had she not locked it last night? There had been the distraction of the shoplifting incident during the day, but she was pretty sure that not only had she closed the door behind her, but she had also locked it securely.

Clare pushed the door open slowly and looked around the shop before stepping inside. Nothing seemed to have been disturbed. The lights were out, and the perfume bottles were all in place. Harbaugh was still looking over the space from his perch on the counter. She stepped into the shop and called out, "Hello?" Nothing. "That was dumb, Clare," she thought to herself, "as if a prowler would answer." She closed the door behind her and locked it before she went into the back. She briefly reconsidered. Should she have left it open in case she had to escape? No, she was just being silly. Nothing bad was going to happen. But she had thought the same thing the night of the launch party.

To be on the safe side, she reached into her bag and took out her trusty pepper spray before tiptoeing into the back room. She slammed on the light switch, which thankfully was just inside the entrance. Nobody was there. Just shelves, supplies, and Frankincense, the taxidermy cat. With her heart banging against her ribcage, Clare briefly considered leaving the building and running somewhere that felt safer, maybe to Ivy's apartment. But nothing seemed out of place, and she had been upstairs not an hour ago. "Clare, stop being so dramatic," she admonished herself as she hung her coat on a hook. When she reemerged from the back room, she noticed a black notebook near the credit card machine. She had not looked at Billy's Moleskine at all yesterday, and it certainly hadn't been on the counter when she closed the shop last night. But there it was on the counter, open to a blank page. A pen rested next to it, as if someone had been about to jot down a note. Clare then noticed that the little stack of papers next to the suggestion box was askew. She peered into the box to see if there was anything inside, though she knew it had been emptied the previous morning. There was a card. It had no name, just a suggestion. "Consider keeping the guests alive?" Not the kind of suggestion they were looking for, but it was certainly a valid one.

Clare was spooked. Who had broken in last night, and how had they found Billy's notebook? She flipped through it, scanning for anything torn out, but nothing seemed missing. Since she'd never examined it in detail, she wasn't sure what had been there all along. The notebook, bursting with extra pages and sticky notes, gave nothing away. She stashed it back in its hiding place under the counter and distracted herself with shelving some of the new fragrances that she had ordered in NY while hoping Ivy wouldn't show up too late.

Ivy stumbled in the door five minutes late with her usual apology and giant coffee. She also had a shopping bag from one of the local bakeries with her.

"What's this?" Clare took the bag from her cousin and began rummaging through it.

"Since tomorrow is Thanksgiving, and we'll be stressed out of our gourds—like what I did there? gourds?—I thought we might want to do our stress eating in advance. I'm not sure I'll have the appetite for it tomorrow, what with the Leights being there and all."

"UGH! I wish you hadn't reminded me of them." She pulled a white bag out of the shopper and opened it. "I think I might just start with this pumpkin danish, if you don't mind. Unless you want half?"

"Nope, I got two because I knew neither of us would be in the mood for sharing."

Clare felt better after demolishing the danish and went into the back room to get the box of holiday decorations. "I think we should get this done today, because hopefully we won't have time for this on Black Friday." She made a face as she dragged out several feet of mangy plastic evergreen garland. "Might be time to buy new decorations. This looks like it's from the 1970s." Shoving it back into the box, she then unearthed a plastic Santa with a moth hole in his hat. "Yuck. I wish I had looked at this stuff earlier. Now I have to go out to buy more."

Ivy had gone into the back room while Clare was talking and emerged with another box. "This is the stuff we used last year. That ratty stuff must have belonged to Grandma." She opened the box and took out a selection of poseable elf dolls, both male and female. "See, we had these cute things you bought at Valley View Farms last year." She pulled out some nicer garland and neat burgundy bows. "We used this stuff on the counter, and around the edge of the console. And the elves, of course, went on the shelves!"

The cousins festooned the shop with merriment while steadily eating their way through the shopping bag of pastries. Ivy stood back at one point, hands on hips, and appraised the progress they had made on the decor. "Ya know, putting up Christmas stuff always gives me the feels, like I'm a kid again."

"Me too. In fact, I was thinking about the old days recently, and it gave me an a-ha moment over Billy's name change. 'Guillermo Flares' seemed familiar, but I couldn't quite figure out why. My original theory was that it was the name of a little-known perfumer, and he adopted it to appear more, I dunno, famous? But that would have been dumb. I know he wanted to be famous in his own right. And then I remembered Mrs Filipowiak, who lived next door to the Leights. She always had the prettiest little garden in front of her house on Streeper Street, with marigolds and pansies and some trailing ivy planted in big pots. Billy liked to play with his action figures in the dirt, hiding them in the flower stems like it was an alien jungle. Mrs Filipowiak would come outside and yell at him to get out of her flowers, though the way she said it with her heavy Baltimore accent it sounded more like 'gerama flares.'"

"Ah." Ivy understood. "So, in essence, that had been his name since he was a kid. I get it. It's not that different from when my older brothers called me 'sissy.' I might have had a boy's 'equipment,' but I was always their sister."

Clare wasn't sure that Brandon and Arthur meant it that way, but she didn't want to burst Ivy's bubble. She agreed with her. "Yes, you have always been their sister. And my favorite female cousin."

"Awww. I love you, too."

Just then, the front door opened abruptly, violently setting off the bell above it. The UPS man pushed a large box through the doorway, then reached behind him on the sidewalk for a couple of smaller boxes, which he slid across the floor toward them. "Thank you!" Clare yelled as the door slammed behind him. "Must be some more perfume deliveries! Just in time!"

The rest of the afternoon was spent unboxing and inventorying the new additions. Not long before they were ready to close up shop, Clare's high school chum Lina came in.

"Hey Clare, I finally remembered to bring in the sample of *Barenia* for that nice old gentleman. What was his name?"

"Walter Barnard."

"Old Man Barnard was in here?" Ivy looked up from writing a description for one of the new scents. "What did he want?"

"You know him?"

"Sure. He lives around the corner. My brothers liked to ring his doorbell and run away before he opened the door. One time I was with them, and they hadn't told me to run, so it looked like I had done it. Man, I got a chewing out. He didn't believe I was innocent. I mean, come on, look at this face." Ivy steepled her hands under her chin and raised her eyes heavenward. "An angel, right?"

Clare chuckled. "Right. I'll call Mr Barnard now, so he knows to stop by next time he's in the area."

Ivy stood up to stretch and glanced out the window. "Aw, crumbs! There's that little thief! Fudgesicles! She's coming in here!"

"Um, hello?"

The door had opened, and Emily, one half of the prior day's thieving duo, stepped into the shop. She was holding the stolen tester out in front of her like an offering.

Ivy sneered. "They always return to the scene of the crime."

"Ah, I'm so sorry about what happened yesterday. It was my friend's idea. I've come back to return the tester she grabbed. And, I'd love to buy a bottle of that salty scent you put under my nose. I think I should probably carry a bit of it in my purse for times like that when I feel like I'm going to pass out. It's way better than smelling salts, which smell of pure ammonia. And I could wear it, too."

Clare stopped draping the center console with garland and went to stand next to her cousin. Ivy looked behind Emily. "Where is your friend?"

"I parked on Thames Street and told her to wait in the car. I didn't want you to think we were back for more trouble. Again, I apologize. It was a stupid idea." Emily paused. "I hope you haven't called the police?"

"No, I didn't call the police. It was just a tester, and we do have another one. I'm surprised nobody tried this earlier, considering that *Lycoctonum* became a collector's item literally overnight. I've heard that there are bottles listed on eBay for over a thousand dollars." Ivy thought for a second and put both testers behind the counter. "I'm not saying it's right, though."

Clare had gone over to the shelf that held the bottles of *Sel Noir* while still keeping an eye on Emily. She picked up a bottle and brought it to the counter, hanging on to it firmly as Ivy rang up the sale. While packing Emily's purchase, Clare also dropped a small empty sample vial into the bag, saying, "You can use this to keep a bit of the scent in your purse, for next time."

"Oh, thank you! Again, I'm sorry for pulling such a stupid stunt. This is a lovely shop, and I hope one day to stop by again."

"I'm not so sure that's a good idea." Clare went over to the door and opened it, signifying that the transaction was over.

Ivy spoke up. "Oh, and by the way, Thames Street is pronounced with the 'h' and the 'a.' It's not 'tems.' We fought a war against the British so we don't have to pronounce it their way."

As Clare shut the door after Emily, she smiled at her cousin. "That's not why we fought the war."

Ivy shoved a piece of pecan pie croissant in her mouth. "I know. We fought over tea or something. Whatever. It's 'thaym es.'"

Twenty-One

THE HOUSE SMELLED LIKE stuffing, sweet potatoes topped with marshmallows, and of course, roast turkey. Terri always stuffed the cavity of the bird with a whole onion and an apple, which both perfumed its flesh and removed some of the gamy funk, a tip she had picked up from watching the Food Network. Ivy was putting the finishing touches on the dining room table, which was beautifully set with mismatched vintage china, some of which came from Busia Manya, and the rest from her maternal grandmother, whom Clare barely remembered.

"Can I put the football game on, Mom?"

"No, Clare. Our guests will be here shortly."

"I'm not sure that inviting Billy's parents to dinner was such a good idea. It's going to be awkward." Clare was removing the top and bottom from a can of cranberry sauce so it would bloop out in one corrugated cylindrical piece. She had a thumping headache and would have preferred staying home in bed.

"Maybe so, but it's nice to support people during the holidays. I'm sure they'll appreciate the company."

"Even if it's us?" Ivy had come into the kitchen from the dining room where she was inserting napkins into pumpkin-shaped napkin rings. She eyeballed the tray of rolls that were ready to warm in the oven before snatching one and taking a bite.

"Don't spoil your appetite, Ivy!"

"As if I could. You're such a mom!"

The doorbell rang, and Terri narrowed her eyes at her niece before hustling to open the door.

"Bob! Amanda! Welcome! Welcome! Come on in. Let me grab your coats." Terri turned and yelled over her shoulder, "Clare!"

Her daughter took a cleansing breath and plodded into the hallway, as if meeting her executioner. "Hi Mr and Mrs Leight," she said, taking their coats and walking away. She wondered if anyone would notice if she went out the kitchen door and kept on walking.

Amanda held out a store-bought pecan pie to her host. "I'm sorry, but I'm not much of a baker."

Ivy swooped in and took the box from her hands. "Any pie is good pie, Mrs Leight! This will be totally amazing warmed up with a scoop of vanilla ice cream. I brought Häagen-Dazs." She disappeared back into the kitchen, humming off-key to the Motown playlist that could be heard emanating softly from a speaker in the living room.

Terri put her arm around Amanda's shoulder and let the couple into the living room. The Leights sat together on the sofa, shoulder touching shoulder, as if they were a unit.

"Can I get you a drink before we eat? We have red and white wine, mulled cider, and I can make up a batch of Manhattans if you'd like something stronger."

Manhattans had always been the Buchowski's default Thanksgiving cocktail. Terri's father-in-law had started the tradition in the 50s when it was the mid-century adult beverage of choice, along with martinis and old-fashioneds. Her husband continued the practice when he was still alive, and sometimes Terri made a batch for old times' sake. Personally, she preferred a cup of warm cider with a slug of bourbon in it but occasionally partook of the stronger beverage. This was going to be a multi-beverage night for all parties.

"Oh, a Manhattan sounds great, doesn't it, Mandy?" Bob turned his head to look at his wife of 38 years.

"Sure Bobby. I'll have one if you will."

As Terri mixed up a batch of the drink, adding a bit more rye than she normally would, Ivy held up a second cocktail shaker. "If a Manhattan isn't your thing, Mrs Leight, may I offer you a Chamomile Spritz? A little tea, a little cranberry juice..."

"Oh, no thanks, dear. That doesn't sound quite strong enough to me. I think a holiday like Thanksgiving deserves something a bit heartier."

Her husband nodded in agreement. "Definitely something stronger."

Nobody knew quite what to say. The group made polite small talk about the uncommonly chilly November they'd been having, and Bob brought up the Orioles' most recent disappointing season. Clare desperately wanted to put the football game on—at least that would add some energy to the room—but she was probably the only person in the house who enjoyed the sport. Even the usually lively Vetiver wasn't much fun.

"Oh, what an adorable dog!" Mrs Leight had spotted Vetiver snoozing on his bed in the corner of the living room. "What's his name?"

"Vetiver."

"Oh, that's unusual."

"It's a grass that's used as a perfume ingredient. It smells woody, smoky, a bit green." Clare should have known when she gave her dog his name that she'd be explaining it to everyone. Vetiver had raised his head slightly off the pillow and squinted at the room, as if he realized he was being talked about.

Mrs Leight was up off the couch and heading toward the dog. "Sweet doggy, hi!" As she reached out to pet him, Vetiver jumped up and started barking maniacally. Amanda jumped back in alarm.

"Um, Mrs Leight," Clare shouted over the barking, "Vetiver's not a people-person. He really only likes other dogs. He's such an embarrassment around company. I could just murder him sometimes."

Amanda Leight became very still. Clare closed her eyes, realizing what she had said. "I'm so sorry. I didn't mean..." Amanda turned around and walked back to the couch stiffly.

"It's ok. It's not ok. I..."

Mr Leight put his arm around his wife and pulled her close as she wept quietly. "We're just going to have to get used to it, my love. We can't expect people to censor their conversation around us." He kissed the top of her head.

Clare was mortified. She knew something like this was going to happen today. Maybe she should just keep her fat mouth zipped for the rest of the evening.

When the oven timer went off, Terri, Clare, and Ivy jumped up simultaneously. Terri quickly said, "I'll call you girls if I need any help," before trotting off into the kitchen with Vetiver hot on her heels.

"We're so grateful that Terri invited us to dinner." Amanda looked at her hands folded in her lap as she spoke. "I wasn't sure what we were going to do. Not that we haven't spent the holidays just the two of us for a good number of years already. But I was pretty sure that I wouldn't be able to conjure up enough of that festive feeling to prepare the big meal this year. To be honest, I've been having a hard time making breakfast most days." Bob reached for his wife's hand and squeezed it.

Clare nodded. Ivy stood up and went into the kitchen. She came out a few minutes later with a plate of rolls in one hand and the bowl of cranberry sauce in the other. "Clare, can you help Aunt Terri with the turkey?" Clare hated carving the turkey, but she was more than happy to do it this time.

"So," Bob said after a long silence broken only by the clink of forks and the soft scrape of serving spoons. "The stuffing is incredible, Terri. Is that, uh, chestnut?"

"Dried apricot," Terri responded, beaming. "With rosemary and sourdough. I saw it in a food magazine and figured I'd fake my way through. I don't like to follow recipes to the letter."

"It's really good," Ivy mumbled, poking at her portion but not really eating.

Amanda nodded politely, her wineglass in hand. "It's lovely."

Clare hadn't said much since sitting down. She had hoped the wine would loosen things up, but the second bottle had only seemed to thicken the tension, like the gravy congealing in the chipped gravy boat that had belonged to her maternal grandmother. Across the table, Amanda was dabbing at her mouth with the corner of her napkin, even though she hadn't eaten anything in minutes.

Ivy reached for the cylinder of cranberry sauce. "I know Clare worked hard on this part of the meal." Clare smiled awkwardly. The silence was deafening.

Terri tried again. "So, Clare, what's going on with your neighbor? The one with the constantly barking dog?"

"Still barking, Mom. Still constant." Clare's headache was intensifying.

Amanda gave a short, surprised laugh.

"Neighbors, right?" Bob said as he cut his turkey into smaller and smaller pieces. "We're currently experiencing leaf blower wars with ours. I'm a rake man myself. Much quieter, and it requires only human power."

"When I was away at school, the neighbors in the next apartment practiced their drumming like Animal auditioning for a thunderstorm," Clare offered. "We moved."

That got another laugh from Amanda, more real this time. Ivy took a sip of wine and raised her glass in a miniature toast. "To strategic relocation."

Amanda raised hers too. "To better neighbors."

Clare clinked glasses with them both, even as something twisted in her stomach.

Bob reached for another helping of mashed potatoes; the motion deliberate. "You know," he said, spoon hovering, "I read potatoes aren't technically a vegetable. They're tubers."

"Sounds like propaganda from the anti-tuber lobby," Ivy said, not looking up from her plate.

"I'm serious," Bob said, grinning. "I saw it in Smithsonian. They said you should serve more proper vegetables, like spinach, to—what was it? 'Diversify your phytonutrients.'"

Terri leaned forward, eyebrows raised. "So, you're claiming this meal isn't balanced?"

Clare stared at her plate; a single green bean lay skewered on her fork, abandoned in a glob of mashed potatoes. "This is the most cheerful conversation I've had all week," she said.

Terri picked up the gravy boat and offered it around with the forced brightness of a game show host. "Who wants to make this meal slightly less awkward? How about some liquid gold?" Clare waved her off, smiling without really meaning it. Amanda shook her head. Ivy said, "Sure," and drowned her plate in the now-cold gravy.

The candles flickered. Someone's chair creaked. Outside, the wind rattled the windowpane, and Clare imagined it sounding exactly like a sigh. Bob cleared his throat.

"So, uh... what's happening at the shop? Still busy with all that perfume stuff?"

"Business has been steady," Clare said. "We're mostly ready for Black Friday tomorrow. Well, inventory-wise, that is."

Amanda was quiet again. Her gaze had dropped to her plate, where the cranberry sauce had bled onto the turkey in a slow, red bloom. Clare noticed. Ivy's fork scraped once against her plate, then stilled. Bob cleared his throat. "Every year, Billy would try to eat all the crescent rolls before we noticed they were gone. And then he wondered why he always had a stomachache halfway through the meal." Everyone nodded. Amanda wiped under one eye but said nothing. Then she reached for the wine and poured herself another glass.

The meal was more than half over when the doorbell rang, followed by insistent knocking. Startled, Clare jumped out of her seat. Putting her hand to her chest, she said, "I'll get it." The knocking continued until she opened the door. "Oh, it's you." She let Stephanie in and closed the door behind her.

"We're almost done eating. Put your coat in the hall closet and come into the dining room." Clare felt no compunction about being rude to the latest guest to arrive.

"Sorry I'm late," Stephanie announced loudly, not sounding at all sorry. She held up a jug of cloudy brown liquid. "I brought a remedy for grief. I suggest everyone take a shot." Nobody moved. Stephanie looked at each person before pulling out the empty chair next to Ivy, scraping its legs on the floor noisily.

"Hello to you too, Stephanie," Bob said eventually, with the wary tone of someone speaking to a possibly feral dog.

Amanda didn't look up. "I didn't know you were coming."

"I wasn't sure either." Stephanie set the jug down in the middle of the table, where it sloshed ominously. "But then I thought, why not? It's not like Billy would've wanted everyone to sit around being sad and eating canned gravy."

Terri, who had in fact served canned gravy, sniffed.

Amanda finally looked up. "Do you want a plate?"

Stephanie shook her head. "I didn't come to eat." She tapped the table with her fingernails. "So... what are we pretending tonight? That this is a normal holiday? That Billy's just off somewhere not returning calls?"

Bob rubbed his face with both hands.

Amanda took a gulp of her wine. "Why did you come, Stephanie? To once again show us how much better you are than everyone else?"

"I'm trying to process that my brother's dead," Stephanie said, reaching for the wine. She didn't ask before pouring herself a glass. "You're not the only ones who lost him."

Bob opened his mouth as if he might say something calming, then apparently thought better of it.

"I don't believe a word of it, and I don't think anyone else does, either." Amanda bit out. You bullied him his whole life, and now that he's gone, you regret it? Why? Because you lost your plaything? Your toy to kick around?

"You know what I remember most about Billy?" Stephanie ignored her mother and went on, voice gaining volume. "He was always the favorite. Every award, every art show, every dramatic personality reinvention, you just clapped and handed him more love."

Amanda's eyes flashed. "And you hated him for it."

"No," Stephanie snapped. "I envied him. There is a difference."

Ivy started stacking plates just to have something to do. Clare sat frozen with her hands wrapped around her wineglass, pulse rising with every word.

"You're twisting this into something petty," Amanda said. "You always do that when you feel left out."

"I was left out."

"You left yourself out," Bob muttered. "Every time we tried..."

"Every time you tried, it came with conditions," Stephanie cut in. "Be nicer. Smile more. Stop criticizing his decisions. Don't question why he only called when he needed something. Maybe if I'd been a little more perfect..."

"...he'd still be dead," Amanda said, voice flat and final.

The silence that followed was heavy and immediate. Terri's fork clattered onto her plate.

Stephanie blinked hard. Her jaw set, but she didn't speak. Clare, heart and head pounding, pushed her chair back and stood. "Okay. That's enough."

Amanda looked up at her. "Clare..."

"I said enough." She took a deep breath, then let it out slowly. "You're all hurting. That doesn't mean you get to shred each other to pieces over dinner."

Stephanie shrugged. "I think coming here was probably a mistake on my part."

"Yes," Clare said, meeting her eyes. "Maybe you should leave." She stood and rubbed her forehead. "I have had the worst headache all day, and it's just getting worse."

Stephanie rummaged in her purse and pulled out a small screw-capped bottle. "Here, take two of these homeopathic tablets. They are great for headaches." She tapped two of the tiny pills into Clare's hand.

Clare stared at the contents of her right palm for a few beats before leaving the room.

"Well, bye all. I have places to be, people to see," Stephanie said as she put on her coat. Ivy handed the untouched jug of her grief remedy to her as she walked out the door, slamming it behind her. Clare, who had just walked into the hallway, closed her eyes tightly at the sound.

"Maybe another glass of wine will be enough to let me forget about the headache," she thought to herself as she went back into the dining room. "Who wants pie and ice cream?" Ivy was already on her way into the kitchen.

Twenty-Two

"WHY DO FAMILIES DO this to themselves?" Clare wondered aloud as she put three tablespoons of Baltimore Coffee & Tea Tanzania Peaberry into the basket of her Mister Coffee and flipped the on switch. Vetiver gave a short bark as if to say, "beats me." Clare had awakened the day after Thanksgiving with a bit more than the usual feeling of post-holiday regret and shame. As usual, she had eaten far too much. She drank too much. Family get-togethers can be a lot to handle, and when they involve a whole other family, especially one with members that have been known for drama, well, the wine was bound to flow. "Do they get together because they feel it's a requirement? That if they spend time together eating turkey and pumpkin pie that somehow everything will be right again? At least for one day? Are they delusional?" Another bark from Vetiver. "You are absolutely right, boy. People are delusional."

As she sipped her soul-sustaining caffeinated elixir and picked at cold, leftover sweet potatoes topped with toasted marshmallow, Clare thought back on the prior day. She had expected more crying and carrying-on, at least from Mrs Leight, but she had really held herself together well. She snapped at Stephanie, though that was completely understandable. Both she and her husband drank an awful lot though. Between the five of them, three batches of Manhattans, two bottles of red wine, and two bottles of white had been demolished, and she was pretty sure Bob had snuck a little flask out of his pocket to embellish the coffee he had with pie. She wouldn't have been shocked had anyone had picked up a bottle and drank straight from it for the mercifully brief time that Stephanie had been there.

After taking Vetiver for a quick walk, Clare braced herself for the workday. She had appreciated "Black Friday" back when hangovers were minor inconveniences. She and her friends never camped outside big-box stores, but they were in the mall bright and early, forging their way through Nordstrom Rack, trying on hideous shoes that were on sale because nobody wanted them at full price, and waiting in lines that snaked around half the store. Then it was off to Forever 21 to do it all over again, hunting for cute, cheap sweaters. It had been a game, a fun challenge.

Now, as a shop owner, she hated it. Good Scents did well on Black Friday—sales often surged despite the discount—but she resented that shoppers expected bargains for fragrances they couldn't find anywhere else. Some years, she'd offered a BOGO 20% promo, which nudged earnings up by nearly half. This year, she felt decidedly Scrooge-like. The only concession she'd make: free gift-wrapping, advertised on a hand-lettered sign in the window. Gift wrapping was always free at Good Scents, but only when requested.

From the first customer to jangle the bell, Ivy was impossibly perky with her, "Good morning! How may I help you!" The night before she had drunk mostly water or the concoction she called a "Chamomile Spritz" made with herbal tea, cranberry juice, and a splash of sparkling apple cider. It was disgusting. Clare thought it would be much more palatable with gin and may or may not have tried it that way. She couldn't remember. She was glad that Ivy was such a kind friend and employee and had thought to bring her an extra-large coffee and a big bag of chocolate chip cookies on her way into work that morning. The cookies were from the grocery store, so they were not tasty, but the sugar rush was all that really mattered at a time like this.

Customers came in steadily all morning, ringing the bell somewhat violently. Clare made a mental note to smash the bell with a hammer once her head stopped pounding. Her old friend Jorge swanned in, wearing round oversized baby blue sunglasses and a huge orange plaid scarf wrapped haphazardly around his throat. The remains of a lavender latte trembled in one hand as he waved the other in a general greeting to all those assembled.

"Tell me this place still has caffeine," he said.

"I have half a cup, but it's cold." Clare held out the coffee Ivy had purchased for her.

"Same," Jorge touched his cup to hers. "To late nights and too much hooch!"

"Ivy?" Clare smiled at her cousin inquiringly.

"On it! I'll go upstairs and make a pot."

"Better yet, bring the coffeemaker down here. I need you on the floor."

Jorge fanned himself with the edge of his scarf, accidentally hitting himself in the face with the fringe. "My hero!" He leaned into Clare and kissed the air somewhere vaguely near her cheek. "That one is god's gift to a dissipated old queen like me." He pulled his sunglasses up and squinted at Clare. "Girl, you look rougher than me. But then I put on a triple coat of under-eye concealer."

"I can tell. It's settled into the creases."

"Oh, you cut me." Jorge dropped his glasses back into place. He looked around the room before floating across the shop like a scent-seeking missile to a woman in an extremely large puffer coat. She had been sniffing a tray of vanilla-forward testers indecisively for some minutes.

"What are you into?" Jorge asked, voice smooth. "Warm and cozy? A little toasted sugar? Something that smells like you took a lover by the fireplace in a cabin in Vermont?"

The woman blinked. "Um... yes?"

Jorge reached for a bottle at the back of the shelf. *Fumé de Câlin* was from an obscure brand Clare had brought in on a whim and immediately regretted.

"You're not ready," he warned, then sprayed a blotter and handed it to her. The customer sniffed. Her eyes widened.

"Oh wow," she said. "That's like... smoky, but also, like, comforting? A little nutty?"

Jorge nodded, sage-like. "It's divine. Like eating burnt pecan pie while wearing suede gloves."

"I... I... I love it." She looked at Clare. "Do you have more of it?"

"Just two bottles. Well, now one."

"I'll take them both."

After the customer left, Jorge turned to Clare, smug. "You're welcome. That bottle's been crying on your shelf since May."

Ivy returned to the shop with the welcome announcement that a fresh pot of coffee was ready. Jorge charged into the back room ahead of Clare and poured some of the hot brew into his takeout cup. "I don't normally drink black coffee, but desperate times and all that."

Clare helped herself to some java and leaned against a stack of boxes that she hadn't had time to open yet. At the rate things were selling, she should do that right now.

"So what's been going on at Good Scents, my friend? Smell any ghosts lately?" Jorge was teasing, but Clare nodded.

"Maybe, but I don't want to talk about it right now. I'm still trying to figure things out."

"Ah, still playing detective. Why don't you let the real police figure it out, Clare? Clearly, you're not getting enough sleep."

"I know, but I feel responsible somehow. Like I should have sensed it coming. We had Billy's family over for Thanksgiving. They were polite, but I know they are in a lot of pain. It's eating me up. I know that doesn't make sense to you, but it does to me. And I have so many questions."

Jorge raised an eyebrow. "Like what?"

"Like how did that shrine get started between my finding Guillermo's body and returning to the store a couple hours later?"

"Oh, that's an easy one. You know Damarion's sister Trina works at the hotel, right?"

"Wait, what? No, I didn't know that."

"Sure. Trina's been there for years, currently the housekeeping supervisor. When she saw the hubbub in the hallway outside his room, she poked her head in to make sure it wasn't any of her staff causing trouble. She recognized Guillermo on the floor and hightailed it out of there. And you know that woman can keep a secret about as well as you can hold your liquor."

"Not very well, I'm guessing." Clare was pretty sure she didn't know that Trina had worked at Ferguson's Wharf. But then Damarion didn't talk about his family much. He'd discuss perfume all day but revealed little more than his opinion on the overabundance of gourmands on the market and why heavy bottle caps annoyed him. "She told Damarion, and he spread the word?"

"I saw it on his Instagram account around lunchtime the day you found him."

"That checks out. I would have been at the hotel talking to the police." One mystery solved. But if Damarion knew about Guillermo's death, why hadn't he called her? He couldn't have known she'd grown up with Guillermo—she hadn't known herself until recently. And maybe Trina hadn't seen her in Guillermo's room. Still. He knew she'd hosted Guillermo at Good Scents the night he died. So why didn't he pick up the phone?

The next morning, as she took Vetiver on his first walk of the day, Clare pondered Jorge's revelation. Of course, he would have known something about the origin of the shrine. Jorge was a notorious gossip—one reason that Clare enjoyed his company so much—and knew pretty much everything going on in the local perfume scene. It didn't hurt that the scene was so tiny. She supposed he had not mentioned Trina Washington earlier because he thought Clare already knew. After all, the shrine was in front of her shop. She made a mental note to spend more time perusing Instagram, so she wouldn't miss anything else in the future. Or maybe she could get Ivy to do it for her.

What else did Trina know? Clare wondered. Perhaps she should pay her a visit.

"Ivy, can you run the shop for an hour or so while I pop by Ferguson's Wharf? I want to talk to Trina Washington."

Ivy was studying something on her phone and didn't look up. "Only if you bring me a pastry and maybe something else to eat. And a coffee."

"Deal." Clare thought for a second. "We drink so much coffee, I think I need to invest in a coffeemaker for the store."

"How about an espresso maker? Maybe a microwave and a mini fridge?"

"We could get a popcorn machine and open a snack bar, too." Clare quirked her mouth to one side. Her cousin looked up and studied Clare's expression.

"A coffee maker is a great idea."

Clare wasn't even sure Trina would be working on a Saturday, but she was impatient and itching for more information. It was a nice day for a walk through Fells Point. The holiday decorations had started to appear, so Clare did a little window shopping for holiday gift ideas. Christmas was a month away, and Clare had been too busy to even think about presents. She didn't want to resort to ordering things off the Internet, but that might be how things went again this year.

The same bored employee was at the front desk as the last time Clare visited the hotel, again watching something on her phone. Clare cleared her throat, and the desk clerk looked up at her suspiciously. Narrowing her eyes, she said, "I remember you. The last time you were here, someone found a dead body."

"Yep, that was me, always causing trouble." Clare continued, "do you know if Trina Washington is working today? The head of housekeeping?"

"She's the housekeeping supervisor. Mr Owens is the head of housekeeping," the clerk responded.

"Whatever. Is Trina here? If so, where could I find her?"

The clerk waved her hand vaguely to her left. "Mr Owens' office is that way. If she's not there, he'd know where she is."

"Um, thanks." Clare looked in the direction in which the clerk had waved her hand and headed down a hallway. Beyond the elevator, Clare spotted a janitorial closet with an open door. As she was about to peek around it to see if anyone was inside, Trina emerged.

"Oh, my goodness," Trina put her hand to her chest, "you startled me." She tilted her head to one side. "Clare! I haven't seen you in forever! How have you been?" Trina reached out for a hug, which Clare reciprocated.

"I've been busy. Holiday stuff, you know. I'm sure it gets busier here around the holidays, too?"

"Meh, not so much this year. We had a little bad publicity from that dead perfumer, you know."

"That's exactly what I wanted to talk to you about, Trina. Guillermo Flares. Is there someplace where we could sit down and chat? Do you have a minute to spare?"

"Sure thing. Mr Owens isn't here, and we're not busy today. Let's go into his office."

Trina led Clare further down the same hallway to her boss's office, unlocked it, and motioned for Clare to take a seat in one of the chairs facing the desk. Trina herself sat in Mr Owens's seat. She bounced up and down in his chair, then leaned back and put her feet on the desk. "Practicing for when I get his job." Trina smirked. "Now what can I do for you?"

Clare loosened her scarf and unbuttoned the top button of her jacket as she spoke. "You probably already know this, but I was the one that found the body that day." Clare related how Guillermo was supposed to return to the shop the morning after the event to pick up the rest of the bottles of his fragrance, and when he hadn't, she went to the hotel to check on him. "Your front desk clerk…"

"Britney."

"Huh?"

"Britney. That's the clerk's name."

"Ah, ok. Britney took me up to his room and then left abruptly. I found the body in the bathroom, called 911, and spoke to both the police and paramedics. When I got back to my shop a couple of hours later, I found the beginnings of a shrine on the sidewalk out front. I had no idea how it had gotten started so quickly, since the only people who knew about it were me and those who had responded to the emergency call. But Jorge said you had posted about it on Instagram, most likely while I was still in the building."

"No, I told Damarion about it, and he posted it. That social media stuff and I don't play."

"Sorry, I got that mixed up. I'm not big on social media myself."

"Yeah, I went upstairs because I saw the paramedics and, well, you know I'm nosy." Trina chuckled. "But I also wanted to check out the crime scene. I'm shorthanded and wanted to know what I was going to have to clean up. You know. In case it was messy, I was going to need to call in reinforcements." She chuckled again, this time uncomfortably.

"Well, if it had been a messy crime scene, it would have been sealed off for a while so investigators could come in and do their thing." Clare was so glad it hadn't been messy. She had a hard time finding a neat crime scene. "You saw the body. But you didn't see me?"

"No, Clare. I did not see you. When I found out later that you were there, I knew for sure I had been right. The dead guy was that perfumer that nobody liked."

"What do you mean, 'nobody liked?' How did you know that?"

"He was that guy who used to post on that internet thing that you frag freaks used to play on forever ago. Damarion said he used to say terrible things about perfumes most people liked. Like this dude wanted to be a perfume critic when he grew up. His name was something like 'Mirr-' 'Mur-'" Trina stopped talking and squinted her eyes shut, as if she was trying to see his screen name, "'Mercury.' Like the stuff in thermometers."

"Wait? Billy Leight was Myrrhcury?"

"Who's Billy Leight? I thought we were talking about this Guillermo guy?"

Clare explained the perfumer's name change to Trina, then asked how she could have recognized him.

"Damarion used to show me his videos. Him sitting in the shadows, all moody-like, talking about perfume like it was the most important thing in the world. My brother would make fun of him. Like, 'ooh, look at me, Mr Pretty Boy. I'm so special,' and he'd hold his phone up in front of his face and bat his eyelashes at it. Damarion could be funny sometimes. He called him 'Mercury,' and told me about what a butthead he had been back then."

Clare digested this information. She knew Billy had formed a second persona over the years, but she hadn't realized it had started as early as a decade ago. And somehow Damarion had known Myrrhcury's identity and never told the rest of the group? Personally, Clare had never had any problem with them; she figured they were just an internet troll, though an exceptionally intelligent one. Jasmine, however, had all sorts of issues with Myrrhcury and had even been banned from the forum for taking arguments too far. And clearly Damarion Washington wasn't too fond of him, either. Or was he jealous?

It looked like a trip to DC was in Clare's future.

Twenty-Three

Clare emerged from the back room carrying a cup of coffee, pleased the new machine had brewed something decent on the first try. She handed it to Ivy, who tasted it like a wine critic. She finally nodded.

"It's not bad. But can we get some flavored syrups to make our own gingerbread lattes at Christmas? I was just looking at them online, and we can get a mixed case of flavors for not a terrible amount of money."

"Oh, like you need more sugar. But sure. We can do that." Clare then noticed the piece of mail on the counter. It was a flat, brown paper, envelope-style package with Italian postmarks that had been hand-addressed to her. She grabbed the box cutter, carefully slit the side of the envelope, and pulled out a small Moleskine notebook, almost exactly like the one she already had. Clare even looked behind the counter to make sure the original was still there. Ivy snatched up the envelope and shook it.

"What are you doing?"

As a slip of paper fluttered out of the package, Ivy responded: "There's gotta be a note, right?"

Clare picked up the paper and read it out loud. "Guillermo Flares wanted you to have this."

"Is it signed?"

"Nope. Guess it's from Parker's counterpart in Italy." Clare flipped through the second Moleskine. "Huh. This looks just like the other one. Scribblings in code. It doesn't seem to have any added sticky notes, though. And it's not as battered as the original."

"Efraim thought maybe Billy had had more than one over the years. Maybe he just copied information from one into another."

"Maybe…" Clare's brain was spinning. "Maybe he didn't like carrying a copy with him, so he had identical copies at all the various locations that he might be."

"Because the information inside was too valuable to carry on the street? Or maybe he was just paranoid?"

"I have no idea, Ivy. I'm just trying to make some sense of any of this."

"I'm pretty sure it's not going to make sense."

"Now what am I going to do with two of these things?"

Ivy grabbed the second Moleskine from Clare's hand and jammed it under the counter next to the original copy. "At least keep them together, huh?"

Clare let herself linger on the sight of the twin notebooks for a moment, then pushed the distraction aside. She had another question burning in her mind. Picking up her phone, she called Damarion, careful not to give too much away.

"It's been too long," he said. "Let's meet for dinner. There's a cool speakeasy just down the street, and I've been looking for an excuse to get back there. I think you'll like it."

Clare agreed, thinking that over drinks she might finally get some clarity about Guillermo and the mysterious Myrrhcury connection. But Adams Morgan. Hmph. That meant multiple forms of transportation. People always said DC was easy to get around thanks to the Metro, and it was, especially compared to Baltimore's sad excuse for a subway. Unfortunately, every place she wanted to visit in that area still required a bus ride, sometimes on top of the Metro. She hated driving into DC, so she'd just have to take Amtrak and call a rideshare from Union Station. Honestly, what she wanted to ask Damarion could just as easily be done over the phone, but she hadn't seen him in almost a year. He was always good company, and she missed that.

After they had placed their drink orders and engaged in a little "long-time-no-see" small talk, Clare got down to business.

"I was surprised to find out from your sister that you've known the identity of the *Cognoscented* troublemaker, Myrrhcury, for years now."

"Is that what this is really about, Clare? I thought you just missed my handsome face and charming company." Damarion put his menu down and folded his hands over it. He examined Clare over his steepled fingers. "Sure, I knew that the stuck-on-himself, fancy, Instagram-famous perfumer Guillermo Flares was Myrrhcury. What of it?"

"I'm just surprised you said nothing to me."

"Why would I? What's your connection to him, besides hosting that launch party?"

"If you knew Myrrhcury was Guillermo, then you know Guillermo was William Leight."

"Right. We went to Calvert Hall together."

"And Billy and I grew up together. He was my childhood best friend."

"Ohhhh...Clare. I swear I did not know that. Believe me, if I had, I would have told you a long time ago. Seriously, I wouldn't have kept that from you."

"He used to hang out at my grandmother's shop. That's where he got the idea of becoming a perfumer." Clare felt a little better that she hadn't been lied to. Her friend just hadn't known there was any reason to share this information with her. "So how did you find out that he was Myrrhcury?"

"He essentially told me. He privately messaged me one day and said we knew each other. But he wouldn't tell me outright; he wanted me to guess who he was. Always a game-player, that one." Damarion relaxed in his seat and draped his arm over the back. "It wasn't that hard to figure out. We had been in the same English class for three of the four years we were in high school, and I remembered he had a particular style of writing. Kinda flighty. Used a lot of big words. Loved wordplay and sophisticated puns. His username, Myrrhcury, is a good example of that. I asked him once why he was so darn mean, and he said it made him feel better. That he pretended the strangers he was attacking were his bully of a sister."

Clare nodded at that. She got it. It wasn't a nice thing to do, but she understood.

"When he showed up again as Guillermo Flares, it was so ridiculous I almost laughed out loud. I remembered him telling me about that incident, when his cranky-ass old neighbor shooed him out of her flower bed in her Baltimore accent. And Bill was such a snob about that. He hated being from Baltimore and tried so hard to hide it. Yet he embraced it with his choice of name."

"He used to tell that story all the time. I know Busia Manya was tired of it, but she was so patient with him. Sometimes I think she loved him more than she loved me." Clare looked down at the tabletop.

"That's impossible, Clare. Your grandmother thought you hung the moon. Why else would she let you take down that gorgeous 1960s floral wallpaper and paint the shop grey?" Damarion threw his head back and laughed at the memory of the wallpaper.

That made Clare feel warm and fuzzy inside. She had always been just a bit jealous of the attention Busia Manya had paid to Billy. Their heads were always together, conspiring over some perfume concoction or another. Maybe she already knew what Philomena would learn some years later: that Billy wasn't famous perfumer material, and that he needed extra help. Some things were beginning to make sense to Clare.

The next morning, after she had fed and walked Vetiver, grabbed a yogurt for breakfast, and opened the shop, Clare did a little poking around in the life of one Rafael Campos, Perfumer, whom she had forgotten about until she saw Damarion. Clare dragged her laptop over to the little round table she had set up at the far end of the room in order to facilitate any perfume consultations on the scale of the one she had with Ayanna a few weeks earlier. She still hadn't advertised the service, but this time of year was always busy. Clare had spotted the cute bistro set at the thrift shop around the corner and thought it would be the perfect fit. For now, it was a good place to park herself and do some sleuthing while keeping an eye on the shop.

According to the internet, Mr Campos was a perfumer from the Philadelphia area, trained in Grasse, and creator of several fragrances with listings on *Scentology*. Mildly impressive, as she had even heard of one of them. *Winter Psalm*. She scrolled down the fragrance's page to read the comments and was struck by one older one in particular.

"I wanted to like this scent, especially after I read on *Cognoscented* that it was 'the olfactory equivalent of being locked in a piano teacher's mothball-ridden parlor.' I felt sorry for the perfumer. But damn if Myrrhcury wasn't right, as he usually was. *Winter Psalm* smells like my grandmother's choir robe, hung in the back of a cedar closet since 1978, with a bag of cough drops in the pocket."

"Wow," Clare thought, "cruel." And there was that name. Myrrhcury. Clare didn't think it was a coincidence that Campos had shown up at the launch party. He must have known that Billy was Myrrhcury. But why had he come? Clare had kept an eye on him the entire night, and he didn't get very far past the door. It's as if he just wanted to see the man who had savaged his fragrance so many years ago. Perhaps he wanted to watch him fail, but with the crowd that night, it was clear that he was doing anything but failing. Disappointed, Campos had left. Where had he gone afterward? If he was a perfumer, then he was another person to have access to potentially poisonous substances. And being the victim of one of Myrrhcury's cruel takedowns might give him motive.

Clare was behind the counter when Rafael entered the boutique.

"Raphael, hi. I didn't think I'd see you so soon.

"Clare," he said, with a tired nod. "I hope I'm not interrupting, but when I got your email saying you wanted to talk, I thought I'd stop by the shop. Anyway, I had a meeting with a potential investor here in Baltimore." He gave a wan smile. "I see you weren't fooled by my calling myself Damarion."

"Not at all," Clare replied. "I'm glad you came by. I wanted to ask," she continued, keeping her tone light, "why you came to the launch party. You and Guillermo weren't exactly... close."

He exhaled softly and leaned against the edge of the counter, glancing at the bottles neatly lined on the shelves. "I wondered how long it would take for that question."

Clare waited.

"I came," he said, "because Guillermo invited me. And because I knew he would think it was a small, poetic victory if I showed up. You know how he was. Everything had to be dramatic. Performative, even."

"It wasn't out of spite? And why did you use a pseudonym?"

"Good God, no." He laughed, but it was hollow. "I told him I'd come, not that I'd make a scene. The party was crawling with bloggers and gossipers. I used a pseudonym so I could get a look at him, at the scent, without winding up as a hashtag. I didn't want anyone to think I'd waste a decade holding a grudge over a blog post."

She tilted her head. "It was more than a blog post, though. Myrrhcury was... brutal."

He didn't flinch. "Yes. He was. But you know what?" Rafael shrugged. "I reread the review last year. And it was right. He caught something real, as evidenced by the many other negative reviews that came afterward. Sure, I know some of them were copycats, but in retrospect, that scent wasn't my best work."

Clare studied his face. "Did you ever confront him about it?"

"I did. Once. In Florence, years ago. We had too much wine. We yelled at each other in the street, like lunatics. And then... we moved on."

Clare softened. "So, no lingering resentment? Nothing that would make you..."

"Kill him?" Rafael interrupted quietly. "No. I don't have it in me. Honestly, I pitied him more than anything. He was all fireworks all the time. I kept waiting for the implosion."

She let the silence stretch.

"You don't believe I had anything to do with it, do you?" he asked gently.

Clare exhaled. "No. But I needed to ask. You understand."

"Of course," he said, straightening his collar and standing up straight. Rafael reached into his coat pocket and pulled out a slim, cobalt bottle. "I made something new. Thought you might like a preview."

Clare took it, uncapped the sprayer, and let a cloud settle on a test strip. Saffron. Hay. A distant hum of fig wood.

"Lovely," she said.

He smiled. "It's called *Afterlight*."

It had been weeks since Billy's death, and though Clare had removed it entirely a few weeks earlier, the shrine had reappeared and was still going strong. She noticed that it had been freshened up occasionally, as if someone had been maintaining it. The spray-painted teddy bears seemed newer, and there were some fresh flowers tucked here and there among the fake ones. It almost seemed to have a sense of design about it. A mylar balloon depicting a teddy bear with a rose and the words "happy birthday" had appeared last week, but that was now gone. Removed because it didn't fit the theme, Clare thought. Billy's birthday was in mid-August. She thought about what he had said to her back in September, during his first visit to the shop: "I wouldn't be surprised if a memorial was erected here to commemorate the occasion." She was pretty sure this wasn't what he meant.

Today, there was a new addition to the somber black heap in front of Good Scents: a professionally printed sign, similar to the ones advertising political candidates found on suburban lawns. This one read, "Myrrhcury will be avenged."

"Clare, what the heck does that sign mean out there?" were the first words out of Jasmine's mouth when she entered the shop that afternoon.

"Whassign?" Ivy had just taken a bite of a cheese danish, so her words were muffled. She swallowed and repeated, "What sign?"

Clare frowned. "You haven't noticed the professionally printed sign that says, 'Myrrhcury will be avenged'?"

"To be honest, I don't notice the shrine at all anymore. It's just become part of the sidewalk." Ivy shrugged and took another huge bite.

Clare turned to Jasmine and said, "I don't know where it came from. It just appeared."

"But why does it mention Myrrhcury?" Jasmine's brain was attempting to process the information. "Was Billy... Guillermo...Myrrhcury? Clare?"

"Um, yeah, about that. Apparently, he was."

"Holy... Clare. You know I was kicked off *Cognoscented* because I argued too much with that fool, right?"

"That's what you told me years ago."

"He stirred up something in me that I just couldn't control. Thoughts. Opinions. He made me angry. Ooohh...just thinking about it makes me mad." Jasmine stomped around the store a bit, fists balled at her sides.

"But that was like ten years ago, right? You were still in college." Ivy took a sip of latte to wash down the latest bite of pastry. "And I was still in grade school. This was forever ago. And he still makes you mad?"

"You had to be there, Ivy. Myrrhcury was infuriating. Insulting, holier-than-thou. He thought he knew absolutely everything there was to know about perfume, so that qualified him to slam some of the best perfumes ever created. Some of my favorite fragrances. He had a way of making every comment a personal attack. I hated him." Jasmine was ranting, waving her arms and breathing heavily.

Clare went into the back room to get a bottle of water. Then she guided Jasmine to the bistro table in the corner of the shop, made her sit, and handed her the open bottle. "Ivy's right, Jas. That was forever ago. And the man is dead."

"I feel like I should be on your suspect list, Clare," Jasmine said between gulps of water. "Had I known at the launch party that Guillermo was Myrrhcury, I would have punched him in the face."

"But you didn't, and you didn't. And you certainly wouldn't kill him." Clare looked at her friend with narrowed eyes. "Would you?"

Just then, the door opened and old Mr Barnard shuffled in.

"Miss Clare! I hear that a sample of that perfume is in for me."

"Yes, indeed. Let me grab it for you."

As Clare went into the back room to retrieve the sample, Mr Barnard studied Ivy.

"Miss, do I know you? You look very familiar."

"Here you go, Mr Barnard. One sample of *Barenia*," Clare had emerged from the back with a small paper bag in her hand. As she handed it to the elderly gentleman, Ivy ducked into the back room. She was in no mood to be chewed out for something she hadn't done 15 years ago.

"Thank you, young lady! And please tell the other young lady who left this for me I appreciate her kindness. Now. Let me smell this."

Clare gave Jasmine a look as if to say, "We'll continue our conversation in a minute." She was thankful that Mr Barnard had come in at just the right time to defuse the situation. Perhaps Jasmine would calm down in a few. Clare grabbed a new blotter from the cup on the counter and held her hand out to Mr Barnard.

"Let me spray it for you."

He handed her the bag, and she extracted the small spray vial. Slowly, as she wanted to give Jasmine time. Clare spritzed the blotter thoroughly, shook it, and handed it to the elderly gentleman. He held it under his nose and inhaled.

"Oh my. This is not what I expected." He sniffed again, held the blotter away from his face and grimaced. "No, this will not do." He handed the blotter back to Clare.

"Don't you like it?" Clare sniffed the blotter herself, expecting the classic leather the name promised. Instead, *Barenia* unfolded like something entirely different, a fruity patchouli scent that was also a chypre. But a modern chypre, which is not quite the same animal as the classic type. Still quite lovely and unique. Clare thought she might want to wear it herself.

"I thought it would be more floral. More lily. I don't think my wife would have liked this. At all." the man sighed.

"Can I show you some of the floral fragrances we stock, Mr Barnard? We might have something more to your liking?"

"I'm afraid not, miss. Perhaps when I get over my disappointment, I'll come back." He patted Clare on the arm. "Thank you for all your trouble."

"We'll be here when you're ready, Mr Barnard. Come back anytime."

Clare watched the old man shuffle out of the store before turning back to Jasmine. Rather than having calmed down while waiting for the transaction to end, it seemed her friend's anger had ramped up once again. Jasmine stood.

"Are you positive Guillermo was Myrrhcury? Absolutely positively?"

"Yes." Clare paused, considering her next words but realizing there wasn't anything to lose at this point. "Now, promise me you won't flip out, but...Damarion has known all along."

"WHAT?" Jasmine looked around the room for something to smash, realized she'd have to pay for anything she broke, and closed her eyes. She took a deep, shuddering breath through her mouth, then let it out slowly through her nose.

"I wish I had known, Clare."

Jasmine turned abruptly and left the shop, slamming the door behind her. Ivy had crept back into the shop after hearing the door close behind Mr Barnard.

"Um. Wow. That was totally unexpected." Ivy shrugged. "Just goes to show that everybody has a secret."

Twenty-Four

After Ivy's comment about secrets, Clare realized she still had not hidden Billy's Moleskines somewhere safer than under the counter. She paced the small back room, looking up at the shelving units for a good place to stash the notebooks. The shelves were packed with the necessities for running a retail establishment: silver-on-grey Good Scents-branded shopping bags in three sizes, silver tissue paper, rolls of receipt tape, a postal scale, a small inkjet printer for packing labels, and empty cartons in various sizes for shipping. There were also a few empty shelves upon which backup perfume stock normally lived. Clare hoped they would be full again before the holidays came barreling in like a runaway sleigh. Finally, there was a box with the detritus of the many takeout breakfasts and lunches eaten in the store—spare utensils, sugar packages, and the like. "We don't need to keep all this junk," she thought. As she removed the box from the shelf, something rolled out from behind it.

"There it is!" she said out loud. The lab bottle of *Lycoctonum* that she had not seen since the day of the launch party. Clare thought it had been thrown away accidentally during all the mayhem of the evening, but apparently it had just been misplaced. She removed the cap and suddenly was overcome with the sensation of yellow flames and heat. She brought the bottle to her nose and sniffed cautiously. The dark herbal rose scent was still there, but it had been tainted by something else. Something...poisonous.

Clare was sure she had just found the murder weapon. She capped the bottle tightly and slipped it into a plastic zip-top bag. After sealing it, she washed her hands thoroughly once, then again, just in case. Billy must have stumbled across the bottle here in the back room and applied it, never realizing it had been tampered with. But by whom? And when would they have had the chance? Maybe it hadn't even been meant as a murder weapon. Perhaps someone had been tinkering with the formula, or pulling a reckless prank, never suspecting that what they added to the mixture of fragrance oils and alcohol was lethal.

The police needed to see this, but for now, she'd keep it safe until she had a moment to call Detective Briscoe. She gathered the lab sample and Billy's Moleskines, sealed in their own bag, and carried them upstairs to her apartment. The old trunk that held Busia Manya's tome seemed the most logical hiding place.

While Clare was rustling around in the back, the bell over the door chimed softly. A woman in her sixties stepped inside, unbuttoning her coat. She looked around the shop slowly, as if she'd walked into a memory. Ivy stepped out from behind the counter, offering a warm smile. "Looking for anything in particular today?"

The woman smiled back. "Not really. Just... something new. Something for myself. I used to wear *Mitsouko* years ago. My daughter says it smells like her childhood."

Ivy lit up. "A classic."

"She got me something modern last Christmas. It was... fruity. I didn't hate it. But I didn't feel like myself in it either."

Ivy nodded. "You're looking for something with roots."

"Exactly." The woman tilted her head. "You don't look old enough to know *Mitsouko*."

"I inherited the obsession," Ivy said, laughing. "Want to smell a few things that might feel like a cousin to it? We've just gotten some brand-new inventory that I'm excited to show someone." Ivy guided her toward the shelf with chypres and classic-inspired blends. As they sniffed through blotters—one mossy, one peachy, one with a wisp of smoke—the woman's face softened.

"Ooh, I like this one. It's warm. A little salty? There's...is that fig?"

"Very good nose. That one is called *Soft Architecture.* It has fig leaf, nutmeg, orris root, a little driftwood, some labdanum and patchouli. No moss, bergamot, or peach, but it still moves like a chypre."

"It's lovely. Can I try that one on?"

"Of course." Ivy gently spritzed the back of the woman's left hand. She then showed her a few other new perfumes that had arrived in the last few days. *Library of Rain* smelled of heliotrope, black tea, incense, cedar, and wet paper. It had a slight melancholy about it, a whisper of florals, and a restrained sweetness. The woman also liked *Autumn Word*, an elegant fall scent with pear, saffron, patchouli, bitter almond, and suede. This one was one of Clare's new favorites.

"I think I'll take *Soft Architecture.* It feels like a memory, but not one I've actually had."

"Sometimes that's the best kind." Ivy said.

Ivy wrapped the bottle carefully and tucked it into a Good Scents tote bag. As the woman left, she turned at the door. "Thank you. This was the first real treat I've given myself in a long time."

Ivy watched her go, a warmth settling in her chest. No mysteries there. Just scent, and memory, and a moment of someone remembering who they were.

A little while later, as Clare was putting newly arrived stock on a shelf of predominantly floral fragrances, the door opened again. She turned, and there was Jasmine, sunglasses on despite the cloudy sky, lips pressed into a straight line. She hovered near the entrance, like someone walking into a crime scene she wasn't sure had been cleaned up. Clare said nothing. Just raised an eyebrow and waited.

Jasmine slowly peeled off her shades and exhaled. "Okay," she said. "So maybe I overreacted."

Clare gave a neutral hum. "Maybe."

"Don't push it." Jasmine glanced around the shop, as if expecting someone to materialize like a spirit. "I've just been… thinking."

She stepped further into the store, her tone quieter.

"I don't want to rewrite history. I was a jerk. So was he, but… I didn't hate him. Not really." She looked down at her hands. "I actually had a thing for him." Jasmine confessed that she and Myrrhcury had chatted personally and that they had gotten along…mostly.

"I didn't know they were male, but I had hoped. Our conversations were…stimulating. And I hoped we'd meet someday. Then I was banned, the forum ended, and so did my relationship with Myrrhcury. We had never exchanged personal information. And then to find that he was someone I'd meet, only to lose him again so quickly, well, it hit me in all the wrong places."

"It's hard, isn't it?" Clare looked at her feet.

"I'm sorry, Clare. Yours was a bigger loss than mine."

Clare hugged Jasmine. "It's okay. He was one of those people who drifted through lives like perfume in the air," she said softly. "Vivid, unforgettable, but never meant to linger. He didn't belong to anyone."

After her conversation with Jasmine and the continual reminder of loss, Clare realized that important call to Detective Briscoe was far too important to put off any longer.

Twenty-Five

GOOD SCENTS WAS CLOSED on Mondays, so Clare had a whole day to putter around her apartment without the interruption of customers or her cousin. The past several weeks had been stressful, and she decided it was high time for a "me" day. Sleeping in, taking a long walk with Vetiver, an afternoon nap, and a filling, carbohydrate-loaded dinner was on the agenda. She knew it wasn't a good idea to make plans, because, as the saying goes, life always happens when you do that. And on this day, life involved Vetiver needing to go out at 7am. "So much for sleeping in," Clare thought. "Might as well take the long walk now, since we're up and the neighborhood is still mostly quiet." She threw on a warm hoodie over her sweats and sneakers and walked Vetiver down to Harbor East.

Clare could remember her grandmother talking about the many changes the area had gone through in her day. Not long ago, the neighborhood of Harbor East didn't even exist. It was a neglected plot of land in the industrial zone bordered by the Inner Harbor, Fells Point, and Little Italy before developers had their way with it. Now it was home to financial institutions, Johns Hopkins University's business school, and a Four Seasons hotel. As Clare and Vetiver walked past Kneads Bakery on the way back home, she made a mental note to pop by there for a treat sometime soon.

It was too early for a nap, and she hadn't eaten breakfast, so Clare decided to pamper herself with homemade waffles with a side of bacon. By the time she finished eating and had the kitchen cleaned up, she was ready for a nap on the couch with Vetiver.

Clare had never been a good napper, and after about forty minutes of futility, she hopped up off the couch. Vetiver looked at her as if to say, "You don't know what you're missing out on, lady," and promptly began snoring.

"Show-off."

It was barely lunchtime, and Clare was bored. She could have tidied the apartment, but it was already clean since she seldom seemed to be there. What she really wanted to do was something she had put off for a while and had promised not to think about: flip through Billy's Moleskine. Er, Moleskines. She made herself a pot of rooibos tea and took it into her bedroom.

"It's time for me to really look at these things." Clare knelt in front of the steamer trunk at the foot of her bed, the one that her great-grandmother had brought over with her from Poland. It was full of family mementos like ancient baby shoes, scraps of embroidery, children's drawings, and photos of relatives from "*moj kraj*," as she had referred to Poland. My country. Clare didn't remember her great-grandmother at all, but she had heard enough stories from her father and Busia Manya that she felt like she did. Babcia Aniela, like her daughter, lived to nearly 100, and had practiced the art of Polish folk medicine, following in the footsteps of at least three generations of women before her.

After Clare removed the plastic zip-top bag that held Billy's Moleskines and put it on her bed, she lifted her family's heavy tome from the trunk. She had kept it just as Busia Manya had, wrapped in an old homemade pillowcase decorated with an embroidered rooster and flower motif. Clare ran her fingers over the antique stitching before carefully unfolding the case and removing the thick book of ancient remedies.

The original leather binding was worn and cracked. Legend was that it had been stitched together by the hands of her fifth great-grandfather. The book had been meant to hold only so many pages; extras had been added over the years, causing the spine to split in multiple places. In order to keep pages from falling out, the book had originally been secured with several sturdy pieces of twine, which had eventually been replaced with duct tape. It did the job but lacked the dignity the book deserved. Eventually, Busia Manya made a new cover out of cardboard and a festively patterned cloth, but that, too, was wearing out. Clare put the tome on the bed next to the Moleskines and heaved herself off the ground. She poured herself a mug of tea from the pot and sat cross-legged on the bed before pulling Billy's notebooks out of their bag.

Though they weren't exactly diaries, some entries were dated. As she flipped between the books, Ivy's theory that Billy copied stuff from one book into another seemed sound. Much of their content appeared the same. The one with the sticky notes and added pages that Parker had given her was clearly the older book, which made sense. Billy's time in New York came before his time in Italy. The book that had arrived with Italian postmarks had no sticky notes. It also had entries that were dated as recently as September. It would seem that the second book may have been left behind in Italy intentionally. Perhaps Billy was being cautious, or maybe he just didn't want to carry it with him. Either way, it was clear he'd arranged for both books to reach her if anything happened. Two pieces of the same puzzle, sent from different corners of his life.

The first few undated entries in both books seemed to contain things he might have learned when he was a student. Short lists of perfumery ingredients and the scents they could create: "citronellol - rose, geranium, floral, waxy" and "geranium nitrile - rose, geranium, woody, sandalwood." Other entries seemed much more recent and the work of an adult perfumer. There were also blocks of what looked like computer code, strings of numbers. Clare smiled to herself. This was the secret code that she and Billy had used when they passed notes in school. If other kids had intercepted and read the note, they wouldn't have understood what it said. Once, however, because the note was full of numbers, some smart ass took it to the teacher and accused them of cheating on a math test. That put an end to their use of coded messages in class.

They had used a simple grid code, in which letters of the alphabet, except the letter K, were arranged in a 5x5 grid. The letter A would be in the first square of both the 1st row and the 1st column, so would be given the designation 11; the letter S was in the 4th row and 3rd column, so would be represented by the number 43. Clare quickly scribbled the code on a piece of scrap paper, so she could refer to it as she paged through the Moleskines.

Among the older notebook's pages, a few spiral-pad inserts appeared, scribbled in a childlike hand, with the occasional sticky note tucked in. Rather than the names of aroma chemicals, these additions listed notes. "Rose, geranium, oakmoss," and "castoreum (beaver butts) leathery, musky, fruity." Several of the added pages also bore the letters "BM," which Clare figured was a way of notating a common fragrance chemical.

As the pages went on, the notations got more complex. Some pages were perfume formulas with lists of ingredients and the amounts of each in grams. Several of them were straight-up diary entries. Like the one dated January 7 from a few years earlier. Using her code grid, Clare read:

"I cannot get it right. I chase the hellebore accord, and it chases me back. It wants to be louder. No, stranger. Not animalic, not bitter, not merely green, but off-kilter, as if the skin can sense something is wrong even if the nose can't name it.

I tried swapping ink for costus. No. Too animal.

Tried a ghost dose of cumin—unforgivable.

Tried Ambrocenide and almost blacked out the accord entirely.

But then! A trace of Blackcurrant Sulfide + Safraleine + Angelica CO2 = the thing I was looking for: a shimmer at the edge of dread.

It's far more difficult to create fragrances on my own than I had anticipated.

Good thing I don't have to."

Next to this entry was a page torn from a different notebook, clearly written by another person. It was not encoded and contained a list of perfumery ingredients.

Hellebore Accord (85g total, compound added to main formula)

Violet Leaf Absolute 12g

Vertofix Coeur 10g

Ink Note (blend: ISO E Super + Suederal + Aldehyde C11) 8g

Ambroxan 8g

Evernyl 8g

Angelica CO2 8g

Black Pepper Oil 8g

Absinthe (Wormwood EO) 4g

Safraleine 4g

Methyl Pamplemousse 4g

Hydroxycitronellal 4g

Ionone Beta 4g

Aldehyde C-12 MNA 2g

Blackcurrant Sulfide 1g

Ah! The mysterious "hellebore accord" was no longer so mysterious. But why was it not in Billy's handwriting?

Clare felt like a spy discovering enemy secrets. Or, more accurately, a peeping Tom, witnessing Billy's soul laid bare. Or was it Guillermo who created *Lycoctonum*? Were they even the same person? She wasn't sure anymore.

The next coded entry was one of the last.

"This one kept me awake. There were nights when I thought I could smell it in the walls. A portrait of the beautiful wrongness of nature...that was the goal. No safety. No pastel musk or shy petals. Lycoctonum is

wolfsbane in flower. Not literal, of course (I'm not trying to kill anyone), but a perfume that hints at danger through a green so strange it nearly hums."

What followed was a list of ingredients, this time in Billy's hand: Rose Damascena Absolute, Galbanum Resinoid, Clary Sage oil, and synthetics like Cashmeran and Iso E Super. The combination didn't wow her, but the last component, "Hellebore Accord," confirmed it was *Lycoctonum*. She rifled through the older notebook again; no other complete list of the accord's ingredients appeared. The newer Moleskine offered nothing similar, though an entry included the rest of *Lycoctonum*'s ingredients. Only the slip of paper, in someone else's handwriting and tucked into the older notebook, contained the hellebore accord formula. Did Billy not create it? And if not, who did?

The more Clare looked at the ingredients for the main part of *Lycoctonum*, the more familiar it seemed. She put the Moleskine aside and pulled her grandmother's book onto her lap. She carefully opened it to the first page, on which were written the names of the women who had used it over the generations. Before Busia Manya had given it to her granddaughter, she had added Clare's name to the bottom of the list. Clare felt like a fraud when she saw that, as she had no plans to go into the folk remedy business. She had no desire to be a healer, only a perfumer. Because of her accident, that wasn't going to happen, but she had accepted years ago that her fate had changed.

She wasn't sure what she was looking for in Busia Manya's book, but she figured she'd know when she found it. She thought back to Dr Lavender's brief and disjointed lecture. Had she seen something in the book many years ago about alchemy? While most people know alchemists attempted to turn various metals into gold, it is less well known that these people also attempted to find elixirs to cause immortality and others to heal all sickness. So, in effect, these people played a role in developing the science of chemistry, though their beliefs in mysticism weren't particularly scientific at all. As a trained chemist herself,

Clare wondered why generations of failure never stopped these people from continuing their staggeringly ambitious trio of pursuits, though it may have been the small successes along the way that kept them going. Certainly, some experiments done in the name of eternal life ended up killing their subjects, but there also must have been some that cured an ailment or at least made it seem better.

Busia Manya had the benefit of over 100 years of experimentation before her. The decoctions and potions she made for her customers had been tested and proven many times over the years. But had the original authors of the book Clare now had in front of her ever dabbled in alchemy? She wished she could read any of the early inscriptions that had been written in many languages. She could identify the Polish alphabet and Cyrillic, but there were also lists of mysterious symbols. Did any of them have to do with alchemy? She realized she was grasping at straws, but she felt that somehow there was a connection between her grandmother and Dr Lavender and the mysterious citrinitas aspect of alchemy, and they all had a connection to the substance that had poisoned Billy.

Clare called her mother.

"Ma, do you recall Grandma ever talking about alchemy?"

"You mean turning lead into gold? I don't think so. I'd like to think we'd have a lot more money if she could figure that out." Terri laughed. "Wouldn't that have been nice?"

"I didn't think she practiced it. I just wondered if there was anything in the family book about it?"

"I wouldn't really know, honey. She was your father's mother. I spent a lot of time with her, sure, but we never really spoke about the 'family business.'"

Clare sighed. She knew it was a long shot, but it was worth a try. "But you can read Polish a little, right? Better than I can."

"I don't know about that. Since I haven't had to speak it for so long, it's going to be very rusty. I had the same language thing with your grandmother that you did. She spoke to me in Polish, and I answered her in English."

Clare had a thought: “what about Aunt Lou? She spoke fluently, didn’t she?” Her father’s sister was a few years older than he would have been.

“You can ask. I don’t think she’s all there most of the time, though. Early onset. How about Uncle Peter, Ivy’s dad? Busia Manya was his mother, too.”

“Yeahhhh...but we don’t talk to him. I mean, Ivy and I don’t. After the way he treated her when she came out as trans, we really want nothing to do with him. I’ll take my chances with Aunt Lou. Do you have her phone number handy?”

Twenty-Six

As Clare climbed the marble front steps of Aunt Lou's narrow, brick Highlandtown rowhouse, she felt bad that she hadn't visited in over a year. Her father's quirky older sister had been her favorite babysitter. Louisa Buchowski had never married and always seemed to have time to watch Clare when her parents needed a date night. And now, according to Terri, she was exhibiting signs of dementia. Even so, Aunt Lou seemed delighted to see Clare and ushered her into the kitchen. "Sit, sit," she encouraged. "I'll be right with you." Lou then scurried off to another room.

At the kitchen table, Clare eased her grandmother's ancient tome open with care. The spine complained at every turn, while the margins spilled over with looping notes in Polish and Russian. She had stared at them for so long that the letters resembled actual chicken scratches.

Aunt Lou breezed back into the kitchen wearing one of her signature ensembles: black-and-white striped wide-leg pants, a men's black v-neck t-shirt that had faded to mid-grey, and an oversized knit cardigan the color of mustard, accented with a brooch shaped like a radish. Or maybe it was an actual radish. She was carrying a mug that read, "Tea First, Then Prophecy."

"Who are you, and what are you doing here?" she asked Clare.

"Aunt Lou, it's me, Clare. You just let me in a few minutes ago. I came here to talk about this." She waved her hand over the large book of folk remedies and potentially alchemical formulae.

"Ahhh! Don't do that!" Lou stepped back dramatically. "You might conjure something."

Clare wondered for a second if that could be true. She tapped a page full of diagrams and yellowed ink drawings of roots and stars. "There's a section I'm trying to understand. When I was in New York several weeks ago, I attended a lecture given by a man who called himself Dr. Lavender. He talked about the stages of alchemy and mentioned three of them—nigredo, albedo, and rubedo—but he just skipped citrinitas. Said it wasn't important."

Lou made a noise like a chicken sneezing. "Ha! Classic Lavender. That man once told me chamomile had no medicinal properties. Do you know how many angry bees I had to consult to disprove him?"

Clare blinked. "You... consulted bees? And you know him?"

Lou sat down on one of her other mismatched wooden chairs. "We might have dated briefly in the 80s." Lou fiddled with the handle of her mug. "He was quite the dandy, that Norman."

"Norbert," Clare corrected.

"Norbert." Lou parroted. "Yes, he was quite the natty dresser, that one was. He was the bass player for the band The Paracelsus Saints. We met at a basement dive bar in Greenwich Village in 1981. He was wearing eyeliner and screaming about post-industrial alienation, and I had just been dumped by my girlfriend." Clare's eyes boinged wide open at that revelation.

Aunt Lou paused reflectively before continuing. "It was love at first sight. He was wearing a black t-shirt that had more holes than fabric, and his hair was this long." She made a chopping motion with the side of her hand against her opposite bicep. "Not sure he had washed it recently. Or ever."

Clare wrinkled her nose as she interrupted, "I thought you said he was a dandy and a natty dresser?"

"I didn't say that. I said he was a ratty dresser. And he sure was randy. All the time."

Clare did not want to imagine her Aunt Lou with Dr Lavender. She gave a tiny shake of her head to dismiss the mental image. Lou abruptly got up from the table and went into the other room. After about a minute, a dreadful noise, possibly the sound made by tortured souls in the very lowest circle of hell, emanated from the other room.

Lou came back into the room, sat down, and began moving her shoulders around in a jaunty manner. Chair dancing. "Isn't this great?" She yelled over the din. "This is The Paracelsus Saints' biggest hit, "Sulfur Kisses (In the Ashtray of God)." Aunt Lou closed her eyes and started singing along in a thin, wavery voice.

"C-c-c-calcination! Desolation! No salvation! Just transmutation! Yeah!"

Clare couldn't speak. She might have made a small squeaking sound, but was otherwise simultaneously shocked, transfixed, and appalled.

Aunt Lou opened her eyes and sighed happily, as if remembering something satisfying. "This was on their debut album 'Recrudescence of the Black Sun,' which I have on vinyl. If you want to borrow it, just ask."

"Er, thanks, Aunt Lou. Will let you know. What about the angry bees? You said you consulted angry bees?" Clare had a feeling she might not want to know the answer to that but couldn't help herself.

"Now, why would I do that? My medium was tea leaves. I consulted teas. They were seldom angry."

Clare sighed. She was pretty sure she wasn't going to get anywhere today.

Lou got up and began rooting through a drawer full of tea packets, used twist ties, and expired fortune cookies. "Citrinitas. That's the yellowing stage, isn't it? Enlightenment. Awakening. The part where everything starts to make sense, just before you set it on fire to make it true."

"That's... surprisingly coherent."

Lou shrugged, pulling out a lemon verbena tea bag. "Your great-grandmother wrote a whole essay about it, I think. Called it 'the moment the herbs whisper.' Though that may have been a metaphor."

Clare looked back at the page. The ink shimmered faintly in the light. "So citrinitas isn't about transformation exactly... it's more like insight?"

"Insight with teeth," Lou said, slapping the kettle on. "It's when you see the pattern, the shape of what's coming, but you're not quite ready to name it yet. That's why people skip it. Too uncomfortable. Too... yellow."

Clare was surprised to find that she understood completely.

Aunt Lou reached out, slid her mother's book out from under Clare's gaze, and arranged it on the table in front of her. She flipped through a few pages to a section roughly in the middle of the book. She ran her bony finger down the page and moved her lips as she read the text.

"Ah! Here it is."

"Here's what?" Clare was almost afraid to find out.

"This is the section you were looking for. My great-grandmother Jadwiga didn't just continue the family business. She was a perfumer as well as an herbalist."

Lou pointed to a list of words and numbers. "This is a formula for a rose perfume with blackcurrant and clary sage." She turned the page and pointed to a similar list. "Here's another. This one has rose, oakmoss, and angelica root."

"How did you know I was looking for this section?"

"Your mother told me." Lou rubbed her chin. "You know, these perfumes could be quite good, but they still need something to give them a little oompfh."

Clare thought, "like a hellebore accord."

Aunt Lou abruptly stood and went to the stove. "How about some tea, hon? I can do a reading for you. Then we could look through my photo albums and you'll see what Lavender looked like in the 80s." Lou smiled as she was momentarily lost in thought. "Did I mention he was a real looker in his day? Especially in my fishnets. Woo boy. Now that was a turn-on."

Clare shook her head. All Lou had to do was mention Lavender in tights, and Clare could envision it. She didn't need the actual image burnt into her retinas. "No, thanks, Aunt Lou. Not today. But I'm very grateful for your help." Clare kissed her aunt on the cheek, slipped Busia Manya's tome into her tote bag, and left the premises.

Clare sat cross-legged on the floor of the shop's back room, surrounded by photocopies, herbal indexes, and Billy's Moleskine. A week of digging through citrinitas, yellow symbolism, ancestral notes, and alchemy, and all of it was feeling like...nothing. She had thought briefly of contacting Dr. Lavender, but after her visit to Aunt Lou, she couldn't help but think of him as a dirty-haired punk in a hole-ridden t-shirt. And fishnets. She shuddered at the thought and shook her head to rid it of the thought. Again. She had found herself doing that a lot. It was very distracting to what she was trying to achieve. But what exactly was that?

The book lay open beside her to a page she had marked with a yellow post-it on which she had written:

"Yellow = transition? Insight? Or a warning?"

She stared at it until the handwriting blurred. There had been yellow flames. Heat. Danger. She'd felt it in her bones. Surely that meant something. Surely it was connected to the citrinitas phase of alchemy. The yellowing. The dawning clarity.

Clare picked up the Italian Moleskine. There was still one coded message at the end of the book that she had not yet read. It was time.

"Clare, apart from Busia Manya, you are the only person who can understand that I became who I am because of my sister. She thought she was helping me, but she only created a monster. The weak and untalented Billy had to go, so I became the much stronger Guillermo. Unfortunately, no matter what I call myself, I am still a fraud. I hope you can forgive me, my oldest friend. My only true friend. I am truly sorry."

She read it twice. Then once more. And then it hit her, not with emotion, but with logic: Clare had been chasing a ghost. The heat she'd sensed on Guillermo's body, the yellow aura she'd seen in her mind when she smelled the lab sample of *Lycoctonum*. It wasn't alchemical. It wasn't symbolic. It was just the way she perceived the poison. It was a physical reaction; a warning her subconscious had recognized before her conscious mind had caught up.

For a moment, it felt like her reaction had special meaning. But it was only her own weird brain chemistry. She'd wanted it to be mystical, poetic. A sign. But it wasn't. It was just...death. Darn that Dr Lavender for putting that alchemical nonsense in her head.

There was a knock on the doorframe. Ivy leaned in, holding a white bakery bag and raising an eyebrow. "Did you just solve something, or unsolve it?"

Clare gave a small, bitter laugh. "Neither. Just... eliminated a theory."

Ivy handed her a snickerdoodle. "Yellow's a tricky color. Too much hope attached to it."

They sat for a moment in companionable silence, surrounded by notes that no longer mattered. And slowly, gently, Clare said, "It was never about symbols. It was about what had been done to him. Not how it felt to me."

Ivy sipped. "So what now?"

Clare closed the tome. The pages gave a soft sigh. "Now," she said, "I stop chasing ghosts and wait patiently for that tox report."

Clare didn't have to wait much longer. The next day, she found the toxicologist's report in her inbox, thanks to Ayanna. Now Clare knew exactly what had killed Guillermo Flares and who had done it. Her next, and hopefully final, step would be to get her suspects together and force the guilty party to confess.

She ran her plan by Detective Briscoe, who said, "Name the place and time, and I'll be there."

Twenty-Seven

"WINTER IS DEFINITELY ON the way," Clare shivered as she poked around in her drafty closet. "I need an outfit that says 'capable, calm, and collected,' but is still comfortable." Certainly, her favorite t-shirt wasn't going to impress anyone. As she slid wire hanger after wire hanger along the closet rod, the sound echoing in the otherwise quiet room like horror movie music, she realized it was the proper soundtrack for her fashion sense. Aunt Lou would feel very much at home wearing Clare's clothes. She finally settled on a pair of black jeans and a black turtleneck sweater. As she appraised herself in her full-length mirror, she felt she looked bland and boring, but at least she appeared to be an adult. Didn't she? She fluffed her curly brown hair with her hands and made a face at herself. Lipstick might help. And earrings. Clare made a mental note to ask Jasmine for some fashion tips once the holidays were over. That one always looked impeccable.

Terri had already picked up Vetiver for the evening. All Clare needed to do before the guests arrived was choose her fragrance. She wanted something somber and elegant. *Last Light on Velvet* by The Recluse was perfect, with its quiet notes of iris, antique paper, peppered vanilla, suede, and myrrh. She dabbed it behind each ear, across her wrists, and once at the base of her throat. The scent bloomed slowly. Crushed iris. Faint pepper. The paper of old letters never mailed. It didn't comfort her. That wasn't the point. It set the tone.

Clare had closed the shop an hour early to get the place ready. "Ugh, it looks like Christmas threw up in here. Maybe we should take down a few of the more cheerful decorations, at least for the evening?" Ivy stood, hands on hips, and surveyed the shop before stomping over to the counter to snatch the miniature Santa hat off Harbaugh's head.

"Probably a good idea. It does seem a bit too festive for a memorial service. Definitely for a 'whodunit' reveal."

"You're living the dream, Cuz. Baltimore's very own Miss Marple."

"Not my dream, believe me. I wanted to live a quiet life, with my beakers and pipettes, creating beautiful fragrances."

Ivy jumped up and down, full of nervous energy. "Still not going to share your thoughts on the murderer with me?"

"Nope, you'll just have to wait until the big reveal."

Smooth jazz played softly in the background, eliciting an "ew, gaaahhh," from Ivy. Wine and wine glasses occupied the counter; surely someone would need a drink before the night was over. There were also tiny dishes of chocolate-covered espresso beans and candied ginger, just in case someone needed a bite of something bright and acrid to counter the emotion of the evening. This was a cover, of course, to hide the real purpose of the gathering.

Clare wanted everyone's eyes to be on her as she revealed to them all who had killed Guillermo Flares, so she and Ivy had rearranged the shop to meet this goal. The console table that normally commanded the center of the room was pushed to the side wall. In its place was a semicircle of chairs, each bearing a name card. The heavy grey curtains on the front window had been drawn to keep out any prying eyes, and the shade on the locked front door was down. The room was intentionally stuffy and uncomfortable, made only more so by the potent scent of *Lycoctonum* in the air. It felt like a haunting was about to occur.

A few moments before 7 o'clock, Ayanna Briscoe arrived with her ever-present matcha latte. Only Clare and Ivy knew she was a police detective. Stephanie arrived next, breezing in as if this were a casual occasion. As the rest of the guests arrived, Clare offered them wine. Only Philomena took a glass. Jorge and Jasmine stood together and chatted quietly, but the other invitees stood apart from each other, seeming uncomfortable and unsure of what was going to happen next. It struck Clare that she and Ivy were possibly the only people in the room who had met each of the suspects. She was pretty sure that Philomena and Stephanie had never met, and that Efraim only knew Guillermo's wife and sister from what he had been told by his boss. Jasmine and Jorge were there for moral support, as of course was Ivy. Clare wasn't sure what she would do without her cousin. She was a bright light in her life, someone she could always count on.

By 7:15, the guests had all arrived. Clare tapped the side of her wineglass with a pen to get everyone's attention. "Please, could everyone take a seat?" After each guest found their place, Clare stood before them and cleared her throat.

"The man who came into this world as William Leight was someone with whom we each had a deep connection. Friend. Sibling. Lover. Rival. He left us as Guillermo Flares, perfumer. Someone who none of us knew particularly well."

"I'm going to call him Billy, as that is the name by which I knew him best. For most of his life, he desperately wanted to be a perfumer, someone whose creations would bring enjoyment to strangers all over the world. And despite having attended perfumery school and apprenticed at one of the most highly regarded fragrance companies in the world, LuxeOne, by the age of 30 he hadn't yet reached the pinnacle of fame that he sought. One might say that he was an impatient man. Such things do not happen overnight. So, when he finally produced a scent that he felt would launch his career into the stratosphere, he was ecstatic." Clare cleared her throat again and took a deep breath to calm the flutter of nervousness.

She continued, "He didn't create that fragrance on his own." After a moment of increasingly uncomfortable silence, Clare went on.

"I have gathered you all under false pretenses. We aren't here to celebrate the life of Billy Leight, also known as Guillermo Flares. We're here to find out who killed him."

Efraim twisted uncomfortably in his chair. Philomena raised her eyebrow at Clare, amused. Stephanie sat calmly, looking straight ahead, her arms folded over her chest. She snorted and said, "Well, that explains why mommy and daddy aren't here."

"Go on, Clare." Ivy made a shooing motion with her hands. "Keep talking."

"I was saying... that Guillermo had quite a bit of help in making *Lycoctonum*." Clare shifted her weight from one foot to the other. "I have two of Billy's Moleskine notebooks, filled with notes on various formulae he'd been playing with, along with slips of paper and sticky notes added over the years. One of which, labeled 'hellebore accord,' was written by someone other than Billy." Clare paused and looked at the perfumer in the room.

"That was your doing, wasn't it, Efraim? You created the accord that made *Lycoctonum* the beautifully haunting scent that it is. The mysterious 'hellebore accord,' a combination of aromachemicals meant to evoke the scent of something that doesn't have a fragrance, a plant that is as poisonous as it is lovely."

Efraim had started to perspire some minutes earlier. He mopped his face with the hem of his shirt and glanced up at Clare. His right leg was bouncing up and down nervously. Finally, he answered.

"Yes, Guillermo—I didn't know him as Billy—was struggling with making his fragrance truly unique. He already had a good base, but it wasn't special. Not for today's fragrance aficionados." Efraim stretched his head back on his neck, realizing he had nothing to lose by revealing the truth. He took a deep breath. "*Lycoctonum* was based on a formula that he had copied out of your grandmother's book of remedies when he was a teenager. I don't know if you knew this, Clare, but someone in your family was a perfumer. While your grandmother was an expert in folk remedies, she only dabbled in fragrances. Her perfumes were pretty, but basic, mostly combinations of essential oils and alcohol. But your great-great-grandmother, Jadwiga, did more than dabble. According to Guillermo, there were several sophisticated combinations of fragrance components in the book you like to refer to as 'the tome.'" Efraim shifted in his seat.

"Yes, I know that my great-great-grandmother, Jadwiga, had been a perfumer, thanks to a recent conversation I had with an aunt. And that explained why so many of the notes in Billy's book bore the initials 'BM', which stood for Busia Manya: they had come out of the family's book of remedies."

Efraim nodded and continued. "Guillermo was particularly enamored of a combination of rose, blackcurrant, oakmoss, clary sage, and leather, and he fiddled with it incessantly, trying to make it into something it would never be: the next Shalimar. A worldwide best seller. Seeing his frustration, I played with the formula myself. Secretly. I was just his helper at the time, his perfume assistant. This was before he started treating me like his flunky. His errand boy."

Efraim shot a look at Ivy, who gave him an encouraging smile. "I put together a combination of ingredients that, when added to his base, turned it into something special. At first, I wasn't sure if I should give him the accord, not knowing whether it would damage his fragile ego to realize that someone he considered beneath him could come up with the solution to a problem that had been haunting him for years at that point. But I felt that the scent had potential that was too good to ignore, so I presented him with the formula. To my great surprise, he was thankful that I had gone to the trouble. He called it the 'hellebore accord,' knowing full well that it referred to a poisonous plant. He thought the name would make the scent seem that much more mysterious."

Clare then said, "Your addition gave *Lycoctonum* a depth it wouldn't have had otherwise. But why did you let him take full credit for the creation of the fragrance when you had done the most important part?"

Efraim cleared his throat, "because I had a secret that he threatened to expose."

"But Billy also had a secret. *Lycoctonum* was more of your creation than his. What could beat that?"

"I'm not sure exactly what his problem was, but clearly Billy had some mental health issues." Upon hearing those words, Philomena nodded. "Within a few days of successfully creating a batch of the perfume, he totally convinced himself that he had created it entirely on his own. Without my help or the help of Jadwiga. So, in his mind, he had no secrets. And no need for me as a lab assistant. Instead, I was sent to do his grocery shopping."

"Then why," Clare paused and looked at Ivy, "did you break into the store? You took nothing. Rather, you left something behind. And just a day after I had seen you."

Efraim shrugged. "Yes, I broke in. I had taken one of the store keys that you left on a hook in the back, one night you were away. That night Ivy and I went out to dinner. She wanted me to smell something, so we came back to the shop. While she was distracted, I grabbed it. Then, when I had the chance, I let myself in. I wanted to make sure that you had the whole formula for *Lycoctonum*. Jadwiga's base had been noted in there, but I was pretty sure my accord had not. Guillermo worked from my notes for that, and I still had them. So, I copied down the formula on a piece of notepaper and inserted it into his Moleskine. It wasn't hard to find; in fact, it was in the first place I looked, under the front counter." Efraim tsked. "Really, Clare, that was not a safe place."

Clare nodded. "I don't think I knew how valuable it was." She paused for a moment.

"Why did you add the formula for the accord? It belongs to you."

"Clare, *Lycoctonum* is your great-great-grandmother Jadwiga's as much as it is mine. Therefore, it also belongs to you. If you ever want to make more, you have my permission." Efraim closed his eyes and nodded. When he reopened them, he added, "I think you're the only person Guillermo wouldn't have minded knowing he was a fraud."

Clare looked around the room to gauge the reaction of her audience. Jorge had removed his hat and was fanning himself with a handful of blotters. Stephanie was still sitting with her arms folded tightly across her chest, legs crossed at the knee, foot waving gently, but she now wore an ugly smirk on her face. Philomena had removed her jacket and was pink in the face from the wine and the heat of the room. She wore a sad expression as she stared straight ahead. Detective Briscoe was taking notes. Efraim still seemed nervous. Once again, he mopped his face with the hem of his shirt. Clare addressed him one last time.

"When I told you that Guillermo and Philomena had married, you seemed surprised."

"Yes. That was something else he was in denial about. He maintained they had gone out on one date, that it was a disaster, and that he spent months avoiding her. Apparently, none of that was true, except that the first date was a mess." Efraim looked at Philomena, who smiled weakly.

"Yes," she admitted. "I was a bit of a trainwreck that night. But we went out regularly after that, and after a few months of dating, we got married. He said I was one of the few people who truly understood him and his passions. And that he couldn't live without me."

Clare looked at Philomena, who was shredding a tissue in her lap. "But then he changed his mind, didn't he?"

"Yes. He changed almost overnight. One day, he was charming, shy, not-quite-sure of himself Billy Leight, the man whom I had encouraged as we worked together. He needed that support; I knew he wasn't particularly talented."

At that, Stephanie Leight snorted and twisted her face in a semblance of a smile but said nothing.

"Go on, Philomena," Claire coaxed the woman who had been Billy's wife.

"I had hoped that there was a great perfumer in there, waiting to burst forth. But he was merely… okay. He could do the assistant's work just fine. He measured ingredients and made notations and tweaked formulae, but it didn't seem like he was ever going to reach the echelon of perfumers that he admired." Philomena paused, as if gathering her thoughts. "Then one day, he decided he no longer wanted to be William Leight. From that moment on he would be known as Guillermo Flares, master perfumer. As if by changing his name, he could change himself. And he did change himself, but not in the way he wanted. He didn't become more talented; he just became more of a wanker." Nobody laughed at that. Apart from Detective Briscoe and Clare's *Cognoscented* friends, everyone in that room experienced his change for the worse in some way.

"I don't know how much of that was him, and how much of it was because of the cult he joined in Rome. Part of changing his character meant that he no longer wanted to be married, nor did he want to live in New York, so he packed his bags and moved to start a new life as a star." Philomena made air quotes at the word star.

Efraim had raised an index finger as if he wanted to correct Philomena about the whole cult thing, then dropped it just as quickly. Clare thought it made little difference what Guillermo's wife believed at this moment and gave him an upside-down smile before turning back to Philomena, who had resumed speaking.

"And to some extent, that happened. When he came back to the States, he was an Instagram celebrity who spoke beautifully about perfume as he batted his eyelashes and charmed his growing legion of fans."

At this point, Stephanie sighed dramatically. "I honestly don't know why I'm here. Billy and I never got along. We barely spoke to each other for the last ten years. And when I came to his launch, he practically threw me out of the store."

Philomena spoke up, "He used to talk about you all the time, Stephanie. You were his older sister with the makings of a talented perfumer, and he admired you and your talent. He was jealous and wanted to have what you had. And instead of encouraging him, you switched his work with yours behind his back and got angry with him when he took credit for it. He didn't know that you had been messing around with his experiments. Billy was convinced that he had done all that great work, and felt betrayed to discover what you had done. It was cruel, and he didn't deserve it." Philomena choked back a sob. "Part of him thought you were lying, that you only said you had made the more refined versions. But another part of him understood you were the better perfumer by far."

Stephanie laughed. Then she shouted, "And I was! I am a better perfumer!" Stephanie turned slightly in her seat. "Why is it fine when that guy there," she pointed to Efraim, "can do the same thing I did—tinker with Billy's experiments and make them better—but when I do it, I'm a villain?"

"Because I let him take the credit. I didn't need to. I saw that he was struggling. I was his assistant after all. And...I'm a nice guy."

"Nice? Nice! And where did that get you, huh?"

"No regrets. I have no regrets." Efraim shook his head slowly from side to side. "None at all."

Clare had been pacing the room while people were talking. She was nervous and hoped that she could pull this off. First, she needed to bring the conversation back on track.

"Stephanie," she said, "you're not currently a perfumer, are you? You weren't particularly interested in it, except to bully your brother. You were more into home remedies, like Busia Manya."

"Yes! I was fascinated by what your grandmother did, healing people. I would have loved to get my hands on her book of remedies. The one you threw away." Stephanie made a face. "I don't know how you could do such a thing to a family heirloom."

Clare smiled. "I lied. Of course I wouldn't throw it away."

"I need that more than you, Clare. How much do you want for it?"

At that point, Detective Briscoe spoke up. "What do you do for a living, Ms Leight?"

"I practice homeopathy."

"Ah, so you have a medical license, Ms Leight? You do know that only those who hold a valid license to practice medicine in the state of Maryland can also practice homeopathy?"

Stephanie dropped her head. "I'm an herbalist."

"What's that, Ms Leight? I could hardly hear you."

Stephanie turned to speak to the detective. "I am an herbalist."

"And what does an herbalist do, Ms Leight?"

"An herbalist is someone who uses plants for healing."

Clare half expected Ayanna to say, "no further questions," but realized this was real life, not an episode of *Law and Order*. She had a question of her own. "Stephanie, what were those pills that you gave me at Thanksgiving?"

"You said you had a terrible headache, so I gave you one of my favorite homeopathic remedies, aconite, which is great for headaches and anxiety, which you also seemed to exhibit. It worked well, didn't it?"

"Actually, I didn't take them. When you put them in my hand, I felt and saw heat. Yellow flames. It turns out that aconite is one of those substances that I cannot smell, but that I can feel through my other senses working in tandem." Clare realized that only her close friends and Detective Briscoe understood that statement, and it didn't really matter if her suspects did. She looked at her friend's sister with narrowed eyes. "You also put aconite, also known as wolfsbane, in the lab sample of

Lycoctonum that was in the back room the night of the launch party."

Stephanie looked pleased with herself as she clapped with delight. "Clever Clare! When I saw the little bottle of *Lycoctonum* in the back room before I left the launch party, I knew it was my chance to prove myself. I had brought with me a few bottles of my favorite homeopathic ingredients, er, herbal tinctures, so I added a couple of drops of this and several drops of that to the perfume, shook it up and put the bottle back on the shelf. I hoped you would apply the scent and realize that not only did it smell good, but it also made you feel so much better. You seemed very tense that evening." She turned to the rest of the group and clarified, "I've been trying to convince her that wellness fragrances are the future."

Detective Briscoe had another question. "And what were these 'drops of this and drops of that' you added to your brother's perfume?"

Stephanie explained that she had used tansy, which she claimed calmed the mind and eased anxiety and depression. Also, she had added aconite, which she described as a "wonder drug" because of its ability to treat headaches and fevers, as well as anxiety. The detective had her phone out and looked up each substance as it was mentioned. "Are you aware that both plants are toxic?"

"Everything is toxic," Stephanie said smugly. "You don't want to know what's in that coffee you're guzzling. Or even in the air around you. And don't get me started on fluoride in the water."

"It's green tea, actually. Matcha. *Camellia sinensis* for you folks who like to pretend that you are scientists. It's great for metabolism support and cognitive function and has antioxidant and anti-inflammatory properties. And it just tastes so darn good with a bit of frothed milk. But my beverage consumption habits are not what we should be questioning. I ask again, do you know that both tansy and aconite are highly poisonous?"

"Tansy is not at all poisonous."

"Where did you say you received your certification in homeopathic medicine?"

"Erm, I'm an herbalist. And as such, I am not required to be certified or licensed."

"Right, an herbalist." Detective Briscoe tapped away at her phone. When she looked up, she explained slowly, as if talking to a child, that there are two kinds of tansy: *Tanacetum vulgare* and *Tanacetum annuum*. *T. annuum* is also known as blue tansy and is generally safe. *T. vulgare*, however, can be poisonous.

"Aconite, or wolfsbane, if you prefer, is toxic not only when ingested but also when absorbed topically." Detective Briscoe continued. "If too much of it just so happened to end up in a tiny bottle of perfume which was then applied to one's wrists, and one rubbed those wrists together to distribute the scent, then that substance would be more readily absorbed by the skin and potentially cause side effects that include dizziness, and cardiovascular problems." She paused. "Oh, and death."

Clare let that hang in the air for a moment before she broke in. "According to the toxicology results supplied by the Baltimore City Medical Examiner's office, Billy had been poisoned..."

Stephanie interrupted her. "I wasn't aware you were on the police force."

Detective Briscoe spoke up. "She's not, but I am." Stephanie turned to look at her with narrowed eyes. Ayanna gestured to Clare with her cup. "Go on with what you were saying."

"The tox report found *Aconitum napellus* in his system, along with *T. vulgare*. The lab sample was also analyzed and found to contain large amounts of both aconite and tansy." Clare swallowed audibly. "Before Billy left the shop that evening, he must have applied *Lycoctonum* from that sample bottle, not realizing that someone had tampered with it by adding poisonous substances."

Stephanie stood. "That can't be! I've used those herbs many times before, and they were always beneficial." She turned to Detective Briscoe. "Both aconite and tansy are known for their healing properties."

Clare broke in. "Would you like to see the toxicology report, Stephanie? I can go in the back and print it out for you."

"Yes, I would very much like to see it." Stephanie said sharply as she turned back to Clare, red-faced.

Clare looked her in the eye. "How many drops did you add? Certainly not just a couple."

"I have always hated you, Clare. I don't understand why my brother seemed to prefer being around you more than spending time with his own sister."

"That's easy. Because I was his friend, Stephanie. I understood him and encouraged him in his dream of becoming a perfumer. And you just wanted to feel superior to him because you had to compete for your parents' attention."

"You don't understand, Clare," Stephanie whined. "You're an only child. Not only did you have your parents, but you also had your grandmother. I would have killed to have Busia Manya on my side. I'd like to think she would have been proud that I followed in her footsteps and became a practitioner of the healing arts."

"Well, you did accomplish some of that. You're an only child again. And you've killed. Healing arts, not so much."

"The wrong person died!" Stephanie shouted. "You should have applied the *Lycoctonum*, not Billy." Stephanie sat down suddenly and sobbed when the realization hit her. In an uncharacteristically small voice, she said, "I didn't mean to kill anyone."

"Ooh, that sounds like a confession!" Jorge whispered to Jasmine a little too loudly.

Clare gave him the stinkeye.

"Indeed," said Detective Briscoe. She went to the door and opened it, admitting two uniformed police officers. Stephanie stood and glared at the detective before allowing the officers to read her rights and cuff her.

As Stephanie was being led away, Philomena said, "You might have been a better perfumer than Billy, but you are a rotten herbalist. And a terrible person." She stood and went to Clare. Putting her hand on the shop owner's arm, Philomena said, "Thanks for this. It was hard, but I feel better. It's not closure exactly, but it's something. I still may never know what happened between us, or what happened to Billy in Rome, if that was where he was, or why he became Guillermo." Philomena trailed off and went to the counter to refill her wineglass.

Efraim rose and stood by the widow, who had downed half her wine and topped it up again. "Philomena, perhaps I can fill in some of the missing pieces. I met your husband in Rome, at the perfumer's workshop where he was apprenticing."

"Thank you. Let's go somewhere we can have a proper drink."

Detective Briscoe drained the last of her matcha, scanning for a trash can. Clare held out her hand. "I'll toss it for you."

Ayanna smirked as she passed it over. "You know, Clare, the department could've cracked this without you. Would've taken longer, sure. And it would've been a whole lot less entertaining."

"I'm touched," Clare smiled, almost shyly. "Honestly, I wasn't sure about Stephanie until Thanksgiving, when she gave me those tablets and I felt the same... heat... as when I found Billy and the tainted lab bottle." She shook her head. "I never thought she had a real motive. More like she let her ego drive without a license."

"That's one way to put it." Ayanna slung her bag over her shoulder. "The courts can figure out intent. I'm just glad I don't have to interview any more perfume bloggers."

"Hey, they're delightful," Clare protested. "Mostly. Anyway, I've got new stock coming in next week. If you're lucky, I might even let you smell it before Ivy misplaces the testers."

Ayanna's smirk softened into something closer to a smile. "I'll hold you to that."

For a moment they just looked at each other before Ayanna gave a small nod and headed for the door. The bell above it chimed as she left, a faint swirl of matcha and tonka trailing in her wake before melting back into the layered hum of Good Scents.

Twenty-Eight

"PART OF ME FEELS like closing the shop tomorrow. The last two months have been a lot to process. But then another part wants to jump right into the holiday season with both feet. Get back to something that feels normal." Clare folded the last chair and leaned it against the counter with the others. Ivy and Jasmine were dragging the console back into place in the center of the room while Jorge fanned himself with the sign for the suggestion box. "I'm getting rid of that shrine once and for all. Once the word gets around that Guillermo Flares was a big fraud, there shouldn't be any new additions."

"I feel so bad for the Leights right now. First, they lost their beloved Billy, and now they're going to find out that their awful daughter is the one who killed him. Accidentally, but still." Ivy grabbed a chair and dragged it into the back room. When she came back out, she was carrying a box of holiday decorations. "We need to put this stuff back up tomorrow, Clare."

Clare nodded. Ivy dragged another chair into the back.

"I can imagine Mom will want to invite them over for Christmas, too, now. Because Thanksgiving was so much festive fun."

"I think your mom deserves a bit of credit here. If she hadn't invited the Leights over for turkey day, you'd never have almost been poisoned by Stephanie's special homemade headache remedy." Jasmine had a point.

"Great. Maybe she'll invite an axe murderer to Christmas dinner."

"Can we leave now? I've been having hot flashes all evening." Jorge had taken off his navy-blue velvet blazer and was standing there in a cropped tank top. "What? I've been having a relationship crisis. I haven't had time to do laundry."

After Ivy had dragged the last chair into the back room, she switched the music from the jazz that had been playing softly in the background to something more aggressively dance-y.

"Wait. Do you know my phone's passcode?" Clare noticed the switch.

"Sure. It's your birthday. 1108."

"Remind me to change that."

"Won't matter. If I make a scary enough monster face, the face ID works."

Clare made a fist and shook it at her cousin in jest. She was pain in the butt, but a loveable one.

"It's a shame Efraim left before we found out what his big secret was. The thing Guillermo held over his head." Ivy said as she shuffled her feet and did a spin.

"Oh, honey," Jorge and Clare said at the same time.

"What's with the 'oh honey' all the time? It's like you pity me."

As Clare shook her head sadly, Jorge went over to Ivy and put his arm around her. "Because he's more my kinda guy."

Ivy shrugged off Jorge's embrace. "Huh? Also, ew. Sweaty."

Clare gave her a look.

Ivy stood there with her mouth open, her eyes darting back and forth. One could almost hear the hamster on the wheel in her head. "Ohmigod. You're totally right." She blew out her breath. "Poop. I really like him." She thought for a few beats. "But why does that need to be such a big secret?"

"In some places, it's not just frowned on, it's dangerous. And he might not want his family to find out." Jasmine looked up from her phone.

"Ugh. People are terrible." Ivy looked disgusted.

"Yes, they are. Good thing we have perfume to make us happy."

"Amen to that! Now let's go indulge in some unhealthy eats and drinks."

"I think Stephanie might have left that big jug of her grief remedy in the back room...."

"No!"

If you enjoyed *Killer Sillage*, let's keep in touch!

https://katlague.substack.com

When you join my newsletter, LaGue's Clues, you'll get:

- Sneak peeks at upcoming books
- Exclusive bonus stories and extras
- Behind-the-scenes looks at Clare, Good Scents, and Baltimore life
- Fragrance chatter, cozy fun, and first access to giveaways
- PLUS! Coming in December, a new, serialized, holiday-themed mystery!

You can also sign up at my website, https://katlague.com

Author's Note

For a long time, I've enjoyed writing nonfiction. I love stuff like digging into facts, doing research, and telling true stories. But at some point, the pull to create something more imaginative became impossible to resist. Writing fiction was a new challenge for me, especially in finding the right balance of dialogue. Unlike nonfiction, where the facts do the talking, fiction needs characters who sound real and conversations that flow naturally. That's tricky, but also a lot of fun.

I've recently become a fan of cozy mysteries, those charming stories set in bakeries, yarn shops, or bookstores where the community feels like a friend you haven't met yet. But I wanted to bring something different to the genre, something that reflects one of my own passions: perfume.

My fascination with fragrance began in my early twenties. I was never the "signature scent" type, more like a fragrance explorer, always eager to sniff anything I could find. In the mid-2000s, I discovered an online forum called *Perfume of Life* (the inspiration behind *Cognoscented* in the book) and a twice-yearly perfume event in New York called Sniffapalooza. These communities introduced me to fellow "perfumistas" and the world of niche fragrances—a universe I hadn't even known existed.

Baltimore, Maryland, isn't exactly known as a perfume lover's city. At least not yet! I grew up in Fells Point, a neighborhood full of character: cobblestone streets (which can be a pain when you're walking but are so charming), cozy boutiques, and inviting restaurants. One of my favorite childhood spots was the Recreation Pier, now home to the Sagamore Pendry Hotel. Before it became a hotel, it stood in for the police station on the TV show *Homicide: Life on the Streets*. But when I was a child, it was a place to play. I have fond memories of swinging on the rooftop swings with my mom and my younger brother, just as the detectives did on the show. These little touches of history and community are what I wanted to bring alive in my fictional version of my hometown.

Thank you for stepping into this world with me. I hope Good Scents becomes a place you want to visit again and again.

With gratitude,

—Kat LaGue

Glossary

A Note on Pronunciation

Some Polish words pop up in this story, and since they're close to my heart, I wanted to make sure you say them right. Polish pronunciation can be tricky, so I've included simple guides here to help you feel like you're part of the family, whether you're whispering *babcia* or softly saying *na zawsze w naszych sercach.*

Babcia *[бабця]* **BOB-cha**
One of many ways to say "grandmother" in Polish.

Busia Manya BOO-sha MAHN-ya
Busia is a Polish-American word for "grandmother," likely a shortened form of *babusia* (ba-BOO-sha), which means "grandma" in both Polish and Ukrainian. Though the character this name refers to was named Mary Buchowski, *Manya* is actually a diminutive of *Maria* (pronounced MAH-ree-uh, not ma-REE-uh). In the author's family, several women legally named Mary in the U.S. were affectionately called Manya.

Eliksiry *[ɛ'lik.siri]* or **ee-lik-SIH-ree**
Polish for "potions" or "elixirs."

Gołąbki *[gɔ'wɔmpki]* or **go-WOOMP-kee**
Polish cabbage rolls. The word *gołąbki* also means "doves" or "pigeons."

Jadwiga *[jad'viga]* or **yahd-VEE-gah**
A traditional Polish name, most famously associated with Queen Jadwiga of Poland, who reigned in the 14th century and was later canonized as a saint.

Mój kraj *[muj kraj]* or **moy cry**

"My country" in Polish. The author's grandmother never referred to Poland as "Poland"—only as *mój kraj*. (*Mój* is the masculine form of "my." Like many Slavic languages, Polish words and phrases change depending on the gender of the noun.)

Na zawsze w naszych sercach
['zafʂɛ v 'naʂɨx 'sɛrt͡sax]
or **nah ZAVH-sheh VNAH-sheh SAIR-tsah**

A Polish phrase meaning "forever in our hearts," often seen on memorials or gravestones.

Acknowledgements

Let's start with my husband, Neal Patterson. He's the real writer in this family, the one with the chops and the discipline. When I started writing fiction, he gave me honest, thoughtful feedback and (to my great delight) admitted he was surprised at how quickly I took to it. Turns out all the blog posts I've written over 20 years were sneaky practice. Thank you, Neal, for being patient and encouraging, and for never once rolling your eyes when I launched into yet another book ramble.

Huge thanks to my beta reader, Diane, who kept me honest with smart suggestions, and to everyone else who listened as I talked incessantly about "my book." Extra love to my brother David, who's always in my corner and has perfected the art of nodding supportively at my endless brainstorms.

A quick nod to the Seans at Buchart Colbert, who gave me answers to my questions about the indie perfume biz. (Their perfumes are excellent. You should try them.)

Now—Perfume. I'm a fan, someone who adores fragrances and how they make me feel when I wear them. And yes, it would have been magical to feature real indie perfumers, but I wasn't up for the job of asking permission for so many scents. (A decade ago, I was wrangling recipes from chefs; I still have dents in my forehead from banging it on my desk.) And honestly, not everyone wants their life's work tangled up in a fictional murder. So instead, I teamed up with AI to invent the perfumes sold at Good Scents, keeping things imaginative and a little whimsical.

Thank also to my readers, for giving *Killer Sillage* a spot on your shelf (or your e-reader). For me, it's about more than perfume and puzzles...it's about sharing a little magic with you. I'm so glad you're here.

Meet Kat LaGue

In Kat LaGue's cozy mysteries, fragrance meets foul play. Her debut novel, *Killer Sillage*, introduces Clare Buchowski, proprietor of Good Scents, a Baltimore perfume shop where every scent tells a story--some of which are worth killing for. The second book in the series, *Savage Gourmand*, expands Clare's world to include the bakeries of Fells Point... and of course, more murder. Book three, *A Bitter Accord*, is scheduled to drop in the fall of 2026.

A lifelong perfume obsessive with a 30-year collection (and still hunting for the perfect Earl Grey scent), Kat brings a nose for detail to everything she writes. As a graphic designer, she's spent years understanding how mood lives in color and shape. As a nonfiction writer covering Baltimore's food scene, she's honed her eye for place and flavor. Fiction lets her stir it all together: mystery, scent, beauty, food, plus a healthy dose of humor.

Kat hails from Fells Point, the historic waterfront neighborhood in Baltimore, Maryland that serves as the backdrop for her fictional world. It's a place she still calls home and one she knows intimately. When she's not writing or tinkering with her latest handmade jewelry design, you'll likely find her sipping a perfectly brewed cup of coffee, doting on dogs, cooking something delicious, or nose-first in a bottle of interesting perfume.

She writes cozies because they celebrate women with creative lives and strong communities, and maybe also the stubbornness to solve a murder.

A Sneak Peek

Hello again, dear reader, it's Kat LaGue, your guide through the deliciously dangerous world of Clare Buchowski and her merry band of mischief-makers. You've already witnessed how deadly a perfume bottle can be, but in this next adventure, while the stakes are dusted with flour and glazed with sugar, you'll see that even sweetness can be dangerous.

Baltimore's bakeries are full of charm and family recipes, but also rivalries layered thicker than puff pastry. And butter! Whose croissant reigns supreme? Whose "secret ingredient" might not be so sweet? And when a body turns up among the sticky buns, Clare and Ivy discover that the line between comfort food and cutthroat competition can be razor-thin.

Savage Gourmand is a feast of flaky grudges, sharp twists, and mysteries. You might want to grab something warm and sweet to savor while you read. Sneak to the kitchen for a cookie, a slice of cake, or whatever will make you smile. Trust me, it makes the mystery even more delicious. Consider this chapter your amuse-bouche—no poison, I promise—just a taste of the drama to come.

So pull up a chair and settle in. Clare and Ivy are about to show you that even the sweetest pastries can hide the sharpest secrets, and I, for one, can't wait to see how you savor every crumb.

Savage Gourmand Chapter 1

"OH BOY. WE'RE IN big trouble," Ivy Buchowski declared, stumbling into Good Scents with her arms full.

"What's wrong? Did something happen? Are you okay?" Clare had been rearranging the shelves in her Fells Point perfume boutique. The warmer weather called for lighter fragrances, so she was bringing more citrus- and tea-based perfumes into the front for spring. She jumped down from the stepladder she'd been using and hurried over to her cousin.

Ivy dumped her collection of small white paper bags onto the counter, where they formed a crinkly heap. She waved her long arms dramatically. "Fells Point has never seen problems like what's coming. You think it's hard to find a parking space now? Well, mister, it's only going to get worse."

Knowing her cousin's flair for exaggeration, Clare folded her arms and waited for Ivy to finish her tirade.

Ivy stopped shouting long enough to open one bag, pull out a donut, and take a big bite. Powdered sugar cascaded down the front of her camo-patterned T-shirt. With her mouth full, she continued, "It's the end times..." Her eyes widened. "Ohm yfudging... this is SO GOOD!" She stared at the donut, oozing marshmallow filling onto the floor. "This is real marshmallow! Not just sticky white frosting."

Clare bit her lip to keep from laughing. "And this is what's going to cause parking problems and the end of the world?"

"Clare, you don't understand. A new bakery just opened around the corner. In another week, a second one will open down the street. And we already have Pitango and Sacré Sucré. It's going to be mayhem. More influencers, more lines for pastries. There'll be TV crews filming 'Battle of the Fells Point Bakeries.' People will pick favorites, and there'll be arguments over whose croissant reigns supreme. I can see it now. There will be bloodshed."

Ivy paused to take another enormous bite of her donut, leaving a blob of marshmallow on her nose. She wiped it off and sighed dramatically. "This neighborhood's about to go all to biscuits."

Clare didn't bother holding in her laughter. "You don't think having four bakeries within four blocks is a good thing?"

"Hell no, Cuz." Ivy patted her slender midsection, leaving a powdered sugar handprint. "I'm going to have to buy a whole new wardrobe to accommodate my pastry baby."

Clare rolled her eyes and started rummaging through the bags. "So what weapons of mass destruction do we have here? Did this come from The Rolling Pin?" She pulled a thick wedge of brownie out of one bag, took a bite, and chewed thoughtfully. After a second bite, she said, "This is one fine brownie." The rich fudginess made her think of patchouli's chocolatey undertone, the same note that could register as earthy elegance or hippie cliché.

Ivy grabbed the bag and looked into it. "You left the frosting behind."

Clare snatched the bag out of her cousin's hand and swiped a finger through the blob of chocolate stuck to its interior. "Ooh, it has chopped nuts, too."

Just then, the door opened and Clare's best friend, Jorge, stepped in, his bright floral shirt half-tucked into trousers that had clearly never met an iron. He took one look at the powdered sugar and chocolate on the faces of the Good Scents staff and folded his chubby arms over his stomach. "Now, what have we here? It looks like a little afternoon delight has been taking place right on the shop floor."

Ivy squinted and looked heavenward for a moment. "I thought that song was about..."

Clare broke in. "There's a new bakery around the corner, which will apparently bring about the destruction of mankind and Ivy's waistline. We're just enjoying ourselves before the inevitable zombies come for our brains." She held out a bag to Jorge. "Join us?"

"Don't mind if I do." After selecting a double chocolate donut, he glanced out the window and said, "You might want to clean yourselves up. I see customers."

"Ooh, be right back." Clare grabbed Ivy by the sleeve and dragged her into the back room where they hurriedly washed their hands and dabbed at their faces with a damp paper towel.

When they returned to the shop, Jorge was attempting to scrape marshmallow off the floor with a square of waxed paper from one of the bags, but the result was a smeary mess. Clare dropped her damp towel in front of him and was drying her hands on her pants when the bell above the door chimed softly. There he was: tall, with dark hair that caught the light just right, and eyes that seemed to hold a secret smile. He also brought with him a whisper of vetiver, which Clare caught beneath the scents of flour and coffee.

Her hands froze mid-air, a faint blush creeping up her neck. She resisted the urge to smooth her hair, which had never fully committed to either straight or curly, and was suddenly aware of the freckles across her nose. Did her heart just skip? So unprofessional. She had the unsettling feeling her life had just gotten more complicated.

Calm down, Clare. It's just a customer.

Ivy, sensing that her cousin was in some sort of handsome-induced trance, cleared her throat and said to the visitor, "Welcome to Good Scents. What can we help you with?" Clare was still standing there, staring. It was getting embarrassing, so Ivy poked her in the shoulder.

Clare started and gave a shaky smile. "I was just looking at what was going on outside. There was this... man... and he tripped over the cobblestones and dropped his coffee. Happens all the time, actually." She mentally slapped herself across the face.

The visitor smiled, and time stood still.

Jorge sensed that the situation could get even more awkward if he stayed, so he popped up off the ground and said, "Well, gals, I'll leave you to it," before bolting out the door.

The stranger spoke. "I'm Julian Partridge. I own Crème de la Crème up the street, which I hope to be opening in the next few days. I've been so busy with turning that old building into a modern bakery that I haven't had a chance to meet my neighbors. I had a few spare moments today, so I thought I'd come by and introduce myself and invite you to my grand opening."

"Hi." Clare said, somewhat dreamily. Ivy stepped in front of her and offered her hand to Julian.

"Nice to meet ya, Julian. Can I call you Jules? My name is Ivy Buchowski, and this one here is my cousin Clare. She owns this shop. I just have the privilege of working here."

Julian shook Ivy's hand and cocked his head at Clare. "Is she okay?"

"No worries. She's got a condition. Sometimes she freezes up like that." Ivy snapped her fingers in front of Clare's face. "Cuz? Do you need to lie down? Want me to bring you some water?"

Clare shook her head. "No, thanks. I'm fine." She tried not to look directly at Julian, but couldn't help herself. He looked just like the man who had been appearing in her dreams recently. Surely it was a coincidence?

Clare's sleep had been disturbed for the past few weeks. On the nights she could drop off at a fairly reasonable hour, she woke up after only one or two sleep cycles. Rather than resort to taking any sort of medication, she went to her Aunt Lou to see what she might put together from her grandmother's book of folk medicine.

Clare's perfume shop, Good Scents, had once been her grandmother Mary's herbalist shop. Not only had Clare inherited the building, she also had custody of the family's generations-old book of remedies. Clare referred to it as the "tome" because it was chock full of, well, *stuff*, much of it written in Polish or Cyrillic, neither of which she could read. However, Aunt Lou, Busia Manya's daughter, could decipher things well enough. After her mother's death, she had even appointed herself the family's official unofficial herbalist—a role Clare suspected gave Lou a certain authority, particularly now that the family had begun whispering about her eccentric behavior.

After poring over the book for several minutes, Lou determined that a cup of tea made from chamomile, valerian, and lavender would help. Lavender always reminded Clare of the fougère scents in the shop, which held sharpness in the opening but dried down into something soft as flannel. She also suggested that Clare eat more magnesium-rich foods. "Personally, I like a good peanut butter and banana sandwich with a sprinkle of those mini chocolate chips," she had said. "Magnesium up the wazoo, and it's great for pretty much any meal of the day."

Clare took the advice to heart, eating a peanut butter sandwich for breakfast every day and sipping the tea before bed. After a couple of days, she was back to sleeping normally. Except now she was having lots of vivid dreams. And she could swear that the man standing in front of her figured largely in several of them.

She didn't want to seem rude, so Clare attempted to be cordial to her new neighbor despite her current disorientation. She held her hand out to him, realized it was sweaty, and instead tucked it into the opposite armpit. "Sorry about that. I haven't been sleeping well lately. As Ivy mentioned, I'm Clare, and this is my shop. It's nice to meet you. Welcome to the neighborhood." Clare looked at her cousin and smiled. "Actually, we were just talking about your bakery. Not directly, just discussing what impact two new bakeries will have on the neighborhood when there are already two that are pretty well-regarded."

"I noticed that you've already sampled my competition's product." Julian swept his arm over the small mountain of bakery bags on the counter. "What do you think?"

"We've only tried a donut and a brownie, but we thought they were pretty good. Isn't that right, Ivy?"

Ivy's attention was on the baked goods. "Um, sure. I think I need to try more before I write a formal review."

"What's that? A 'formal review'?" Julian looked at her with interest.

"I'm a food blogger." Ivy fluffed her unruly brown curls. "*Bite Me, Baltimore*. You've probably heard of it. I track all the foodie gossip: hidden recipes, secret menu items, um, bakery battles... the works."

Clare rolled her eyes. Ivy had been a blogger for all of two months at this point. A spirited conversation with a friend, perfume blogger Jasmine Reed, sparked a stubborn little fire that wouldn't quit until the world had heard her take on pastries, sauces, and everything in between. Jasmine pointed Ivy toward a blogging platform, and Jorge helped her with a banner. So far, she'd written a handful of posts, including ones on Asian-fusion restaurant Ekiben, and another on Sophia's Place European Deli in the Broadway Market.

Julian grinned, but before he could tease her further, the bell over the door jingled again. A tall woman swept in, her thick blonde hair tied back in a neat braid, a dusting of flour still visible on the front of her dark apron. She looked friendly until she spotted her rival. With a voice edged in sugar and spice, she said to Julian, "Wasting time already, charming the neighbors, while I'm up to my elbows in *pâte à choux*?"

Julian's smile disappeared. "Heather. I didn't realize you'd be wandering so far from The Rolling Pin."

Heather arched an eyebrow. "I don't need to wander. News travels fast when a so-called French bakery decides to set up shop practically in my backyard."

"'So-called'?" Julian crossed his arms, mock offense in every line of his body. "I studied in Lyon."

"Mm," Heather drawled. "And yet, last I checked, Lyon isn't Paris. Croissants require Parisian finesse. But perhaps your customers won't notice."

Clare blinked, glancing between them. The air was suddenly thick with competitive heat. Julian's vetiver brightness was colliding with Heather's cloud of vanilla and yeast, like the awkward olfactory equivalent of two rivals squaring off. Ivy, wide-eyed, whispered, "Ohmigod, this is better than I thought. The Battle of the Bakeries has already started. My blog is going to go viral!"

Heather finally turned her gaze on Clare and Ivy. "Just a word of advice, ladies. Don't fill up too much on Partridge's pastries. You'll want to save room for the real thing."

"Don't listen to her," Julian cut in smoothly. "I'll bring you samples myself, and then you can be the judge."

The air practically crackled. Clare shifted uncomfortably, while Ivy looked like Christmas had come early. Heather's eyes flicked toward the heap of crinkled paper bags on the counter. A slow smile curved across her lips. "Ah. I see you've already had the good sense to stop by The Rolling Pin."

Ivy clutched one of the bags protectively. "We were, uh, conducting research. Very serious, very scientific." She noticed a smear of chocolate on her thumb and licked it.

Heather smirked. "That's what I like to hear. Research." She gave Julian a pointed look. "Nothing like a taste test to prove who really knows their craft."

Julian folded his arms. "Enjoy your head start, Heather. My ovens will be firing soon enough."

Heather laughed, low and confident. "Soon enough? Oh, darling, by then your neighbors will already be addicted to my kouign-amann."

Clare, caught between them, muttered, "I think we might be in trouble," but Ivy's eyes were shining.

"This is gold," Ivy whispered, already digging in her bag for her phone. "Two bakers, one neighborhood, zero mercy. My readers are going to eat this up."

Heather tilted her chin toward Ivy. "Readers?"

"Food blog. *Bite Me, Baltimore*." Ivy puffed out her chest. "I report the truth. Hidden recipes, secret menu items, bakery battles..."

Heather's smile widened, sharp and amused. "Well then, Miss Blogger, be sure you spell my name correctly when you crown me Queen of Fells Point Pastries. It's Heather Newbold. N-E-W-B-O-L-D."

Julian shot back, "Don't get too comfortable on that throne." He leaned toward Ivy with a conspiratorial glint. "Maybe I'll let you sample something before opening day. For... research purposes."

Ivy practically squealed. "Shut. Up. Yes, please."

Heather rolled her eyes and brushed imaginary flour off her sleeve. "Empty promises. Meanwhile, I actually have a business to run." She turned on her heel, then glanced back at Clare. "Don't worry, dear. When you're ready for more of the good stuff, you know where to find me." She flicked a look toward Julian before sweeping out the door, leaving the shop filled with the scent of sugar and vanilla so thick Clare wanted to reach for one of her sharper green florals to cut through it.

Ivy leaned on the counter, fanning herself with one of the empty bags and inadvertently sprinkling powdered sugar on herself. "Did you see that? This is huge. I've got front-row seats to Pastry Thunderdome."

"God help me. You're going to turn this into a multi-part series, aren't you?" Clare pressed a hand to her forehead and thought to herself, *If this really was a battle, my money is on vetiver versus vanilla.*

Ivy grinned. "Cuz, this is at least a ten-part saga. Maybe more if someone starts throwing éclairs."

Julian just smiled, clearly enjoying himself. "Guess I'd better make sure my éclairs are worth fighting over." He sauntered over to the counter and plucked a marshmallow-filled donut bag from the pile. "You really should be careful," he said, teasing. "Getting caught with the enemy's pastries is dangerous business."

Ivy gasped. "Enemy? Ooooooh!"

Julian leaned in conspiratorially. "Don't tell Heather, but I've got a few tricks up my sleeve. You'll just have to wait and see."

Clare forced herself to find her voice. "So, are you here to introduce yourself to all the neighbors, or just to scope out the competition?"

Julian's eyes twinkled. "Can't it be both?"

Ivy smacked the counter. "You HAVE to bring samples. My blog demands it. My readers..."

"You've had two readers," Clare muttered.

"Two dozen," Ivy corrected. "And they are hungry for knowledge."

Julian laughed, shook his head, and said, "Alright, blogger. I'll bring something by. Just don't hold it against me if you fall in love... with my sticky buns."

He lingered just long enough for Clare to feel her pulse quicken, then tipped an imaginary hat. "Until next time."

www.ingramcontent.com/pod-product-compliance
Lightning Source LLC
LaVergne TN
LVHW100525110826
845146LV00002B/785

* 9 7 9 8 9 9 9 9 2 1 0 0 0 *